The Beast in the Nothing Room

The Beast in the Nothing Room

by
Kyle Michel Sullivan

KMSCB, Buffalo, NY
Published 2019 by KMSCB

This book is a work of fiction meant for adults only. Names, characters, places, incidents, and situations are purely the result of the author's imagination and are used fictitiously. Resemblance to any persons, living or dead, is purely coincidental. All rights are reserved by the author, including the right to reproduction in whole or in part in any form, manner, or concept.

Acknowledgements

Thanks to Vicki HJ and Sue B for their help in making this piece stay true. Additional thanks to The Depraved Minds Club on GoodReads.com and my Facebook friends for giving me so much support. They help me keep real.

Table of Contents

About the Author

Other Books

The Beast in the Nothing Room

In the Nothing Room

Finn had no idea where he was or what had happened. One moment he was in the woods searching for poachers; the next, he was lying in a room that was dark...yet not dark, for he could see light casting a vague glow off his nose and cheeks. Both silent and not, despite an absence of sound. And it was neither warm nor cool. In fact, he couldn't even be sure it was a room because he was unable to locate any of the walls encompassing him...just like he was unable to find any source for the light shining upon him.

But what was worse? He sensed he was not alone.

He was stretched out on a bed...that wasn't a bed. It felt like there was nothing beneath him but air, simple air holding him up. He knew he was still in his clothes — a well-fitted suit in a fine modern cut, neat tie and Oxfords, completely inappropriate for tramping through the shrubs and sticks of a forest, but being a police officer, he'd had little choice.

The call had come as he was en route to Clayton-Magna to meet some friends, and the male caller's tone of voice was panicked. At least, that's what the call center had said. Strange lights whispering through the forest. Animals scattering away from it in fear. Concern it might be a drug deal going down, or what was worse...poachers. Uniforms were on their way but were fifteen minutes behind him and, since he was a Detective Sergeant, they felt he was best to at least make contact with the person reporting the incident so as to initiate a proper beginning to the investigation.

He'd agreed to do it because he didn't feel it would take too long and could hand it over to another DS, as soon as he arrived. Plus, he knew his friends would be understanding. *The life of a cop*, sort of thing. He'd made a hands-free call to Prue, the woman who'd arranged the get-together, to let her know he was running behind then turned down Mid-Clayton Road to double back for Lower Clayton-Merrill.

He gave a soft chuckle. Prue was the reason he'd worn this particular suit. It was fitted in all the right places, showing off his trim, well-formed torso and colt-like legs, though it was a bit...well...*snug* around the derriere and...um...frontal area. However, he felt very *male-model* in it, and knew she would be impressed. At least, hoped she would be. Since she was a biologist, an unspoken part of that hope was perhaps she'd also now see him as not only a prime specimen of the male figure, but a possible bed partner and, if all went well, eventual husband. He was ready to start a family, having now settled into the area and it being just past his thirtieth birthday. Find a nice cottage someplace local, somewhat similar to the Cotswold's. Not too far from the Criminal Investigations Division and DCI Blethyn, his superior. Base his life from there. They were meeting with another couple, married with a child on the way so he also hoped this was a subtle sign she might be considering him as more than a mere boyfriend. And the idea almost felt cozy and warm.

By using a bit more speed than he should have, considering the narrowness of the roads, he'd arrived to the stated location only to find...nothing. No lights. No fresh tracks from foot or vehicle. No animals, either. The forest was still and dark, despite it only beginning to approach dusk. He'd wondered if he'd gone to the wrong side, but double-checking his GPS showed he had gone to where dispatch had said.

He'd tried to go a few meters into the trees, just to get a sense of the place, but the brush was thick and he could see no path to follow. He hadn't wanted to push in too far because that would mess up his *aren't-I-hot* suit, so he was about to back away when something had struck him.

The forest was completely silent.

No sounds whatsoever.

Not even the hint of a breeze to rustle the tree branches. That had been decidedly odd, especially being this close to the Channel.

Then about a hundred meters to his left he'd seen a light. Not like that of a torch or lamp, just a soft blue glow behind the trees.

Surrounding a lone figure.

Headed towards him.

He'd jolted and begun to back away, saying, "Hello! Police. I'm Detective Sergeant Winterbourne," and the blue light had swirled around him —

And now he was here, with no idea how he got there or what was going on.

"Did I fall? Knock myself out?"

That had to be the explanation; the figure hadn't been close enough to reach him, and there was no indication of a weapon firing, so he'd stumbled, hit something, been struck unconscious and was dreaming. It was the only thing that could make sense.

He tried to sit up...but he couldn't move. Not his legs. Not his arms, which he finally realized were now held behind him by something that felt solid and firm, like thick cuffs. He could shift his eyes around, and could swallow, and he could breathe. That was all.

"Hello?" he called, not so much expecting an answer but only to see if he was capable of speech. He heard no echo in the chamber so figured he probably only thought he was speaking. Now he was certain he was caught in a dream.

Then he felt a whisper of air around him, like the soft caress of fingers...but nothing was there. It traced over his clean cheeks, his fine lips, his bright open eyes, a cool blue under light brown lashes. He felt it on the eyebrows he'd trimmed last night in anticipation of his date. Felt it travel through his thick curly hair, cropped close to keep from becoming too unruly. He wasn't movie-star gorgeous; he knew that, but he also knew his face was well received by most young women...and the nothing-air was touching every inch of it in ways that made him very uncomfortable.

It moved over his chin, well-shaved not an hour ago; he had issues with a light five o'clock shadow, which Prue had once mentioned in her flat Belfast brogue, and he wanted nothing that might prevent any kisses. He had even showered and changed into this suit, at the department.

He noticed the nothing-air was also caressing the back of his head and nape of his neck. Whatever it was he was lying upon made no difference; the sensations merely displaced the feeling of support momentarily as they travelled across his shoulders and down his back...then up his sides?!

What sort of dream is this?

The nothing-air in front was pacing that in the rear as it drew over his chest, tenderly exploring under his suit coat to play with his nipples. Which surprised him. He'd never had anyone finger those, before, and the fact that it sent a jolt of pleasure through him was even more startling.

Then it continued down his fairly taut abs to his groin.

He moaned with both pleasure and discomfort.

Oh...oh, no. This...this isn't real. It's all a dream.

Except it certainly felt real. Especially when the nothing-air traced over his trousers to...to fondle his crotch?!

And massage his ass?!

"What're you doing? What're you doing?!?!" he cried. Or did he merely think it? He still couldn't tell. But it had become deplorably invasive and he wanted it to stop.

After even more intimate caressing, the nothing-air traveled down his thighs and over his calves to his feet, making him cringe and try to pull away as short grunts of disbelief burst from him.

"What is this?!"

Still nothing but silence.

Then he felt the beginning of an erection.

He couldn't believe it. The nothing-air was so sensuous in its touch, he was responding?! His body was enjoying it? He was shocked beyond belief. The one positive was, he'd worn his new tight CK boxer-briefs, and those might keep him from becoming too embarrassed.

He tried to move, again, but still could not; just remained floating in the silent nothingness. He knew this was not sensory deprivation because he could see light reflecting off his face and feel himself being touched. He swallowed, fear starting to build in him.

Then he felt his shoes being untied and removed!

"Bloody hell, what're you doing?!"

No response. No echo. No proof of any sound coming from him. Just off with the shoes and a soft clunk when they dropped to the floor. Then the nothing-air caressed his soles and toes as it removed his socks, a new pair he'd worn because the only other pair that matched this suit had holes in them. Next, his suit jacket was shifted off his shoulders in soft, loving movements that were close to tenderly demanding.

"Stop! What're you doing?! I'm a police officer! Stop! STOP IT!"

His tie was undone and his shirt slowly unbuttoned.

"It's a dream, it's a dream, it's a dream, it's a dream, it's a dream," he gasped. Or maybe he was just thinking it. Hoping it. Wishing it. Because no matter how hard he tried to convince himself otherwise, he could feel every single solitary thing the nothing-air was doing. Each touch was insistent. Each caress was too real. Each movement over him was meant to lead him closer to something carnal and prurient. It didn't help that he'd been going through a dry spell and had been more than hoping Prue would take him to bed, that evening, instead of his hand being his only partner, again. But this?

This!?

Living with his grandmother...his Nan, where his mum and dad had dumped him as an infant so they could follow their own bliss...he'd had a couple of what she called *Emission Dreams*. She'd told him they were completely natural for boys hitting puberty.

"Both of your uncles went through this," she'd said, "as did your father, despite his claims to perfection. Nothing to be embarrassed about. Just make sure to give yourself a good wash." Then she'd taken his sheets and pajamas without further comment.

She'd always been the level-headed one in the family, not typically British in her understanding about sexual needs. She'd lived on a commune in Wales, traveled to Monterrey, California, and even stayed in some temple in the Himalayas for some form of awareness. All of that had carried with her, and he was glad he'd taken more after her than either of his unknown and very self-interested parents. Remembering this helped calm him and let him focus on the reality of the moment.

As soon as he could figure out what that reality was.

To start with, he knew this could not be happening except in his mind. So no matter what the nothing-air did, it wasn't real. It couldn't be. Despite what his body was telling him.

That helped when the nothing-air pulled his shirt open to reveal his undershirt — tight, white, and just a little see-through — then slipped the crisp cotton down and off his arms with a touch that was almost worshipful in its caress. The shirt was softly whispered past his hands even though they were still caught behind him...which made no sense, but that was the reality of this dream.

His breath was coming faster as he fought to keep panic at bay, and his well-formed pecs were causing the undershirt to shift a little over his now tender nips. He was proud of how he'd built himself up, after having been born underweight and sickly, and it seemed the nothing-air agreed, because it ran over his muscles and fondled and flicked and twisted his nipples through the fabric, making them tent against the light cotton, every touch shooting fire into his groin. He was in shock at how lovely it felt. How fantastic it was. How he didn't want it to stop. How a tingle behind his balls was actually making him groan from pleasure.

Christ, is this what I want Prue to do to me?

Then the nothing-air ripped his undershirt open to reveal his smooth, barely tanned skin was laced with a dash of tawny hair that swirled down his abs to his groin. He yelped as the caresses ran across his belly and over his shoulders and along his arms to guide the shirt's remains away in ways that seemed to sear the heartbreaking prurience of its touch into his very soul.

His breath grew sharper. Heavier. Was punctuated with grunts of fear. He fought to keep one thought in his mind.

It's NOT real, Finn, it's not real, it's not real.

But he was losing the battle. The sensations brought on by the nothing-air were too demanding. Too consistent. And on top of it, his dick was growing fat and hard, in response.

Even though he could not move his torso or arms or legs.

Just an emission dream, that's all, just an emission dream.

Then his trousers were unbuttoned!

He fought to picture Prue being the one doing it. Picture how lovely she was. Round in all the right places.

Peaches and cream skin under golden red hair cut just right. That Belfast brogue. He'd been attracted to her the second he met her on a murder case. She'd been a suspect, for a little while, so their beginning had been tainted by that, but it was Blethyn who'd made the accusations, not him. After some stumbling, he'd been able to get her to know him and let him know her, and now...well...using the image of her helped him refocus and make this nightmare into something he could handle. If he was going to be dream-mauled, sexually, at least it would be by someone he wanted.

His zipper was lowered, almost teasing, and his trousers were guided past his hips and rear with the same tenderness and beauty as was done with his shirt. And under those briefs, he was totally ready to go. The nothing-air danced back up to play with his dick and balls through the cotton, not only whispering around them and over them and under them and along them but making the taut material surrounding them feel like something alive and needy. It also massaged the cheeks of his ass as if they were ripe melons. He didn't have a bubble-butt, but it was a nice size and fit him just right. Apparently the nothing-air agreed, for this continued as his trousers were maneuvered down his legs to his ankles while the caresses wafted over the soft down on his thighs and calves. The elegant sensations were beginning to overpower his ability to concentrate.

Then the waistband of his CKs was grabbed...and they were pulled down to his ankles, where his trousers waited, exposing an erection that may not be the biggest dick ever but was certainly above average. At least, none of the women he'd been with had complained. He'd even caught a few lads in the gym casting him glances of either envy or interest, or both.

But now?

Like this?

As he was being violated?

The trousers were gently removed, then off went the CKs with even more caresses over his calves.

And he was now completely naked.

Completely vulnerable as the dreadful intimacy continued.

I'm handling it. I'm handling it.

Then the nothing-air slipped between the cheeks of his ass and touched his rectum.

"NO! STOP! THIS ISN'T RIGHT! YOU CAN'T DO THIS!" he screamed.

He fought to squirm away but his body still would not move. His breath was fast and furious, and while he could shift his eyes to look around and move his mouth to speak and knew damn well he really was yelling and snarling words into the nothingness, he also knew his nips had grown pointy and his balls were happily being juggled and his dick was being stroked while every other part of his body was also being mauled.

Bloody hell. Is this an alien abduction? Are those bloody stories true? No, I have to be hallucinating. I have to be!

Now the nothing-air danced over his nips to send more lightning through every nerve in his body. Caressed the hair on his abs and wandered through his pubes like they were rafting down a river that cascaded into gentle pond. Glided over his ass. Fondled his dick and balls in ways that seemed more like worship than sexual need. Sensations swirled up and down his thighs and calves, adding to the build of erotic need within him.

His dick was now as hard as it had ever been, and he was whimpering at the incessant manipulation of it taking him almost over the edge...but never quite. Stroking. Caressing. Loving it. Holding it straight up so that he could just see the head of his penis if he looked down with his eyes. He felt some form of covering glide over it, like a condom, but so far as he could tell nothing was actually being put on him.

"No, no, no, no..." was all he could murmur, now. He knew his cries and screams and pleading would do no good, but they still jolted from him at each step in the invasion.

Then a form appeared in the dark space above him, shining so bright he had to jam his eyes closed. As he adjusted to its glow, he slowly realized this was another man. Also naked. Lean and tightly muscled, with dark fans of hair over his body in all the places it should be. Nearly black eyes under thick lashes. A two-day growth of beard on his strong chin, surrounding full lips. A couple years older. He saw the hair on the man's body shift slightly, as if he, too, were being caressed.

And he was also sporting an erection, his shaft ripe, his knob red, his foreskin drawn completely back from the head.

The suddenness of it jolted Finn, and jammed one thought into his mind.

I know him. I know him. From where?

The man recognized him, as well. His expression shifted to confusion. Then shock.

"Him?" the man said, in a Geordie accent. "It's him?! No!"

"Newcastle!" Finn said, in shock. "You...uh, you're Hallsworth! Detective Inspector...uh, Joss Hallsworth?"

The man's expression grew pained he said, "Yeah. I know you. Winterbourne, from down South. Conference a few years back, at New Scotland Yard. You'd just gained Detective Sergeant."

"Right, right. What the hell's going on!?"

Joss almost laughed. "If I could explain it, I would. How'd they trap you?"

"Trap? I...I...I got called out to investigate some lights. Caller said...well, he thought they were...uh...they were..."

"Poachers," said Joss. "Bloody hell..."

"No argument there," Finn said...then felt the nothing-air slip up against his anus and he cried out, in shock. "STOP IT!"

"They're all over you. Right?"

Finn had to fight a panic building in him. "I...I'm...I'm dreaming you?"

"No. You're not." His voice sounded mournful. "I...bloody fuckin' hell, not him! Not him!"

Not him?

The nothing-air pushed harder against Finn's rectum. He fought to keep from screaming then gasped, "What do you mean? Are they mauling you, too?"

"This is how they work. Touch and grope and fondle and abuse...and...and nothing's there."

"That's what they're doing to me, but I can't move and...and..." Finn's nips were pinched, making him shout, "WHO THE BLOODY HELL ARE YOU? WHY'RE YOU DOING THIS?"

Then Finn realized he wasn't lying down; he was upright, as was Joss. And they were closer together. Closer. Closer. Until their erections touched each other. Slipped side by side. Held in place as the nothing-air whispered over the both of them. Fondled them, together. And it felt so good...too good...too damn good.

"STOP! STOP IT!" Finn cried. "This is rape!"

"Oh, Christ," Joss said, "I can't...please...not him..."

Finn focused on Joss. "What're you saying?!"

"They're using me. Against you. Against others. Take me whenever they want and...no, don't make me do it, not to him! Please..."

Finn felt the nothing-air surround his ankles and lift his legs up and up, even as his arms remained locked behind him and the caresses and the probing continued all over him.

He screamed, "NO! YOU'RE NOT — YOU CAN'T — NO! THIS IS RAPE! THIS IS RAPE!"

"They don't care," Joss murmured. "They don't follow our laws. Dammit, don't make me, please, not him."

The nothing-air rested Finn's legs on Joss's broad shoulders, his ass now completely open and vulnerable. Then he felt Joss's erection press against him.

"Finn, I'm sorry..."

"NO, NO, NO, NO, NO!"

The nothing-air opened Finn's cheeks wider.

Joss's dick pushed in.

Finn howled in pain.

It kept going in. Slowly. Slowly. Filling him. Deeper and deeper. He felt he was being torn in half and yelled and snarled in anger and frustration. And still he could not move to get away from it.

"I'm sorry, Finn, I'm sorry, I'm so sorry..."

Then Joss's erection was all the way inside, right to the base; Finn could feel the man's pubs against his skin. He felt the covering over his dick begin to pulse up and down, stroking him as Joss began rocking in and back and in and back and in and back.

I'm getting wanked as he buggers me?!

Finn gasped harsh and fast. His eyes slammed shut and he howled. He felt the nothing-air pinch his nips and whisper over his pecs and caress his thighs and toy with his pubes and fondle his balls as the unseen covering stroked his dick, making it harder and harder and bringing it closer and closer to the brink then stopping just before he could let go then starting, again, and it went on and on and on and every push in hurt and every pull back was like fire and he screamed and yelled and cursed and tried to fight but couldn't move as he was mauled and groped and felt up and fucked and pulled at and it kept on and on and on and then...then slowly...oh so slowly...almost exquisitely, to his shock, the pain shifted...and each thrust began to feel like something beautiful and wanted and every nerve in his being was filled with pleasure. Each stroke on his own dick made it grow even harder. His balls became even more tender and quivered each time Joss's pubes brushed against them. His nips were crazed by each light lovely pinch. His calves and thighs laughed with joy from the nothing-air traveling over them. He couldn't believe it.

I'm enjoying being fucked by a man I barely know!? Getting off on being raped?

In and back and in and back, over and over and over, each thrust taking him closer and closer to a stunning nirvana. The passionate demands of it finally enveloped him and he lost all sense of time or reality as Joss kept going in and back and in and back and kept on and on and on for hours and hours and Finn didn't care because he wanted it and needed it and hoped it would never end.

Until he felt a rush build from behind his balls and roll through his body as every muscle in him clenched and joined with the nothing-air's caresses to make him grunt and let out a bellowing roar as the rush slammed down his thighs and across his ass and over his nips and up into his dick and a massive line of cum exploded from him, the like of which he had never experienced. It vanished into the invisible covering as he fired again and again and again, each jolt better than the last, draining him of what seemed like gallons of semen.

Then Joss slammed harder and harder against him and jolted and shuddered and stopped deep inside and cried out...and filled him with his own cum. Gasping and whimpering in both pleasure and horror and joy and pain, he rammed against Finn harder and harder, sending more and more flooding into him. On and on until he was a quivering, laughing mass and could make nothing in the way of a coherent sound.

Finn was so lost in his own overwhelming sensations and feelings and exultation, he was just as incoherent.

After what seemed like hours but was probably only a few minutes, stillness returned to them both and Finn slowly...slowly...slowly drifted back to himself. He found he was able to move his head, now. His arms hung limp, behind him. He looked at Joss, whose eyes were half-closed, his face slack from the intense pleasure as he pulled out. His dick was still dripping with semen.

No condom on him.

Finn's own dick lay back on his belly, fat and clean and satisfied with itself. He was even still erect. Somewhat. And he felt nothing surrounding it, anymore, as it began to shrink back to normal. Then his legs were removed from Joss's shoulders.

The man looked at him, confused.

"You're still here," he whispered, a near smile on his face. "Still here. You're not...not..."

"What...you mean?" Finn managed to gasp.

Joss cast Finn a vague, sorrowful glance as he murmured, "They. They made me. Do this. To others. So many others. Just like us. Till they. Till they let loose, same as you. They all did. But they. They left. Fell away. You haven't. Now I see. So sorry."

"Were you...done like this, too...?"

"I...I'm so sorry. Didn't want this. For you. Sorry."

"Not your fault," Finn murmured.

Joss smiled. "That's what. Rob said. Manchester's finest, he was. Poor bastard."

Then Joss drifted back into the blue light.

Finn felt the nothing-air still caressing him. Fondling him. Probing him. Nips, balls, dick, thighs, ass, back, sides, face, feet...but it was in a manner that seemed sweet and caring. Loving, even.

Which made no sense. Did his assailant think he'd been made love to? Had this really been some bizarre alien abduction and the bastards believed it was a proper sexual coupling of Earth people? That he'd wanted it to happen? Despite his screams and struggles? It had hurt like hell, and he was brutally sore from the fucking...but he had to admit how mellow and easy he felt after having cum like he did. So much so, he almost didn't care about being violated.

That shocked him more than anything — the idea that he had rather enjoyed being raped by Joss!

In his head, he knew this had been a harsh, vicious, cruel, manipulative, painful sexual assault. But a deeper truth also made itself known.

I want it to happen, again.

His unbelievably intense ejaculation at the end of it had overcome the horror of everything else. He felt like someone coming down off his first snort of coke, who wanted more, wanted to regain that high. It frightened him, but also put him at ease.

Which makes absolutely no sense whatsoever.

He felt his CKs being slipped back up his legs in gentle caresses. The tight, white cotton softly surrounded his ass and scrotum as the nothing-air adjusted his dick and balls so he was comfortable. Next came his trousers, socks and shirt, followed by his shoes. The tie was knotted around his neck, and the suit coat came on and the light swirled blue and —

He was lying in the forest, two constables watching over him, one young and fit, the other older and more concerned. The young one was on a mobile phone.

"'E's coming 'round, sir," the man said. "Yes, still needs a medic. 'E looks pretty shaky."

Finn made himself sit up, even though he felt rather dizzy. He glanced at the fit young constable and noticed how the lad completed that uniform very nicely, in every way, his pale blond hair, chiseled features, and strong tanned forearms glistening with golden down adding to his beauty.

Confused, Finn had to make himself look away.

"How long?" he murmured, his voice shaky.

"We got here 'bout twenty minutes, ago, sir," said the older constable. "Saw your car and looked around. Couldn't find you till there was some lightning in the clouds and I noticed you here. Dunno why we didn't see you, before. I loosened your tie."

"Know what 'appened?" the young constable asked.

Finn shook his head and started to get up. The older man held him down.

"I'd stay put, were I you, sir. That's a nasty cut over your ear."

Finn touched a sore spot behind his right ear and his fingers came away with dabs of blood on them. He sighed. So it was all just a dream. He was only sore from having fallen or been hit; he wasn't sure which, yet.

Which was vaguely disappointing.

He almost laughed. He'd never even thought of being with a man, before, let alone getting buggered by one, but here he was, sad that what had happened in his head hadn't occurred in reality. It was madness.

But something didn't add up. He ached in every part of his body, as if he'd overdone his workout, something he never did. Could that be from just a blow to the head? And should his ass hurt like he'd taken a really hard bowel movement? And his nipples, why were they so tender? And why did he feel so...so different, now, as if his whole world had shifted?

That's when he realized his undershirt was gone.

I always wear one.

A weird sort of relief swept over him and he smiled. It really had happened. He felt his balls tingle and his dick shift in agreement, and with it came a surprising hunger. An odd sort of need.

And that lovely young constable would be just the tonic for it.

A thousand questions exploded through Finn's mind. One moment he's dreaming of a night with a beautiful woman; the next, he's focused on the very nice rear and well-formed legs of a man and thinking how much he'd like to have access to them? Really?

So was he queer, now? Had the aliens made him a poof? One of his uncles was gay, and he was the coolest man Finn had ever known. Had he decided to swing to that side, thanks to this?

No, the very idea was ridiculous. One doesn't go gay from a smack to the head, and you can't rape a man into changing his sexual orientation. The whole process would be too traumatic.

The thing was, he didn't feel traumatized. Which made even less sense. He had dealt with rape victims when he was a constable, and there had always been a sense of powerlessness and trauma and anger and pain, involved. Why not with him?

It looked like Prue would have to wait, because he needed to sort this out, and the first step towards doing that would be to track down Joss. Find out what he knew about this whole mess. If he had any form of an explanation. Then would come finding what sounded like a fellow officer named Rob. *Manchester's finest*, as Joss put it. Finn needed to see if his reactions had been the same as his own. If his world had been shifted as much. He bet Rob would turn out to be someone about the same age and as fit as him and Joss.

Poor bastard, Joss said. Perhaps a DS like me, whose world's shifted, too? Confused, too?

Finn began to smirk at the thought. For some reason, he wanted to spend as much time as possible with Rob. To compare notes, of course. Support each other. See if they could figure out why this happened. Maybe they could even sequester themselves in his gay uncle's B&B, near Whitford Park.

For a long leisurely weekend. In a double bed. Engorging on carry-out...and the pleasure of his company. Uncle Niall wouldn't mind.

That thought brought an even more-wicked gleam to Finn's eye. Then he and Rob could go to Newcastle and face down Joss, together. Something about the man's careful choices of words and reticence in answering Finn's questions made him fairly certain there was more going on than he was saying. Especially taking into account how he'd danced around the comment of having been used in the same way as them.

Whatever had happened, they needed to dig up the reason they both had been taken, and why a man like Joss was the one doing the taking. Finn remembered he had a wife and kids. Of course, that didn't mean much; Joss could be bisexual. So they would need to guide him away from the family. To a hotel, maybe. Where they could pick his brain and drag more about the other rapes from him. He had indicated there were others, hadn't he? Other men brutalized like them.

Which sent a shiver diving straight into Finn's scrotum.

He almost hoped Joss would not be forthcoming about the other men.

Wasn't that a cute choice of words?

But it could give him and Rob *justification* to introduce their *unwilling rapist* to the joy of being on the receiving end. Show him what he'd missed by not being used like them.

Get some of our own back. Wouldn't that be fun?

Finn jolted.

A detective Sergeant as sensible and sure as he was, who knew right from wrong, without question, considering breaking a dozen sexual assault laws, *fun*?

What the hell had happened to him? Finn was not a believer in alien abductions, but something ridiculously confusing and intense had taken hold of him and he had no other rational explanation for it. All he knew for certain was, his whole way of viewing sex had been altered, and he now felt not only different and confused but also delightfully dangerous.

He heard sirens approaching. One of them an ambulance. He touched the injury behind his ear. The blood was already coagulating, and he felt no real pain. No headache. Nothing but a soft murmur of a throb. Could that have been the cause of his shift in perceptions? Did something like this happen after a concussion? Should he see a specialist to make certain he wasn't damaged more than he thought?

Yes, that had to be it. He'd been assaulted and struck unconscious, and it had scrambled his brain. He was just thinking he'd worn an undershirt, because he always did, but might not have had a clean one to change into after his shower. Of course. It all made sense, now. He'd probably feel back to normal once he'd had a checkup and good night's sleep.

Except...

A singular thought insisted on bouncing around in his mind.

Me and Rob on Joss. Yes, that would be fun.

And not one iota of his being even considered rejecting the idea.

Finn was back at CID the next day, sporting only a small bandage over his cut, which was really more of a scrape or scratch; hardly worth mentioning. The doctor couldn't even explain why he'd been found unconscious.

"Seems to have been a lucky blow, is all," was the final verdict.

Finn said nothing about the sexual assault because he was still not a hundred percent certain it had really happened. Yes, he was sore, but there was no blood. No difficulty shitting, sitting, or walking. Just a feeling that something had gone on, down there.

He'd called Prue while being tended to and explained, and she had tried very hard to hide how irritated she was.

"It would always be like this, wouldn't it?" she'd finally said. "Make no plans, just hopes."

"I'm sorry, but I am a police officer."

"I know. I knew." Then she'd sighed. "Glad you're fine."

"Thanks. Talk later?"

"Yeah. Talk later. Bye."

Then she'd rung off...and Finn had known it was over. The next time they spoke, it would be to make the break official. But he wasn't sorry.

Which made no sense to him.

He'd really wanted to be with her. Liked the idea of starting a family with her. But now that seemed like years ago. A different life, altogether. In the space of a few hours, his world had shifted in ways he still could not understand. He found himself glancing at other male officers who filled their uniforms or suits nicely, something he had specifically forbidden himself to do when working with a female officer. It was confusing, to say the least.

He was able to track Joss Hallsworth in Reading,

where he was now a Detective Chief Inspector.

He's young for that, but he was sharp in the conference.

He was told Joss was out, so left a message on the man's voicemail. Then with the desk sergeant. Then another voicemail before shifting his complete focus to Manchester.

Fortunately, it was a quiet spell in the crime area, so he spent the rest of his shift scouring inter-departmental files for an officer named Rob...only to find thirty-two of them spread throughout Manchester's recent history. After weeding through them all, he narrowed the probabilities down to three candidates. One had become a DI then transferred to the Met, in London, and now was working with New Scotland Yard. He was an attractive man of mixed race, with a strong chin, big smile and sloe eyes. But he was also well-past fifty and a grandfather.

Doubtful.

The other was a recent arrival from Brixton, who was bright, dark haired with a beard, and had a round, happy face. He was also five years younger than Finn (*one of the youngest ever to make detective sergeant,* according to reports) and could stand to lose a bit of weight.

Attractive, just not...right.

Problem was, the last good possibility was *Robert Paul Hoskins*, who had recently advanced to Detective Inspector. His photo showed a man about the same age as Finn, with strong, ruddy features, a half-smile that bordered on a smirk, deep brown eyes that were beyond intense, and russet hair cropped closer than Finn did his own.

Problem was, he'd been killed, a year earlier.

By a fellow DI named Alwyn Prym.

Who looked one hell a lot like Joss, in the photo Finn was able to scrounge up.

"Poor bastard," he'd said.

That set off all sorts of warnings in Finn's mind.

He spent the evening at CID scouring the official Coroner's report. Hoskins had been investigating a drug ring and Prym, who turned out to be a corrupt officer working with the ring, had arranged for him to be run down by a car when he got too close. The murder plot was unearthed by a fellow DI named Hannah Wilcox. Finn could tell there was much being left unsaid in the report, but one side note caught his eye.

The day before his death, Hoskins had been found unconscious in a cemetery.

It was just one short line in a separate constable's report that he'd almost not bothered to open. Now questions exploded through him. He needed to know more about that particular incident but could find nothing further about it.

And Joss never returned his calls.

He had some leave coming so put in for it as an emergency, using his break-up with Prue as his excuse.

"Just need to clear my head, sir," was what he told Blethyn, "so I'm in top shape."

Mrs. Blethyn had taken his side and he was allowed three days, not one jot more.

"Back on Monday," said Blethyn. "One never knows when murder will erupt." Pronounced *muuuuurder*, in his *BBC Agatha Christie* style. It never failed to bring a smile to Finn.

He hopped an early train for Manchester, with a change in London. He could have driven, but then he'd have had to account for the mileage and he didn't want to deal with that, just yet. Besides, it would have taken him almost as long and been a lot more tiring, while on the train he could gather his notes and thoughts and work out a plan for his inquiry.

When he arrived, he left his bag at a *Motel One* across from the station — convenient and cheap enough, now that his uncle's B&B was not in the cards — had a pint and decent fish and chips at a pub, next door, then hopped a cab for the *Greater Manchester Police-City Centre*.

He checked in at the desk and was introduced to a fellow DS named Laurence Arbuthnot, a pleasant man with a long face and thinning brown hair, sporting a thick wedding band on his pudgy finger. He asked why Finn was looking for DI Hoskins's cases.

Finn played it simple. "I'm investigating an incident and his name came up as perhaps having worked something similar. Then I heard about what happened and considered letting it be, but I began to wonder if he'd left behind any files to look through?"

"What kind 'er case?" Arbuthnot asked in his Scouse accent.

"Drugs dealing," said Finn. "I know he was working on something along those lines when he was killed."

"Yeah, we're all gutted on that."

"Of course you are. Who wouldn't be?"

"The bastard what done him. Whole life term, the divvy's got, but well-protected, inside, thanks t' his *connections*. Bloody quilt."

"Yes. Well, there was a note about another case DI Hoskins was investigating. Drugs being left in a cemetery, if I read it right. The details were minimal."

"Don't 'member that..."

"Just a couple things in the periphery. I was hoping to look through his case files, see if there was anything similar. Other notes. Comments on things to follow up with?"

"His case loads're well sacked off. Maybe somethin' in the records files, sub-level."

He led Finn down to the second sub-floor of a basement, dark and dreary and packed with shelves holding storage boxes of old cases. Arbuthnot helped Finn find a couple with files Rob had worked or been working on.

"These were jibbed on his death," he sighed. "Connected to...to what 'appened. You can look through but all over arse, they are. I'll winnow out any other cases, on-goin', but don't 'old 'ope."

"Thanks," Said Finn. "This is brilliant."

"You can stay till Carter's off duty, ar' the desk. Don't find what you need, back, t'morra."

"Perfect. I'm not set to return to my center till Friday."

Arbuthnot sauntered off and Finn spent the next four hours digging through the files...but nothing least bit interesting was found. It didn't help that Hoskins was not exactly precise in his records-keeping.

He was in the process of putting the folders back in place when he noticed a piece of paper caught under one box's corner fold. He pulled at it...and half of it tore away. So he re-emptied the box then broke it down to get the rest of the paper...and found a couple more sheets that had been ripped from a small notepad and deliberately tucked inside, as if to hide or protect them. The handwriting was rough, but he pieced it together well-enough to read:

Call from centre Lights Bevin Cem Middle of day?

Bevin Cem No lights Arsholes Prank
Why so quiet? Lights. By mausol
Here the "L" dragged off in a line, then:
WTF???? Woke up Uniforms checkin me
Hurt all over Was I hit? Fall on gravestone? Cut behind right ear Not bad
Weird fuckin' dream Prym in it?
Why? Fuckin' hate his arse an' he fucks me? Like he fucked Helen!!
Fuckin' Freud BS this
Arse hurts Sore
No y-fronts?
WTF???

Finn couldn't breathe. By the end, the scribble had become uneven and wild, but no question this was the *Rob* Joss referred to. He had also been taken and raped.

But Hoskins referred to his rapist as Prym.

The man who had him killed a year ago.

Who looked like Joss.

Finn let out a long, deep sigh and sat back, stunned. His mind was caught in chaos. He took several moments to let himself process what the notes said, then absently slipped them into his jacket pocket. It wasn't till he was carrying the boxes over to the desk that he realized he had replaced the files in them.

In order, of course.

Carter, a short squat man closing in on retirement, scowled up to him.

"Done, are ya?" he snapped, not at all happy about Finn's presence.

Finn nodded. "Caught some more notes, but nothing usable. I...I think this was a dead end. But I must say, looks like Hoskins was a good man."

Carter's scowl softened and he nodded. "One o' the best. Whenever he come down here, he brung us a cuppa. Just as I like it. Wasn't s'posed t', but he did. An' we'd chat. Gets too quiet down 'ere. Lonely. You get used t' it too fast."

"I'm sorry he's gone," whispered from Finn. He started away then stopped. "Tell me, that thing in the cemetery..."

"Cem't'ry?"

"The day before he — before it all happened. Did you

see him, at all? Talk about it?"

Carter looked at him, puzzled, then he nodded. "Arr, yeah. I 'member it now." He shook his head. "Day he died, was it? That mornin'. Come down 'ere to look up some old files. Still brought us tea. Chatted. But his mind weren't here. Did say somethin' odd, though. What were it? Somethin' like...oh, like, *How d'you know who you really are?* And he were lookin' at his pad when he said it...but not lookin' at it, know what I mean. I asked him if he were right. He sort of laughed and said, *Dunno.* Then he left. Last I saw him. Done in, that night. No one's brought me tea, since."

"May I ask where he's buried? I'd like to pay my respects."

Carter eyed him, a bit wary, then finally said, "St. Stephen's. Cremated but a proper burial. Full dress. By then we knew what'd happened. Line of duty and...and..."

He looked away to clear his throat.

Finn studied his thumbnail, in respect. Then he noticed the vague scent of whiskey and smiled. "Have you a bottle?"

Carter jolted and his scowl returned.

Finn put up his hand, to keep Carter from speaking, and said, "Toast to his memory."

Carter gave Finn a wary look that slowly shifted to a quiet conspiratorial awe. "I...I've only the one cup."

Finn smiled and whispered, "Propriety be damned."

The old man broke into a glorious grin, pulled out the bottle, poured a dram into a chipped mug, rose to his feet, and offered it.

Finn took it and said, "To Rob Hoskins, a good man."

"A good man," Carter said, holding up the bottle.

They downed their drinks at the same time, then Finn gave the mug back to Carter, saying, "Thank you, Constable Carter."

"Thank you...sir."

****

St. Stephen's was a lovely cemetery next to a canal, just outside the city center. It still took the cab half an hour to get there, thanks to GPS insisting the only way to go was down a road that had been closed for work. After five wrong turns, they finally made it in.

Finn had the cab wait as he checked at the office for Rob's grave's location, only to be informed his ashes had been interred in the mausoleum. He found the bronze marker in the building, carved with *DI Robert Paul Hoskins A Good Man Will Not Be Forgotten*. And he saw Rob had died when he was only thirty.

"Life is so bloody unfair," whispered from Finn.

He took in a deep breath, plucked a carnation from a wreath that had been laid close by, and stuck it into the top of the plaque. He smirked at himself for both his petty act of larceny and feeling so melancholy over the death of a man he'd never met. But now he knew they had a bond they could never share.

As he wandered back to the cab, Finn wondered about the others who'd been through the same thing as he and Rob. Joss's comments had suggested as much. He'd have to check. Could it have been other police officers? Men like himself? Could any of them have been killed? He hadn't heard of another officer dying in the line of duty, recently, not like happened in the States. But it still made him nervous, the similarities between his and Rob's experiences, and then the man's death.

The cab dropped him back to his hotel and he finished checking in. He could have taken a late train back to London and made the last connection to Clayton-Merrill, but he was tired. Bone tired. And sad beyond belief. He had no explanation for this except he wished he hadn't made so many childish plans for him and Rob before doing the research needed to see if they would work out.

Besides, he'd have to pay for the room, anyway.

He had a toasted sandwich and ale in the lounge, took a leisurely shower that sometimes drifted into a blankness he couldn't quite explain, wrapped himself in an oversize towel and sat propped up on the bed to dig through the notes on his laptop. But he kept coming back to that photo of Rob. And he finally realized he was feeling exactly what he'd felt when Nan had passed on.

He was at Cambridge and had come home for a bank holiday weekend to find her collapsed in the narrow kitchen, a broken mug next to her, the vague scent of death in the room. She was rigid and cold to the touch, and the tea that had been in the cup had stained its whiteness into the wooden floor; Nan had always used double sugars and a quarter milk. It was a stroke. Massive and sudden. Even with immediate treatment the coroner had doubted she'd have survived. Finn's only consolation was, she had gone quickly.

When he had finally tracked down his parents, to tell them — they were at some retreat in the Andes, and he only found that out by chance; Nan's letters had shown his father had stayed there twenty-odd years before and he'd thought the place might have an idea as to where else he might have gone – his lovely mother and father had said they knew he and his Uncles Cormac and Niall could handle everything. And so they had. And there had been no contact since.

That had almost crushed him.

It had taken Finn years to fully accept their abandonment of him to Nan's care was due only to their selfishness and not caused by him. With her death, those feelings of abandonment had flooded back, and he felt he'd lost the last of his family. He had almost ended his studies, he was so depressed...until he was handed one of those *To Be Opened By Finn, Should I Die* kind of letters. The solicitor handling the estate had forgotten about it until he was doing his last sort through the paperwork and happened upon the envelope, months later. He'd hand-carried it to Cambridge to deliver in person, along with his *most sincere apologies.*

It took Finn a week to open it...to find it was written in her very precise hand.

My Dearest Finley,

I cannot tell you how proud I am to have watched you grow from a confused sickly child - confused through no fault of your own, I might add - to a strong, healthy, handsome, intelligent young man worthy of the name I bestowed upon him. Meaning, yes, it was I who named you and not your mother or father. Since you were born with issues, I suspect they felt you would soon be gone from this world and it was not worth bothering with a christening. While I'm not a firm believer in genetics having total sway over our development, in this case I am willing to accept that you received the best genes my husband, who was truly remarkable, and I could offer — and missed those of your parents. Be glad for this. Their selfishness is not only beyond contemptible, they will never be able to exist in the real world whereas, as your name indicates, you will make it your own.

Remain strong. You are worthy of the utmost respect and admiration...and I say this despite your rather disconcerting love of "graphic novels." Comic books! Who knew they could help establish a solid foundation for one's life?

You will always be my Finley. My dearest Finn. Even when you dress in those ridiculous costumes. I may now admit that I proudly carried a photo of you in one in my purse. All blue and gold. And may I add, on more than one occasion when showing you off to a friend, while remarks were always made about your tender eyes, your healthy look, your sweet, knowing smile...more than a few also popped out about your very well-formed legs. With which I silently agreed, even though I am your grandmother.

Do NOT let yourself go to fat and lose that beauty. Do me proud.

With all my love,

Nan

He had wept for an hour after reading it. Then he'd refocused on his studies, done his third year in Berlin, since he'd also been learning German, and, upon matriculation applied to the police. He'd paid his dues at York and Brighton, where he'd achieved DS, and a year after that he'd been assigned to Clayton-Merrill.

And now he was in Manchester looking at the photo of a man he could never know and feeling the same sense of loss. Rob had the appearance of someone who came from rough, possibly a rural upbringing, but it also suggested that he'd always been strong and in control. Which was probably why he was a DI by the age of thirty. He knew who he was and where he was going.

Until Bevin Cemetery.

Then he'd also wondered if he knew himself.

"I could have discussed this with you," Finn murmured. "We could've worked together to explain it. What happened. Accept it. Found the best way to handle it, since we'd both been worked over by it. But nothing to be done about it, now."

Meaning he'd have to contact Joss on his own and see

what could be gleaned from him. After a visit to Bevin Cemetery, of course. Get a sense of the scene of the crime.

An overwhelming weariness set Finn to drifting. He felt as if he were having to start from the beginning of another murder investigation, where his suspicions had been dismantled over details that were kept secret until forced past a suspect's emotional walls. Never easy. Often demanding. He closed his laptop and leaned back to rest his eyes; it was early, yet, and he had more research he wanted to do. Plus he was still in the damp towel and did not like to sleep nude. But he was feeling too lazy to get up and pull on his sleeping shorts, so he just drifted and dozed and —

Someone was straddling his torso!

Finn's eyes jolted open to find the room completely dark and a black figure atop him. He tried to shove them off, but his hands were shackled to a corner of the bed! Before he could cry out, he was punched a couple times in his sides, startling the breath out of him, then something was shoved into his mouth and his tie was bound around his face to secure it. That made his focus shift to not vomiting into the gag.

"Why're ya here?" It was a man's voice, thick in his Midlands accent. "What the fuck're ya lookin' for?"

Finn muttered something unintelligible, trying to indicate he couldn't speak, but the man wasn't having it.

"Talk 'round the gag. Slow. Enunciate."

Finn fought back his fear and forced himself to slowly form the words, "Checking. On. Case. Like. Other. Cop."

"Rob Hoskins! I know. Askin' questions 'bout a dead copper. Messin' in his old files. Things ya don't know 'bout. Why? WHY?!"

"Case. Similar." Then he coughed.

"Similar!?" The word spat from the man. "What case? How!?"

"Cemetery."

The man froze. His tone shifted to one of curiosity. "Similar?"

Finn took a chance and said, "Blue. Light?"

The man shifted back, wary. His rear now rested on Finn's hips.

Finn was finally regaining his breath and some sort of control. He let the man think. Tried to make out his size. He was wearing a bulky coat. An Anorak? And a balaclava. And he was strong. Damn strong. He probably didn't weigh much more than Finn, himself, but it felt like solid muscle and his legs held Finn in place with what seemed like minimal effort. A hand went to where his mouth should be. He was wearing gloves, and he seemed lost.

The man leaned in, focused on Finn. "What 'bout the lights?"

"Saw. Then. Un...con...scious."

The man seems to shrink, a little. "Dream?"

Finn nodded. "Not. A. Dream. Real. You. Too?"

The man let out a long sigh and slowly climbed off Finn. He sat on the edge of the bed, shaken. Seemed not to remember Finn was shackled and gagged...not until he finally cast him a look.

"Used?"

Finn nodded.

"By...by a bloke?"

Finn nodded.

"One ya know?"

Finn hesitated...then nodded. So it *had* happened to who knows how many others. His curiosity slammed his fear aside. Now all he wanted to do was get this guy to talk and talk and talk.

But all the man said was, "Bloody fuckin' hell."

He rose and undid the tie. Finn spat out what was in his mouth...and realized it was one of his dirty socks. He gagged, gasped and choked in air and shifted his jaw as the man unlocked the shackles. He decided it was best not to say anything, right then, especially since all he'd do is croak. Instead, he sat up, grabbed a bottle of water and guzzled it all down, half gargling some of it. He vaguely noticed it was after four a-m, and that his towel had come unwrapped and he was more than half-exposed. He pulled the towel back in place and made himself sit on the side of the bed. He was still shaky but in control.

The man stood over Finn, watching the whole time, then he collapsed on the floor, cross-legged, and looked up at him, in a combination of confusion and relief as he pulled off his mask.

It was Robert Paul Hoskins.

****

Neither Finn nor Hoskins said a word for the next five minutes. Instead, Finn heated water and made tea to give himself time to wrap his brain around this new reality. It wasn't easy; his mind was whirling so fast, he had to remind himself he was close to naked and should pull on his sleeping shorts and an undershirt. He did so while the kettle heated, then he fixed two cups and set them on the floor beside the man. He took the tray with the little tubs of milk and sugars and positioned it next to the cups, his eyes locked on Hoskins, then sat across from him and leaned back against the bed. Waiting.

Throughout, the man watched him like a wary but curious feral cat. Half lost in thought but ready to hiss and scratch at the least excuse. It wasn't until he picked up the hot cup by its bowl and burned himself that he jolted and snapped, "Bloody fuckin' hell!"

Finn almost smiled. "Careful. It's hot."

"Oh, yeah?" Then he huffed and let a half grin come to his lips as he shifted around to lean against the bed, next to Finn. "Shite. If I had my head about me, I'd of known that." He fixed his tea with two raw sugars and three tubs of milk. Finn did one sugar and the last of the milk. Only when they'd both sipped some did Hoskins say, "I hadn't found anything 'bout you. When'd it happen?"

"Couple days ago."

"Bloody hell. Ya work fast, findin' me. Findin' out 'bout me." He sipped more tea. Finally, he asked, "Were it that easy?"

"For a cop."

Hoskins nodded. "What do I call ya?"

"I'm DS — "

"I know you're a DS, right? And I know your name; I saw your warrant card. But I...I'm...what do I call ya? Finley? James? *Mr.* Winterbourne?"

"Finn's good."

"*Finn.* Right." He let steam from the tea whisper into his face and cast Finn a sideways glance. "You're posh for a DS, ain't ya?"

"What's that supposed to mean?"

"Nothin'. Just yammerin'." After a moment, "Rob,"

drifted from him. Then he murmured, "So it was Monday, Tuesday?"

"Tuesday. Why?"

"We got to make ya safe."

"What do you mean?"

"You're runnin' on borrowed time. I know of three other men, besides you and me. Two died the day after....after it happened. Me and one other, we almost got it, too. Almost."

"Died!?"

"Oh, no, not him, not to him," Joss said.

Rob nodded. "One in a car wreck; the other in a home fire."

"One other survived?"

Rob nodded. "Almost drowned. I'm with him up...up North Scotland. On the islands. We been piecin' it together since I...since I almost...I was almost..." He focused on his tea.

"How did you get away with that? Everyone thinks you're dead."

Rob let out a sharp laugh. "I damn near was, but I come to on the table as the Coroner started to cut me open." He pulled off the Anorak and tugged the neck of his shirt down to show a short scar at the base of his sternum. "Scared the shite out of him. He's a mate of mine. Knew what I was goin' through — "

"He knew about all this?"

"No! Other crap. I hadn't looked into what happened with me, yet. So we worked it out. Unclaimed cadaver. Wax mask of me face. Makeup and blood. I were all mashed up so nobody got close but him. Hid me in Leeds."

"With your injuries?"

"Fixed me good enough to give him time. Knew a surgeon there, took care of the rest."

"I find that difficult to believe."

"Do I look dead?"

"No, but still, that's very elaborate for spur of the moment."

"I was in the morgue two days. On a slab. Sedated. He did it up right."

"And violated half a dozen laws, in the process."

"To protect me! He thought Prym might have a go at

me, again."

"But now the man's imprisoned for life, over murder."

Rob shot a harsh glare at Finn. "Ya gonna weep for him?"

Finn sighed. "I don't know the particulars of the case."

A sharper laugh exploded from Rob. "You talk like Queen's Counsel."

"I hold a degree in law."

Still chuckling, Rob shook his head. "Oh, you *are* posh."

"Will you stop calling me that?!"

Rob looked at him, a genuine smile on his face. "Sorry, but ya got the look of *The City* about ya. I mean, I saw your suit and...and look at how ya talk and...and I...I'm just happy."

Finn was incredulous. "At learning I was also assaulted?"

"Relieved. I know it's mad, but I...I was so bloody scared. Even lookin' at ya lyin' there, asleep...I didn't know what to think or do or anything. I...I'm wonderin' if I been found out and ya were sent after me." He took Finn's hand and touched where the shackles had scraped into his skin, then gave Finn a look of contrition. "That's why I..."

"I understand. I'd probably have done the same."

Rob smiled his thanks. "You're right, y'know. It's a funny way to put it, but I am glad to know somebody else who's lived through it."

"Not funny, in the least. I was hoping the same. But you mentioned another man..."

"Stu. He's a case. He's got a few year on you and me, but what happened...it's messed with him, awful. Fact is, I wouldn't even have come down here were he not in jail."

"He's in jail?"

Rob nodded. "He'll be there till I'm back."

"What's his charge?"

"Oh, nothin'. He...he's just mates with the DCI, and he lets him stay, is all. He feels safe, there."

Finn leaned his head back on the bed. "Christ, every comment you make raises a hundred questions in my mind. I'm more confused than ever about what happened. There's the man who used you and the one who used me. How are they part of this? And why aren't they also dead, if that's an aspect of it? And how *could* it happen the way it happened, with people we know?"

"If ya want answers, I ain't got 'em. Nothin' 'bout this bloody story makes sense. But tell ya what, *City Boy*." He looked at Finn, slung an arm around his neck and pulled him close. "You tell me yours and I'll tell ya mine. Maybe we'll find a way of workin' it out."

Then his deep brown eyes bore into Finn's and he kissed him, full on the lips.

And to Finn's shock...and joy...he kissed him back.

****

They didn't get on the bed. They didn't even undress, not completely. Their lips locked, Rob groped Finn under his shorts as Finn unzipped the man's jeans. Rob didn't even remove his shirt, just pulled it up so the hair on his chest could caress Finn's pecs as their tits connected with little shocks. Rob wore bright blue y-fronts so his dick was hard to release, especially since he was ready to go, by that point. But Finn managed and they ground against each other like wild animals.

Finn couldn't believe the powerhouse sensations screaming through him, and from Rob's grunts and growls he could tell he wasn't the only one feeling them. Fingers dug into skin and traced down backs and groped asses and brushed over thighs to swirl around balls and stroke dicks, driving them both close to madness until Rob grabbed Finn's wrists and pinned his arms above him, to the floor. Finn could have freed himself with no trouble, but the look on Rob's face was so harsh and raw and needy, he kept still...well, as still as he could.

"I dunno why," Rob gasped between heavy breaths, "but I want...ever since Prym buggered me, I've wanted...wanted...but Stu won't...he...he...will you?"

All Finn could do was nod.

Rob released him. They maneuvered his jeans off his rear, and Finn found his cheeks were so smooth and cool to the touch, so nice and round and even, he didn't need to see them in order to know they were gorgeous. Rob sat back, positioned his ass against Finn's groin and gripped his dick. Finn was harder than he'd ever been, before, and Rob's own erection was pointing straight at his face, gleaming and ready, its head ripe and round and red, his circumcision scar giving it a two-tone look.

Finn pulled at Rob's cheeks, making him groan. The man guided Finn's dick to his rectum. And slipped it in. And sat back onto it. And gulped in pain and discomfort but did not stop until Finn's pubes tickled against his scrotum, then he closed his eyes in wonder and awe.

To Finn, the feel of himself inside Rob was overpowering in its perfection, something he had never experienced with a woman. He had loved them and enjoyed them and sought them, but this? This was euphoria.

They remained still, like that, for a moment, then Finn grinned and gave a light little push up into Rob, who let out a gasp of shocked joy and pushed back and began to rock him in and back and in and back as Finn toyed with Rob's nips and his own were pinched and mauled by Rob's strong yet tender hands in ways that sent shrieks of joy through his entire body.

Rob traced his fingers over every inch of Finn's torso while his scrotum rubbed up and down Finn's treasure trail and his nice fat dick bounced around in ecstasy. His groans became animalistic in their need and passion while Finn just breathed harder and deeper at the growing want engulfing him. His fingers dug into Rob's sides then his thighs then his ass then his nips then his chest and back to his thighs in ways that grew more and more demanding, over and over for what seemed like seconds or hours of total bliss until Rob jolted and howled and shot hot streams of cum onto Finn's belly, chest and face as his ass tightened around Finn's dick in in a way that was so sudden and startling and massive, Finn's balls screamed and crashed into him in complete abandon as he also let loose. Like he had when Joss fucked him. Filling Rob like Joss had him. And he was so overwhelmed by the exquisite release, he nearly passed out.

Rob slowly folded down upon Finn, releasing his dick, and did not move, for several minutes, his face nestled next to Finn's, his chest smearing the semen into their torsos.

Finn slipped his arms around him to hold him close. Brushed his cheek against Rob's thick-cropped hair.

Caressed his strong jaw and powerful neck and felt more complete than he ever had with any woman. Rob reacted to his touch like a cat enjoying having its ears scratched.

"I think I'll need another wash," Finn finally murmured, still lost in wonder at what had just happened.

Rob chuckled and shifted to rub his nose against Finn's ear. "So bloody City."

Finn joined his chuckle with, "Stop it. I've an uncle works there. One of the banks, high up. Mates from university, too. Me? I'm just a copper."

A near purr echoed from deep within Rob. "Good copper. Nice copper. Room enough for two in that shower?"

"Let's find out."

Rob whispered a groan as he murmured, "Not just yet. I like bein' here. Like the feel of ya under me. So peaceful, like. So right."

Finn ran his hands down Rob's back, almost purring. "You can stay here forever, if you want."

"That wouldn't do us much good, would it?"

"Then how about till it's your turn to do the buggering?"

Rob drew in a deep breath and chuckled. "Dunno what I got left. But I'd like to. Fit body. Very fine legs."

Finn laughed. "That's what my Nan said."

Rob shifted to caress Finn's ear with his lips. "Your governess noticed your legs?"

"Grandmother. And friends of hers."

"Oooooooooh...sounds kinky."

"Nothing like that! I didn't find out till after she was gone."

Rob traced his fingers over Finn's lips. "Well, they were right. She was. I looked your legs over 'fore I jumped ya. Lyin' there. Even in the dark, they showed good form. Thought a thousand things 'bout 'em."

"That sounds just a bit stalker-like. Almost rape-y."

"Yeah. Confusin's what it is. I notice that about blokes, now. Never did before. But now I check out if they're fit. Wonder what they look like under their clothes. Think about ways...about ways to get them. Get them to be with me."

"I've noticed that in myself, as well. A complete

change in focus. Sexual orientation. Which makes zero sense."

"No shite on that."

"Did you ever...*do* anything about it?"

Rob grunted a *No*. "Ain't much gonna happen, where I am. And I needed to keep a low profile, so..."

"You were saving yourself for me?" He gave Rob a soft wink.

Rob propped himself up on his elbows and caressed Finn's face. "I like the way ya look. How *City* ya are." Finn almost protested but a finger to his lips silenced him. "But not *City*. Too aware for that. Too caring. Skin so smooth. Not too much hair; just the right amount. Angelic face touched with scruff."

"Only because I have to shave, morning and evening."

"But it feels right. Manly. Gives your cheeks character." He leaned on one arm and caressed Finn's profile with his other hand's fingers, light and tender and almost in awe. "If I'd known about ya, I might of come lookin'. Warn ya. Maybe brought Stu with me."

"That would have been...interesting."

"Not for this. It's just...I almost think he might be open to talkin' with ya."

"Hasn't he told you what happened to him?"

"Not much. Just enough. I dunno why, but he stops an' panics when it gets too intense. I *do* think you'd do better than me, 'cause you're as posh as him and — "

"Christ, am I *City* or am I *posh*? Can't be both."

"Why not?" Rob grinned. "I'd still of let ya bugger me."

He leaned in to trace his lips up over Finn's cheek and around to his mouth to kiss him so tenderly and sweetly, Finn ached for him.

When they finally moved apart, Finn could not help but whisper, "I'm glad you're not dead."

Rob chuckled and nuzzled Finn's lips. "So am I."

"I'll do everything I can to protect you. Both you and Stu. Keep you alive."

Rob looked straight into Finn's eyes, his face caught in a thousand emotions, from joy to fear to pleasure to need to even a fair amount of respect, and he nodded.

"So will I, you, *City Boy*. So will I."

A Journey North

There was plenty of room in the shower for them to jostle and goose each other like schoolboys, squirting dollops of shower gel from a dispenser to wash each other's front and back. Gentle suds whispered down gleaming skin and coursed through light hair, followed by playful caresses and happy embraces. Finn saw multiple scars on Rob's lovely torso and caressed them with tenderness as he told Rob everything he'd been through, then Rob shared more of his own time in the nothing room. It mirrored Finn's in every way...except for the man raping him.

Prym had been on the force for some time, so Rob not only knew him well, but hated his guts.

"He were a double-dealin', back-stabbin' bastard," he said as he rinsed soap off Finn's back, "so I were goin' near mad tryin' to figure out why he...why he did to me like were done to you. Said he were sorry, sure, but I knew bloody fuckin' well he weren't. Y'see, him an' Hannah...well, she and I were together when he went after her."

"After her?"

"The bloody quilt fucked her, and her...dammit, she knew I didn't trust him, but still she let him have her because *she was pissed at me for bein' so focused on the case* an' *she was horny* an'...an' all kinds of bollocks. All of it were tearin' me up.

"Then while I'm in hospital, I'm tryin' to figure out what to do, next, when I hear this other patient talkin' about a lad who'd been found knocked out in a field. His name's Finn, too. In his twenties, he was, but a punter. Died in a wreck tryin' to get away from the cops. Him, he was found by his brother just outside town, near a copse. He thought the little bastard got clocked over a bad drug deal, but he were actin' strange. Not all there. Talked about blue lights.

His brother thinks there were damage done to his brain, and that's why he led pursuit on the chase. I pieced the timin' together, and his death matched mine. Twenty-four hours. Thought it might be coincidence, at first, but it got me thinkin'. Lookin' 'round. Cross-referencin' online and newspapers. Located a cop in Munich, found on a riverbed in the city. Said somethin' 'bout blue lights takin' him."

"How'd you find out? Which paper?"

"*Süddeutsche Zeitung*. I know some German."

"*Oh, as do I*," said Finn, in German.

"*That's weird*. Anyway, his house burned down thanks to a faulty coffee maker. Twenty-four hours later."

"But it's been more than twenty-four hours since my assault, so these sound coincidental. Merely accidents."

"One, maybe. But both? On top of Stu and me?" Rob shook his head. "So where were ya, twenty-four hours after it happened?"

"At CID in Clayton-Merrill...which is very well protected." He turned the nozzle of water onto Rob's back to rinse him off. "What about the man who...who *used* you?"

Rob stretched his arms over his head, murmuring, "Prym."

"Did you find anything similar for him?"

"Not from what I can tell, but he were a sneaky bastard, and he's still alive. Yours? Joss?"

Finn rubbed Rob's ass with his free hand, guiding water over it with the shower nozzle, enjoying the feel of his form as he said, "The closest I noticed in regards to an attack on him was a kidnapping during a murder investigation, where he was struck unconscious. Nothing about lights or calls."

"When's that, exactly?"

"Oh...I have it in my notes. About three years ago."

"That punter in Leeds were killed two years back."

Finn ran the shower nozzle up Rob's back. "Which sounds even more coincidental, because Joss was in Newcastle, at the time. He's moved on to Reading. As a DCI. If I hadn't connected with you, I'd have gone down to find him. Sound him out."

Rob stretched like a happy cat as Finn smoothed the water over his skin. "I wonder if it's a good idea, now."

"You may be right. Tell me more about Stu."

"Like I said, he's friends with a DCI," said Rob. "Near drowned, he did. Ferry got hit by a rogue wave and he got washed overboard with four others. Missin' seventy-two hours, he was, and presumed dead." He took the nozzle away, put it back on its hook and pulled Finn close. His hands trailed down Finn's back. "That's why I decided not to come back, once I were healed. There was somethin' weird goin' on, and I didn't want to give whoever's behind it a second go at me. But Hannah were gonna have a baby, and if it'd been mine...well, I might still've chanced it. But me mate snuck a DNA test of her..."

"How was that possible?"

"Her last checkup 'fore the birth. He got the GYN to take a sample of the placenta and...and it weren't mine. So I told him I wanted to stay dead. He weren't happy 'bout it, but couldn't say anything. That's when I went up Scotland. Connected with Stu."

"Did you jump him as you did me?"

"No. First glance told me he weren't doin' well, with it. Him, I stalked. Let him see me. Took a week 'fore I even tried to talk with him. I think...well, it seemed like when he finally noticed me, he knew. An' he got spooked. Took another week for him to believe I hadn't come to hurt him. Then he held me. Like I'm holdin' you. That's all. No...he clung to me. Like I were a life preserver.

"He's got it in his head that if he's outside alone, they might come back for him. So he never is. And by outside, I mean out in the open. His garage is attached to his house. He don't leave unless he's in his car, an' he don't get out of his car unless he's talkin' to someone. He's got a daughter he shares with that DCI. Good cop but kind of thick about things. First time I met him, I thought he and Stu were...well, I figured it was a *my two dads* kind of thing. But Stu's a *Jack-the-lad* who never grew past it. And he never said word one to that DCI; he's got a bit of remove from him. And from me, still."

Rob leaned against Finn, sighing. "Except...he likes me to hold him, at night."

"Nothing more?"

Rob lay his head in the crook of Finn's neck. "Told ya. An' I haven't pushed it. We've been watchin' each other's back, since, but it's been hard. His legs an' arse are killer. Good thing I'm a good wanker."

Finn pulled on Rob's dick, playful, making him laugh, then asked, "No questioning by the locals? About you and him?"

"Put me over as his cousin." He cast Finn a crooked smile. "I'm still Rob, but last name's Haller. Same initials. Worked out well. Got me papers set up with that and everything. The locals think I just come up to use his crap cottage outside Leryll. Build furniture. Which I do. Sell it in Aberdeen. Not much of an income, but it works well enough." He caressed Finn's face and gave a soft chuckle. "Barely know ya an' it's my life story."

"I'm glad to hear it."

"Even though I attacked ya."

"Understandable."

Rob laughed as he said, "You are so very *City*."

Finn chuckled. "Stop it."

They turned off the water and got out to towel each other dry.

"How did you find me?" Finn asked.

"Got a text from me mate, said ya were lookin' into what happened, with me, an' you'd come here. Just made the plane for Edinburgh an' drove down. Couple phone calls as *DCI Richards* an' I got ya." He cast Finn a soft glance. "Ya went to me grave."

"It seemed the right thing to do."

"Thanks."

"You came down here on your own."

"But 'round people. Till I got in your room. Ya sleep real sound."

"God, I don't snore, do I?"

"No...sort of purr..."

"Oh, thank you for that," Finn growled.

"I watched ya for a moment. Lyin' there. So young an' innocent."

"We're practically the same age!"

"But I look it. Hannah said I was born thirty. I believed her. I looked it when I was sixteen. She said I'd look it till I died." He snorted a laugh. "Who knew how right she'd be?"

"How did you get into my room without me hearing?"

"Clerk downstairs. Made like I was drunk an' lost me key, flirted a little, give her your name an' room number."

"How'd you know it?"

"I'm parked on the street, below. Saw you in a window. Not hard to work out. Crossed over with a group of university kids."

Finn whipped the towel around Rob's rear to draw him close. "Well, no need for them, now. I'll not leave your side."

Rob laughed and twisted and slung Finn onto the bed, face up, then jumped on top of him. And kissed him with an intensity that sent shock waves through him. And murmured, "I think I'd like my turn, now. Ya up for it?"

Finn ran his hands down Rob's back and over his ass and around to fondle his dick and balls...and found Rob was growing...and growing...and Finn took in a deep breath. "Yes, I am."

Rob crushed him with a kiss and got down to it.

And to Finn's vague surprise, he loved every moment.

****

After another quick wash, they dressed — Rob now wearing a clean pair of Finn's boxer-briefs and undershirt, which fit him snug but looked amazingly gorgeous — then they had a fry-up in the café and got to Rob's car just as a traffic warden was about to write a ticket. Finn used his warrant card to send her on her way, but not before she gave them both a knowing smirk and shake of her head.

Over breakfast, Finn had used his laptop to look up the German police officer who died – Willem Schröder. This led him to two other men with similar stories, a Police Detective named Christian Hauptmann, in Hamburg, who'd been found passed out by a statue in Munich; and an architect named Bernado Allemenes, in Buenos Aires. He had been found unconscious while overseeing a project in Patagonia. Both were still alive, long after their respective occurrences.

"All around the same age as us, when it happened," Finn had murmured.

"Argentina might be a bit far to check out," Rob had said before loading a fork full of beans into his mouth.

Munching on a slice of toast, Finn's response had remained soft and inattentive. "When I return to Clayton-Merrill, I'll find a way to contact them."

Rob had stopped chewing. "Ya goin' back?"

"Yes."

"But that'll give 'em a clear shot at ya."

Finn had looked straight at Rob. "Not if you're with me."

Rob had put his fork on his half-finished plate. "I can't leave Stu. It's like I'm...I'm responsible for him, now."

Finn had been a bit taken aback. "Might he join us?"

"Clayton-Merrill? South of England from the North of Scotland?" Rob had shrugged. "I can't see it."

"But at CID I'll have the resources I need to get in contact with these other men. Perhaps find more. Sound them out about their experiences."

Rob had given him a sexy grin. "All the salacious details?"

Finn had cast him a shy smile. "I seriously doubt anything they say will equal what you and I have just done."

Rob had shifted Finn's laptop around to look at the information and chuckled, "Christian's a real lad; I wouldn't mind interrogatin' him. But Bernardo? Reminds me too much of Prym."

Finn had nodded, sipping his tea, noting the man looked rather like Joss, as well.

They drove up the M61, Rob doing the speed limit and no faster. Neither of them spoke, but Finn found himself casting appreciative glances at the man beside him. The strength in his arms. The beauty of his hands. His sharp well-defined profile, from forehead to chin and neck. The way his belly was flat, even slouched in his seat. How his legs filled his jeans just right. The whole sensation of just watching him overwhelmed Finn in ways no woman ever had, no matter what her beauty.

He didn't understand it, but the truth was, even Prue was like a piece of a puzzle he'd been trying to work out. Something he figured was meant to be. Now he could see she was more of an abstract. A concept rather than a living breathing creature he wanted to become one with. Build a family with. Rob, however...Finn's connection to him was so intense and all-encompassing, he knew he'd die before letting anything happen to him.

He'd only felt this strongly about one other person in his life — Nan. Because he knew she felt the same way about him. Once, when a fifth form boy he knew, a lad named Trevor, had insultingly suggested Finn was really her bastard child, he had beaten the lying little creep to near unconsciousness...and had been unremorseful when dragged into the head's office.

Nan had arrived shortly after to hear the details. Of course, they were presented in such a way as to make Finn seem a vicious aggressor against an innocent youth.

Her response? She had calmly asked, "So you have no problem with one of your pupils insulting the legal guardian of another pupil? These are the values you instill in your classrooms?"

"Mrs. Winterbourne, Finn's actions far outweighed Trevor's unfortunate comment."

"*Unfortunate comment.* Calling me a whore was merely *unfortunate.* How interesting."

"He is being dealt with."

"Well, considering who his parents are, I know nothing will come of it. What do you plan to do about Finn?"

"An incident such as this calls for expulsion..."

At that last word, Nan had locked her fingers together, and leaned against his desk, and grown very still, her eyes boring into him. The man had actually seemed to shrink, before her.

"*Normally* calls for expulsion," the head had said, quickly. "But in this case, I think two week's suspension is sufficient punishment."

Nan had grown even more still, if that were possible.

The head had actually blushed as he'd stammered, "Which I will cut to one week, since he's not been trouble, before."

Without a word, Nan had stood up, taken Finn by the hand and led him back to their semi-detached home, where she'd fed him ice cream and cake.

"Nice to know you've some of me in you," she'd said, her eyes sparkling with mischief.

A month later, he and Nan were in a Sainsburys when

they saw Trevor and his mother. Finn had wanted to ignore them, but Nan had pushed her cart straight up to them, dragging Finn with her, and said, "Hello, I hear your son thinks me a whore. I have little doubt he got that idea from you, and that you're happy to spread that lie even further. So I've had my DNA tested, along with Finn's and his parents', and it proves he is *their* child, not mine. In fact, his genetic makeup is quite remarkable, to the extent they've asked for more so they can study his structure. Now...I wonder if you would be so brave as to have yours and Trevor's tested along with his father's? Especially considering some of the stories *I've* heard."

Then she had led him away. And he'd heard not one more word about it.

What was remarkable was, he and Trevor had become very good friends, after that, and remained in touch. He now managed a new Morrison's in Sheffield, had grown quite round and happy, was married to a woman just as round and happy as he, and they had four daughters, all of whom were...yes...round and happy.

He smiled at thinking about them.

Rob noticed and grinned, "Wonder what's goin' on in the *City Boy*'s head."

Finn chuckled. "Thinking of an old friend. His family."

"Lots of friends, have ya?"

Finn nodded...then his smile vanished and he looked at Rob. "What about you? All your friends in Manchester, and family..."

Rob's expression grew stony and he said, "I've got a new life, now."

"Rob, it looks like not everyone who's been through this has died. Perhaps these other occurrences *were* coincidences."

"Won't know till we've figured it all out, will we?"

"It's just...I like where I am. Settled in. And I did mean it — you...you could join me. I'd get a cottage. You could build your furniture."

Rob let out his sharp laugh. "Haven't even known me twelve hours and askin' me to move in?"

Finn looked away with a sigh. "Right. It's madness. But I feel connected to you. Which is even crazier, isn't it?"

Rob shrugged. "What about Stu?"

"He's part of this and...and you don't think he'll want to move. Sorry, I didn't think it through and..."

"Finn...I like the idea, but no need to make a decision now, is there? Let's talk more on it, later."

Finn nodded and the rest of the drive was in silence. He decided he'd said too much too quickly, which was unlike him. Besides, Rob was right; they barely knew each other, despite the sex. Best to wait on making such a major decision. Think on it.

But...Finn could still hold out hope.

****

They returned the car and just made the last flight of the day to the island. It was in a small prop-job with single seating on each side, and the ride was not without turbulence, but soon they had landed and were hopping into Rob's 4x4. They drove through a winding village jammed along a narrow road that curved straight up to the police station, an old two-story building that looked like a councilor's office. Rob hurried in to get Stu as Finn waited in the truck, after moving to the rear seat.

He lazed across it, idly gazing down a short hillside to a harbor of fishing boats and pleasure craft along a recently renovated set of piers. The tide was in and the water calm under a soft blue sky barely touched with clouds. Few people were about, mostly squat solid creatures who could survive whatever life threw at them, and the breathtaking silence was so all-encompassing, when another SUV went roaring past it startled him.

Rob finally exited with Stu, who was shorter than him, had thinning silver and black hair, and a scruff of salt-and-pepper beard on a square chin, highlighting a fine mouth. His taut body would be fit for any man and his legs were full and well-formed in his jeans. He even had a hint of a strut in his walk, but his eyes gave the impression of a boy who'd just been struck and didn't want to be hit, again.

When he saw Finn, Stu stopped and grabbed at Rob's arm, pulling him away from the 4x4 until Rob told him, "He's the one I told ya 'bout; one of us." Then he had to add, "I checked him out; it's true."

Stu kept a wary gaze on Finn then said in a light burr,

"I'm in back."

Finn nodded and moved into the front passenger seat. He knew this was so Stu could keep an eye on him.

They drove over rolling hills covered in green and brown, the North Sea glistening in nearly every direction Finn looked. The area felt peaceful beyond belief. Life as it might have been lived a hundred years ago.

They arrived at an old cottage that was long and slung low. Slate roof. Whitewashed walls made of cut stone with chimneys jutting up at each end. Small, dark windows in black frames and two short, black doors. A near ramshackle garage with double-wide entrance was attached in the rear. Wild grass surrounded it, highlighting the piles of aged wood and kindling for a fireplace as well as a rusting tractor and other farm equipment. A rutted dirt drive led up to the garage; behind it was a round hill five times its height. The place looked so much liked a hideaway, Finn almost laughed.

Rob stopped before the garage and nudged Finn. "Help me?"

They got out and dragged the garage doors open, then Stu drove the 4x4 in. They pulled the doors shut and near darkness enclosed them, cut through only by tight shafts of light dancing through splits and holes in the walls.

They wandered into the house through the kitchen, and its interior was more modern than Finn expected. Electric stove. Refrigerator. Power outlets. Countertop appliances. All the utensils in their proper place. The main room had cozy chairs flanking a couch before an open fireplace. Lamps were available for light, and the walls had simple monochrome photographs framed in black, to cut the whiteness between the windows.

Stu went straight to a cupboard and pulled out a bottle of whiskey then poured himself a glass. He motioned to it for Finn, who shrugged a *yes*. A glance at Rob brought a nod, so Stu got two more glasses and poured a dram into each.

Finn held his glass up, half-forced a smile and said, "To new friends, soon to be old acquaintances."

Stu eyed him, raised his glass and downed his shot, as did Rob. Finn sipped half of his, making Rob chuckle and nudge him, "So *City*."

Stu glanced between them and leaned on a stool by the kitchen counter. "Yer together."

Rob jolted then went to him, put his hands on his shoulders and said, "We're *all* together."

Stu eyed him and nodded then looked at Finn. "Ye really been through it?"

Finn responded with a light shrug in the affirmative and downed the rest of his whiskey, afraid to say anything for fear he'd spook the man.

Stu slipped a hand around Rob's neck and touched foreheads, but his eyes remained on Finn. "When?"

It took Finn a moment to reply. "This Tuesday, past." Then he made himself add, "I'm not here to take Rob away from you."

Stu did not move, just whispered, "Tell us yer story."

Finn took in a deep breath then motioned to the bottle. Stu nodded, so he poured himself another glass.

And told him everything.

Stu frowned when Finn described Joss and had him go into greater detail, but he said nothing more until Finn ended at the point where Rob had jumped him.

Stu looked at Rob, hurt. "Ye were taking a risk."

Rob shrugged. "I had to know. Can't be dead if someone's sniffin' out you ain't."

Stu nodded, turning his sad, wary, ice blue eyes on Finn. The impression he gave was of a child seeking forgiveness from an angry parent.

Finn rounded the counter and squatted before him. "I am still a police officer," he said, soft and easy. "Sworn to serve and protect. I will do everything I can to make this right."

"Not possible," Stu snorted, but his wariness was drifting away. He continued with, "The man ye described...who assaulted ye...he's like...he looks like the one who...the one with me."

Rob blinked and pulled away, his eyes locked on Stu. "Yours had the same look? When Finn described him, he looked like Prym but I thought it coincidence. Now with yours?"

Finn rose as he said, "Could they possibly be the same man?"

Stu shook his head. "No, no, mine was an...an old mate

from university. He'd been with men. Called himself ambisexual, he did." His eyes drifted, lost in memory. "Martin Lowenstein."

"But why is that, I wonder? What's the significance in having them all look alike?"

"Dunno," said Rob. "Don't care. I'm more concerned they tried to kill us."

"But it shows we've been researched," said Finn. "Not randomly selected. We were lured to a spot where we could be taken without witnesses and our acquaintance with a person who has a specific appearance was used to complete it. There's a sort of connection here; there must be."

"I've gone over it for the last year, Finn. Found nothin'."

"Now there's three of us looking at the issue, each with the same basic experience. I'm a fresh pair of ears for yours. Perhaps I'll notice something you missed. It's worth a go."

"If you're game, I am," said Rob, "but..." He cast a wary glance at Stu.

Stu's eyes shifted between Finn and Rob, then he closed them, took in a deep breath and shrugged. *"Once more into the breech, dear friends?"* He rose from the stool, crossed to the liquor cabinet and pulled out a liter bottle of Irish Whisky, saying, "I reveal better on a polluted mind."

****

The three of them spent well into the evening going over every detail of their encounters in the nothing-room. Finn made coffee to dollop his whiskey into; Stu and Rob drank theirs straight. By teatime they were all feeling the effects, but Finn was still somewhat coherent. He found eggs, cheese, bread and butter and worked up a massive French-toast omelet, which they devoured as they went over what they'd learned.

All three were assaulted by men who looked similar. All three had their semen taken in the same way. They'd also been out of doors and alone when the figure and blue lights came, Stu having been called to another of his properties near Terlich. Then twenty-four hours later, Stu had been on a ferry that was hit by a rogue wave, leaving four dead.

"I was considered a fifth casualty," Stu said, fighting to keep from sounding like he was drunk. "Current carried me to another island. Only person I could find was a man who hated the world. No phone or telly. Had to wait till his groceries was delivered to make me way back to Leryll."

"This shows the accidents were merely coincidental," Finn said. "No one can predict the future, especially as regards when ocean waters will erupt into something dangerous. Yours, Rob — the attempt to kill you probably came after Prym realized you hadn't been thrown off or neutralized by your attack. The young man in Leeds — "

"Fin-baaaar," said Rob, just as drunk as Stu.

"Yes, he was in trouble with the law and tried to escape them by doing something that never works and often results in catastrophe. The officer in Munich...while we don't yet know the particulars of the case, he might have lived in an older building with bad wiring, or had an appliance that shorted or even set the fire, himself. It's not uncommon to have thoughts of suicide after a sexual assault."

"Know ye anything of the other lad in Munich?" asked Stu.

Finn shook his head. "What we have gleaned is minimal. His name's Christian Hauptmann, another police officer."

"Four cops of six victims ain't coincidence," Rob growled.

"Or seven, with Argentina," said Stu, absently, making Rob nod.

"This is true," said Finn, "but Hauptmann is situated in Hamburg and is still alive. He was only visiting Munich."

"This description of our assailants," Rob growled. "Bloody generic, it is. Tall, dark hair, trim, good-lookin'. *Familiar*. But ya'd only met your Joss once, at a conference. I known mine for years, while Stu's...he ain't seen him since....since...?"

"More'n ten year," Stu said, nodding, fighting to act like he wasn't drunk out of his mind. "He married, second year of uni."

Finn frowned. "Does he have any children?"

"Aye, three. Swap cards at Christmas."

"And you have a daughter. What about you, Rob?"

"None I know of, but Prym's got one, now. Daughter."

"Joss has a wife and five, last I heard. Stu, do you have a photo of your assailant?"

"Nothing recent," said Stu in a sing-song. "Let's Google him." He sat in front of his laptop and hummed a tuneless melody as he searched, and found, Martin Lowenstein on the web. A photo showed a happy, beefy, dark-haired man with his fair-haired wife, two dark-haired sons and a fair-haired daughter.

Stu blinked and moved closer to the screen, to get a better view. "That's how he looks? Has to be an old picture. He was always so fit."

Finn frowned then searched up a photo of Joss from the Police files.

Stu nodded. "That's closer to what he was like when he. When...when he..." His voice trailed off and he grew tense. Rob put a hand on his shoulder and he leaned back against it.

Finn noticed and hesitated then gently asked, "When was your attack, Stu?"

It took him a moment to say, "It's been three year and..." He began to gasp.

Rob crouched down to wrap his arms around him. Held him tight. Stu's hands gripped his arms closer.

Finn sighed, shaken. "You were on your own with this for two years before Rob found you?"

Stu couldn't look at him. He choked out, "Thought it was just me. That I'd imagined it. Or...or put one on and...and got into something crazy. Not exactly what ye share 'round the table, is it? Till I met Rob and...and...he showed me there's others and...I'm still...still..." He was shaking.

Finn squatted next to him, saying, "Stu, listen to me. It's all right. You were the victim of a vicious assault. As were Rob and myself. And as you can now see, your reaction at the time was hardly something you could control."

Stu gasped out, "Wasn't it?"

"If you'd been shot, instead, would it have been your fault that you were injured?"

Stu almost smiled at him and gave a slight shake of his

head, murmuring, "Dunno that I appreciate the analogy."

Rob barked a laugh. "I do! Because it's mad as hell, this is." He bolted up to pace. "Men with children assaultin' and killin' men without? Or one man pretendin' he's them to do it? That makes for a bloody mess."

"We're missing something, here," said Finn, rising. "Something probably so obvious we can't see it."

"My vote's for alien probes," Rob snickered.

"Yeah, right," said Finn. "That's why they need a man to bugger us; they're not advanced enough to get what they want, without it."

"Maybe they're makin' porn. Kinky. Psychotic. Bi-curious."

"No, it's something else," said Finn, not catching the jokiness of Rob's comment.

"There's always...a government...conspiracy." Stu said, back in control but still barely able to form the words.

Finn looked at him. "Were you struck when this happened? Injured in any way, other than sexual?"

Stu nodded and put his hand behind his right ear.

Rob shrugged. "Yeah, I got hit in the same spot."

Finn pulled off the bandage covering his injury. "Tell me what you see, in mine."

Stu staggered to his feet to check it. "Looks like a scrape," he said. "Scabbed over. Shape of a crescent moon."

"Follows the curve of your ear," Rob said, looking closer. He traced where his own injury had been and nodded. "I think mine did, too."

Stu ran a finger behind his right ear, frowning, "I never thought of it, but I don't remember it bleeding much..."

"So they come at us from behind, to the right," said Finn. "When we're alone. Were either of you checked for drugs in your system?"

Both men shook their heads as Rob said, "Nobody knew about it but us."

"Nor was I," Finn said. "Didn't even consider it."

"Could it be like a shot we're give?" Rob wondered aloud. "A Taser?"

"Possibly. But the dream..."

"Maybe it injects a drug into ya, or after...naw, events're too consistent for that."

"Unless we're being fed this fantasy," Finn muttered as

he began to pace. "While in a drugged state. Maybe that's what it is — we're being fed a dream whilst under the influence of some sort of opiate as...as a cover to whatever it was they were actually doing. That we weren't really assaulted; we were only led to believe we were. Because as a constable, I dealt with rape victims, and invariably they were shocked and ashamed of what happened to them. Depressed. Angry. There are also physical manifestations. Shaking. Injuries. I've felt none of that. And the sudden attraction I have for you and other men, that is so completely out of the ordinary..."

"Yeah," said Rob. "Like we been reprogrammed."

"Into being almost happy we were — " Finn stopped short and gave Stu a stricken glance.

"Yeah," Stu whispered. "But I fit the classic pattern for this...this sort of thing, don't I? So there's another theory shot down."

Rob put his hands on Stu's shoulders, like a father would his son, and said, "Maybe ya were a test case, bein' the first."

Stu looked around, lost, then stumbled back to a door next to the fireplace. "I...I've had...I've had too much. I'm...I'm to...I'm to bed."

He cast a look at Rob, who nodded and said, gentle and kind, "I'll set Finn up the couch and be right in."

Stu smiled and wandered into the bedroom.

Finn sank onto a chair. "God, what a stupid thing to say."

"No, it's not," Rob said, not looking at him. "It gives him somethin' to grab hold of. He's got himself convinced it's his own fault this happened. Can't accept it. I didn't even think to suggest he might've been drugged. Reprogrammed. I got stuck on him feelin' better 'bout it since we connected 'cause it showed he weren't alone in this."

He sighed, a deep sadness in his tone.

"I thought...I thought that's why I were able to better handle it 'cause I caught on quick that others were used the same way."

"Rob, it was something to start from instead of nothing, which was all Stu had, before."

Rob's voice took on an odd, nearly hurt tone. "I notice

ya got more out of him, tonight, than I had in a year. Guess I was right. You bein' posh made it easier to share."

"I think it was the whiskey more than anything."

"He's been drunker'n that." He took in a deep breath and patted Finn's shoulder. "So...what d'*you* think of *him*?"

It took Finn a few moments to answer. "What happened hurt him, greatly, and there's more to it than what he's letting on. Perhaps he'll open up further, tomorrow."

Rob nodded. "Just the one bedroom; other room's my workspace. When he's here for the night, we share the bed." He pulled Finn into a quick hug. "Now ya know why I was so hungry."

"I...I'm fine on the couch."

Rob gave Finn a light kiss then went to pull sheets and a blanket from a cabinet. "Need a pillow?"

"Please."

Rob handed everything to him, smiling. "Set yourself up. Washroom's first door on the left, just inside the bedroom." Then he swatted Finn's ass and followed Stu.

And as he closed the door, Finn was overwhelmed by the feeling that while Rob liked him...he loved Stu.

Finn laid out the sheets and blankets, propped the pillow against the couch's arm, stripped down to his underwear and settled in.

But couldn't sleep.

Rob will never be mine, not completely.

It tore into him, knowing that. But he could now see that Rob was too focused on Stu to even think of becoming one with someone else. He'd hinted at it, before, but Finn had noticed that when he was around Stu no one else mattered...which hurt in surprising ways. He had felt a full and complete connection to Rob, and thought it reciprocal. Had wanted it to be. Hoped.

Christ, Finn, one bloody night together and you want to stick with him for life? Could you be more absurd?

He stared at the old brown beams in the white ceiling, letting thoughts bounce around in his head, trying to shift back to searching for an answer to all of this. He had always been able to realign his deepest, darkest thoughts, in the past, especially when faced with an incomprehensible situation.

Like when he'd begun wondering if his parents had abandoned him to his grandmother because he had been born with a defective heart. He was nine at the time, and it took little to convince himself they had regretted having him. He'd remained quiet about his thoughts because he loved Nan and didn't want to hurt her, but he still hoped he could find some way of apologizing to his mum and dad for not being perfect and show them he was much better, now. Maybe even become a complete family.

When his grandmother had finally caught on to what his thoughts were, she'd flown into a startling rage and told him, "It had *nothing* to do with your birth and *everything* to do with your father not wanting to take the trouble to help you! He never grew into adulthood and managed to meet the one woman who could be Wendy to his Peter Pan! It was disgraceful!"

But that had barely made a dent in Finn's self-questioning, so she had handed over the letters his father had written to her, while at King's College. They were lectures, actually. All about *the need to find inner peace, love and understanding*, explaining why he had decided to attend retreats in Darby and the Andes and a dozen other points around the world.

"How he paid for it is beyond me," Nan had said, "but he never asked me for a penny so...it was up to him."

She had still made certain he knew what was in each and every one of those letters...even reading them aloud, to him, when he put them aside. Once done, she had added, "Notice how everything is about him, no one else. Neither of your uncles are like this, as you well know, so I honestly cannot tell from whence this streak of pure selfishness came, but there it is. Finley, dearest, you cannot blame yourself for someone else's actions. You are only responsible for your own."

"But then why'd they have me?" Finn had cried.

"Because your mother wanted you! If she hadn't, she'd have ended the pregnancy; she had the choice. That *spiritual center* she was living in would not have refused her. However, my oldest child worked his reasoning and selfishness into her, and he became more important than her actual child. Between you and me, I consider that unforgivable, and hold it against both of them. You did *not* deserve to be treated like this, and I will *not* have you sink into that vile swamp of believing otherwise."

It had still taken a few years of her cajoling for his self-confidence to rebuild, but now he could see how his parents had left him with the one person who could do the most for him. Unintentionally, perhaps, but still for his own benefit. And he no longer felt any animosity towards them; merely sadness.

And a vague sense of loss.

This led him to wonder if all of the recent events might have something to do with his parents. With all of their parents or guardians. Finn would raise that as a possibility, in the morning. They could then to go through each of their histories in detail to see.

Which might take days.

Finn huffed; he needed to be on duty, come Monday, and he wanted to be. He *did* like where he was and was determined to stay there. But if Rob was right and whoever did this to them might try to kill him, it was best to figure out what was happening, first, so he could be ready for the second assault.

If there was to be one.

While he understood Rob's reason for fearing an attempt on his life, and could not even begin to explain that whole series of what he called *coincidences*, he still wasn't fully convinced that concern was warranted. He'd been out and about on his own on numerous occasions, the past few days, giving his assailant an easy target, but he hadn't even caught a whiff of a repeat action. Then there was Hauptmann still being alive, and Allemenes, and who knew how many others, and Rob had been out and about.

Rob.

Big, bad, beautiful Rob.

So similar to him in so many ways. Protect and serve.

"I'd not have liked him otherwise," Finn murmured.

Lying still like he was, drifting in a vague sadness, the whisky finally began to take over and Finn allowed himself to wander towards sleep, thinking, "It's insane, every bit of it. Maybe it is all just a dream..."

He rolled up in the blanket, murmured, "A damn nightmare," and finally lost himself in slumber and —

He jolted awake to find Stu seated at the table, watching him, glass of whisky in hand, wearing only sleeping pants, no shirt. The room was dark and his laptop was open, and in the light glow from the laptop's screen Finn could tell he had a torso that was tight and trim and fanned with more silver and black hair. The glow also gave his face a deathly hue.

Finn sat up, giving his back a slight stretch, then looked at his phone — 2:05.

"Can't sleep?" he asked, his voice a soft croak.

Stu shrugged, his eyes locked on Finn, his voice soft as he said, "Rob could make it through a rocket attack. Once he's gone, he's gone. Shows a certain level of innocence, I think. It's a funny thing to say, but I love that about him."

Oh, damn...

"Stu, I told you, I'm not here to take him — "

"Take him away from me. I know. I believe ye." His eyes stayed locked on Finn. "But I am glad Rob found someone to give him what he wanted. What he needed. I wish I could of, but I'm still too confused. Hurt. Not like yerself. I don't understand it...you and him, how easy ye are with it. With what happened."

Finn leaned back. "To be honest, neither do I."

"And yet, here ye are...and I'm watching ye...and...and yer as fine as Rob with it all."

He sipped his whiskey, his eyes shifting away from Finn.

"Y'know, when first I saw him, I knew he's out of place here. He's too lovely. I wanted to touch him. See if he's real. And couldn't understand why. He's a man. Beautiful man. And yer almost as fine. That's what I first noticed about ye. Bloody mad, it is.

"Then I got to thinking he's a trap. They'd tried to kill me once; maybe this would be the one that worked. But he said no word to me. Nor tried to catch me. And when I finally got close enough to look at him, I...I near forgot to breathe. The concern in his eyes. The understanding. I could see it. See it all. See what happened, in him. See how strong he was with it. And just holding him, I...I felt strong, again." His eyes shifted back to Finn. "When I look at ye, I almost feel the same. Like kindred spirits. And it doesn't fit with what happened..."

"No argument from me," said Finn as he wrapped the blanket around himself. "Is there anything you want to..." He almost said *tell me* but changed it to, "...to ask me?"

Stu looked at him for a long moment, his need to please obvious even in the midnight shadows, and almost said something. Then he took in a deep breath and exhaled a question. "Is this the man who assaulted ye?"

He turned the laptop to show an image of Joss...and it jolted Finn. He rose and joined Stu, crouching over him to get a better view. Stu's eyes never left him.

The photo was from Monday, with Joss at a news conference before a crowd of reporters, speaking about a murder-suicide. His features were the same, but he looked years older. Gray flecked his hair and his eyes were close to haggard. Nor was he as trim as he'd been.

"That's not a good picture of him," Finn said.

"But it is a current one," Stu murmured. "The one ye showed us, it's from a few year back."

He pulled up the photo Finn had shown him.

Finn nodded. "That's when I met him, at a conference in London. He chaired a panel I was auditing — using DNA in the database to capture criminals. I'd just made DS but had already been involved in solving a murder through DNA referencing. It was a decade old; a young man who'd gone missing and whose body was found on the moors."

Raped and murdered by a priest. Could it be connected in any way? No...no...but...

Stu shifted his focus to the laptop. "Here's what me own assailant looked like." He pulled up a photo of a handsome, buff, strong-featured young man with bright eyes and a bit of scruff, looking so very much like Joss, and yet not quite, sporting a thick mop of dark hair gelled into a pompadour.

"It barely resembles the photo of him with his family," said Finn.

"This is from when I saw him last, at university. This is what he looked like when he...when he..."

Finn looked at him for a long moment. Saw the pain in his eyes. The tension in his neck. He had a feeling Stu wanted to speak but was blocked, so took a chance and said, "You know...I wonder...well, I don't know why, but I get the impression you were...you were hurt more than Rob or myself..."

Stu took in a few deep breaths, not even trying to look at Finn, then nodded...and slowly held up two fingers.

"Twice?" Finn said, squatting beside him. "Lord, no wonder you have issues with — "

"They're not *issues*," Stu hissed. "They're blind bloody panic attacks over what he...the things he did to me...till he decided to kill me..."

His voice trailed off.

Finn put a tender hand to his back, but Stu jerked away, then said, "Sorry."

Finn shook his head. "You needn't be. And don't tell me anything you don't want to."

Stu's eyes shifted back to Finn's, never wavering.

"D'ye still dream it? When ye sleep?"

Finn jolted. "Do you mean, relive it?"

Stu nodded.

"I...I haven't, yet, but I understand that can be a...an issue for people who've been through this." Finn fought himself but finally asked, "So I take it you do?"

"Every night. Made it better when Rob begun holding me."

"He's a good man. Protective."

Stu nodded. "I don't understand how that beast could take such pleasure in what he did. Martin. We were mates since sixth form, so I never would've thought he could...could find such joy in hurting me. Humiliating me. The second time." He shifted his arm to show Finn a scar that looked like a human bite. "I have another on me leg. Left thigh. Drew blood on these two. The others...they faded. All but gone. And...and...the nothing-air, as ye call it...it forced me mouth open and...and now I know what urine tastes like. And semen."

Finn sat on the floor and whispered, "Christ. And you haven't even told Rob."

"Can't. He won't think well of me, letting those things be done. He'll stop wanting what he wants and what I want...and that's what's so damning about it. I do want to. With him. But I can't. Can't do it. Take that final step. Make. Sense. Of it. In thirty-three year I'd ne'er thought of a man in that way, but then this happened and...and sometimes I look at Rob and I want so much more than for him to just hold me, and I can't work out why. I've been trying to since. Trying even harder once I saw it wasn't only me...and Rob discovered others who were killed, like he and I almost were. But it wasn't till I showed ye a photo of me assailant as he is, today, that I realized...when he took me, he...he looked exactly like when I last saw him. What's more, there's something I hadn't thought about — he's Jewish."

Finn blinked. "Your assailant wasn't circumcised?"

Stu shook his head. "But I am, thanks to me Da. Martin — he saw me in the showers and thought I was a Jew, too. I hadn't thought about that. Not till I got to remembering about him and saw the photo of yer man..."

"Joss was not circumcised, but then he wouldn't be. He's Catholic. Told me of his daughter's first communion."

"Yerself?"

"Yes. My father was. My uncles. My grandfather, and great-grandfather. It used to be quite common in England and...and I never really thought about it, but it's not so very common, now. Christ, Rob's even — "

Finn cut himself off and gave Stu a wary look.

Stu just nodded, "I've seen him. His mum's Jewish. When he wakes, we'll have to ask him about Prym...but I'm near certain he'll say the same as we did."

"But...if they're choosing men who are circumcised, why do it in England? Why not go to Israel? Or France? Their Jewish population is far greater than ours. It's even more common in America. And then there are Muslim men, all across the world."

"How do we know they haven't?" Stu asked. "That man in Buenos Aires might be Jewish."

"But...do you think the two men killed were circumcised? A street hood and a German police officer?"

"Don't know how we can find out."

"Christ, that'll expanded our search exponentially. Input *blue lights, male, unconscious, open field, circumcised*, and wade through a hundred million possibilities...if not more."

Stu turned back to his laptop. "Maybe not. This...this detail got me to thinking. When Martin appeared before me and I...and I recognized him, he looked still like he was at Uni. And that photo of yer man, it's years old. Rob's man...his happened all so quick and within one timeframe, I don't think his attacker's appearance would be different. Would it?"

Finn stood, rubbing the nape of his neck. "What are you leading up to?"

Stu rose with him.

"I'm not sure, yet. But I doubt it's extraterrestrials or our government playing with some mental reprogramming. The time between when ye saw the lights and were found is too short for ye to be taken somewhere for that. For any of us, really. And for someone to come do this to us would be seen, by somebody. Somewhere. At least once."

"Yes, I've been trying to work that out, myself," Finn muttered.

"And then there's the accidents that happen the next day. So precise." Stu took a moment to work himself up into asking, "So tell me...Finn...do ye think it might...eventually...be possible for...for man to travel through time?"

Finn half-sat against the table, absently murmuring, "That sounds fantastical," as his expression spun into questioning and contemplating and wondering.

"It makes more sense than anything else," Stu said. "They search for those about to die, pick our memories for someone we know who matches a certain type, go back for him and bring him forward to use in raping us. And the next day we're dead."

"But your assailant was not your Martin, if you judge by his foreskin."

"But I didn't notice that about him till the second time. When he was harsh. When he made me see it."

"Which makes no sense. And to what purpose would they do this? Some bizarre research program? Futuristic gay snuff porn? And why would your attack be so much worse than ours?"

"Me second attack. That's when Martin certainly enjoyed having his way with me. Causing me pain. Especially once I ejaculated. He was kind, the first time, like he was making love to me. And he apologized for it. Apologized after I...I let loose."

Finn all but gasped. "And what happened then?"

"I told ye — he grew rougher and...and..."

"No, I mean, what happened with your semen."

Stu shrugged. "It stayed in whatever condom it was they put on me. Both times."

"As did mine. And Rob's, as well."

Stu let out a short laugh. "What — they're milking us!? We're prize cows, to them? As pleased as I can be with me sexual prowess, I doubt I filled even so much as half a teaspoon."

"But have you ever had your DNA tested?"

Stu tensed then gave a slow nod. "I...I was suspect in a murder, and they took a swab."

"Rob had his done, as well."

"His was just a paternity..."

"But done by the coroner. And mine was worked up when I was twelve...but...that was not through police channels. Damn."

Stu leaned back to look Finn over. "Ye think there's a connection between us through our DNA? We're being picked for that?"

Finn took out his laptop, sat on the couch and pulled up his department's website. "The lad killed in Leeds. Rob said he was a criminal, so he should have his DNA in register."

Stu sat beside Finn, watching as he signed into the department's system, cross-referenced a number of words, and found Finbar Carimin, aged 23, who died while leading the police on a car chase. His police photo showed he had a long face and big sad eyes, with dark hair and a crooked smirk. A bit more cross-referencing found his DNA was on file thanks to his stint in a youthful-offenders prison.

Religion noted as Muslim.

"Muslim men are circumcised," Finn said. "Notice — the coroner's report says his body was burned in the car fire. The officer in Munich died in a fire."

"But I near drowned."

"If your body hadn't been found or was located after a day or two, your injuries would not have been noticeable. And Rob, the scars on his body from being hit by a car..."

"Finn, ye think this could be the reason...the link...?"

"It's tenuous, but we should get Rob. Show him — "

"I am up," said Rob. They jolted around to find him leaning against the bedroom doorframe, still in Finn's CKs, looking sexy as hell. "Been watchin' you two work together, the last fifteen minutes. Not a word to me."

"Ye were sleeping," said Stu, rising. "I like it when ye sleep."

Rob's voice held a snarl as he said, "'Cause I won't bother ya, then, right?"

Stu began to shake, his need to please exploding across his face. "No, Rob, no. It's because ye...ye look at peace. Yer face relaxes and ye seem so calm and...and I envy ye that. And I love that it's possible. And would hate to interfere with it."

Rob grimaced, gave himself a mental kick, then slowly padded over to Stu — his hips swaying like sex incarnate, his legs giving him the grace of a panther — and wrapped his arms around him. "Sorry. An' here I was, hopin' you two would bond. Just didn't expect it so quick or easy.

Unsettled me."

"So you heard what we said?" Finn asked.

"Most." He propped himself against Stu and looked at the screen over his shoulder. One of Stu's hands reached around to caress Rob's right ear as he continued, "We might be connected by DNA. That make this incest?"

"I doubt we're close enough for that," said Finn. "I have no siblings and know all my cousins." He noticed Stu was looking at him, his eyes deep and open. "Would it matter?" he continued.

Rob reacted to Stu's hand like a cat being scratched behind the ears, saying, "It's not like we're havin' kids, is it?"

Finn grinned and rose, saying, "Not from want of trying." Then he grimaced and shot an uncertain look at Stu.

Rob waved his concern off and murmured, to Stu, "I heard what ya said. Taken more than once..."

Stu tensed then nodded. "It happened the night I near drowned. I was...it was brutal, and I...and I was dropped in the middle of the bay, once he was done."

Rob tightened his embrace, his expression shifting to anger. "You were taken off the ferry?"

"Just as the wave hit us. I was on me own and...and it was so much worse. So damn much..."

He began to shake. Rob nuzzled the crook of Stu's neck, letting him regain his center.

"That is awfully precise," said Finn. "And it means they could move you where they wanted. Could someone from the future do that? Even be allowed to do that?"

"I'm not sold on the idea," said Rob. "I think they're of today and messin' with our minds. Maybe we should have an MRI or Cat-scan; see if we've got implants feedin' us these situations. Easier to believe, considerin'."

"I don't know what to consider," Finn said, as he half-sat against the table. "Stu," he finally asked, "I was wondering — would you come with Rob and me down to Clayton-Merrill?"

Stu cast him a wary look. "Why?"

"I'd have access to the forensics labs, there. Could have our blood analyzed. Our DNA compared. I can then use that to research into similar occurrences around the world, through Interpol, the FBI, a dozen other sources. But Rob...we don't want to leave you here, on your own."

Stu looked at him for a long moment then said, "I...I can't answer ye, not now. Let me think." Then he slipped away from Rob and staggered towards the bedroom.

Rob sighed and followed him into the room, sending Finn a quick thumbs-up as he closed the door.

Finn sat back on the couch, murmuring, "Traveling through time? Sounds insane...but if they're coming back to a period where our lives have already been written." He snorted. "Don't some religions say our lives are planned, from birth to death? Perhaps someone finally managed to connect with that thread and follow it. See *what really happened in history instead of what was written by the victors.* Perhaps this is the connection. And our DNA somehow being in the legal system's files is the thread."

He felt the absurdity of it well up inside him as he closed his laptop, lay back on the couch, and settled in, thinking, "Wouldn't that be insane?"

The Beast

Finn drifted awake. Dawn had just begun to make its appearance, outside, and he felt completely at peace. The early morning was so lovely, he didn't want to move; that might break the gentle aura of contentment surrounding him, something he'd felt so rarely in his life since Nan died. He luxuriated in it. Let it tenderly comfort him. He vaguely realized this was what he'd been searching for when he'd considered partnering with Prue – hell, with any of the women he'd known – but it had proven illusory.

Until Rob.

Rob.

A man, not a woman. As strong, if not stronger than him. Not classically handsome but amazingly gorgeous. Supportive as well as open with his own needs. Who could never be his, not completely; he was too dedicated to Stu, but in a way that Finn understood. Yes, it was confusing, but it was also liberating to feel this...this visceral connection to another person.

What was more interesting was how he had also begun to feel hints of that connection with Stu, who was damaged but proving to be resilient. Who was willing to face what had happened to him, head on, even if it hurt him more. Who was fighting to build his own connection with Rob.

Could the three of us build our own little family?

Finn chuckled. The situation was taking on the appearance of a ménage-a-trois. "So very bohemian," as Nan would have put it. "And so bloody what?"

He truly missed her. Especially how she could dare life to try and run her over. Her certainty when she was right. Her unwillingness to back down from an argument. Finn was more the peace-maker who tried to find a common ground. Some way to understanding.

Nan had noticed that sense building in him long before

he headed to university and warned him, "Don't expect to find everyone open to compromise, Finn. There are those who will never be happy unless you are unhappy. It's sad and pathetic, but that's the way of the world. What's best is to find someone who will change your life for the better, and hold onto them as long as they are willing. And if that's for as long as your grandfather and I had, you will be a very lucky man."

His grandfather, dead a year before Finn appeared in the world. Heart attack, despite adhering to a very healthy life. The same issue Finn had been born with. At least he'd left Nan with enough to keep her comfortable the rest of her life.

Fortunately, Finn's issue hadbeen detected and repaired well enough to let him build up his own health. He'd never be able to tackle an Iron-Man course, but he was doing as well as anyone could expect. And he was open and flexible enough in his world to handle any alterations in his life.

"Though I doubt Nan meant something like this," he muttered, "when she spoke of life-changing."

Still he had to admit it was nice shift, the sudden comfort and pleasure in having been with a man he'd only just met. The quiet joy it brought him. Part of him cautioned against becoming too certain about Rob, just yet; they barely knew each other. Same for Stu. But still...he could have lain there the rest of his life and been happy just thinking about them, except for one little detail.

He really needed to pee.

Problem was, the toilet was in the bedroom, and he could hear the soft breathing of Stu and Rob as they slept. He didn't want to do anything to wake them, so he rose, pulled on his shoes and slipped out into the brisk dawn air. Then he took a nice long lovely piss into that pile of wood, grinning as the critters inside skittered about, thanks to his rude waking of them.

A fog was growing and it was still chilly and dark but clear, overhead. To the south he could see thick clouds illuminated by flashes of lightning and had the sense they were headed north.

Probably rain in the morning.

He sighed then focused on the stars above him. Bright

and brilliant. Surrounding a silvery slip of a crescent moon. The trail of his breath whispering from him added to an amazing sense of tranquility, here. He could understand why Stu wouldn't want to leave, and why Rob found it the perfect hiding spot.

He'd experienced the same peace down in Clayton-Merrill on a clear night like this. There were more people about, true, but not to the point of invasiveness. What made it just right was how he could hop a train up to London for a comics and graphic novels conference. Or dinner with Uncle Cormac's family. Or just a night out with his old school chums. Amazing how most had wound up working in *The City* or *Westminster*. Thinking about it, he had to acknowledge their manners had probably rubbed off on him in ways he'd not noticed, until Rob pointed it out.

He let out an impulsive chuckle at the thought of the man. What Finn most liked about him was how they thought alike in so many ways. Saw things alike. Despite having different personas, they approached things the same way — *move forward and find solutions*. And protect others.

Like Stu. Who was nothing like either of them, just a guy in over his head.

Which brought Finn back to a question he might have the answer to, now. *Why had they had been attacked?* They looked very little alike, had never met, and these were hardly rapes of opportunity, where the looks mattered less than vulnerability. These were targeted assaults; he was sure of that now. Possibly something to do with Rob's, Stu's and Finbar's DNA being in the criminal justice database. The sticking point was, Finn's was done through a private lab, so if they were linked by that, someone had to be accessing both sources, which might be a way to narrow down the search. Once they were back to Finn's CID, he and Rob would know how to suss that out and —

A blue light colored the fog.

Finn jolted and looked around to see a figure appear from it.

Joss.

Finn tensed and backed away from the house. No way in hell did he want the man to even think he could follow him inside.

Joss paced him, smiling as he said, "So this is the place."

"How'd you find us?" Finn asked.

"I can find *you* whenever I want. We're linked, now."

"Have you come to kill me?"

"You? No. The other two? Unfinished business."

"You can't have them."

Joss stood still. The blue-tinted fog swirled around him like something dangerous and alive. "You have no say in it. Now that I know where they are, I know when I'll take them and what I'll do, once I have them. It's not like they're of use, any longer. Except to my pleasure. We thought them dead long ago, but it seems no one updated Haller's records, and Hoskins was surprisingly nimble in keeping himself considered deceased."

"You're not making any sense."

"I don't have to."

"I know this has something to do with our DNA," Finn said as he reached the dirt drive. "I've requested a comparison of ours, to see what it is." As he spoke, he scratched *Joss Here Careful* into the ground, using his shoe. He needed to keep the man talking so added, "And I know you use us sadistically. Some *pleasure* you seek — causing pain and terror, then killing us in ways where our bodies won't show the injuries you caused."

"I don't kill anyone," said Joss. "I merely put them back where I know they're scheduled to die."

The chill slamming through Finn was not from the early morning air. "What do you mean?"

"The records show their deaths. I use that."

Finn fought to keep his voice level. "Who are you? You're not Joss Hallsworth, that's for bloody sure."

"He's my avatar."

"No, no, what you did to me was not digital in any way!"

"*Digital*," Joss chuckled. "I haven't heard that ancient phrase in years. No, what's happening between us is a bit more advanced than that."

"You...you control his body?"

"More like, his body becomes mine," Joss said, gazing at him. Almost smiling. "What he experiences, I experience."

"You *are* from the future..."

Joss smiled and —

They were in the nothing room. Finn was frozen in place, his arms caught behind him, unable to speak.

"By nearly five-hundred years," Joss said, grinning as he approached. He caressed Finn's pecs. "Of course, I can't really travel back through time. What I can do is connect with someone of the period and use them as my surrogate to fulfill my dreams and desires."

He pinched Finn's nips through his undershirt, continuing in a near monotone, "And I do desire you, Finn. Which is odd, considering I have always been more attracted to powerful men. Like Hoskins, were his hair darker and his age a bit younger."

His fingers drifted over Finn's lips in a viciously erotic caress.

"Lowenstein was also close to my ideal. Not overly-built, dash of hair, so much fun to use. But he was hurt by what I had him do to Haller, so I dug up Hallsworth. Shifted my connection. He's been easy to control, and he's provided so much fun."

He tore Finn's shirt open then let his fingers fondle Finn's nips before trailing down his sides to drift across his crotch.

"When Haller cursed me as *Martin*, the second time, I allowed it. He fought so hard, I don't think he noticed he was wrong. Same for Hoskins, both times. He thought I was someone named Prym. I looked him up. He'd have been close to what I want, but the connection wasn't there, so Hallsworth it is."

His fingers traced around and over Finn's rear, teasing between his cheeks.

"We have many young men like Hoskins and Lowenstein, in my era. Developed to perfection as soldiers. Warriors. Fighters. Beautiful to behold. Their uniforms fitting their bodies like a second skin. They were made to be desired, but our overlords forbid us to even think of touching them."

Joss bit Finn's nip, hard. Finn growled in furious pain.

"It's too bad I can't have one of my lovely soldiers," he said as he licked at his bite. "But my society is too well-policed for me to use any of them, not without being punished."

Joss dug his fingers into Finn's ass. He grunted in pain.

"That's why taking men similar to them is joyous. I use them by proxy. Feel their quivering flesh under my fingertips. *Hallsworth's* fingertips; as I said, I feel whatever he feels."

Joss's hands curled back around to Finn's groin and slipped inside his CKs to toy with his pubes.

"Of course, you're not my perfect man, but you fit together so nicely. Good proportion. And I do love your ass. Hallsworth sensed I would obsess over you. Which I have. I think he senses I'll never let you die."

"Never?" Finn managed to grunt.

"Never." He groped Finn's dick with one hand, rolling his balls with the other. "You're mine, from now on. I can take you at any time in your life, now that I have the connection."

His hands traced back up to grip the waist of the CKs.

Finn grunted in fear. His breath was sharp and shallow, but he still managed to say, "Don't understand. Why? Doing it?"

"Simple. There is a beast inside me demanding to be fed, and having you makes it happy."

He tore Finn's CKs halfway off, revealing his dick as his balls remained caught by the material.

"Every part of my being tingles from this experience. Not just in my hands and arms and body...but in my heart and soul in a way that takes me out of my own limited existence."

He smacked Finn's dick, rough and demanding, then trailed his fingers down Finn's inner thighs.

"It was quite by accident that I woke this beast. I was assigned to search for a particular strain of DNA when a sample I'd been handed locked me onto a young man about to die in an airplane accident. Hundreds died with him, but it was his terror I found myself living. His last moments watching the aircraft disintegrate into flames and pieces, killing him and everyone else. I jolted back, horrified, but deep within I felt a pleasure I had never experienced, before. Because that beautiful young man's fear had screamed through me, and given me the most explosive orgasm I ever had."

Joss returned to Finn's dick and stroked it, rough and steady. Finn could feel the man's erection pushing between his legs, rubbing under his balls as his chuckle grew deep and evil.

"I told no one of what happened. Instead, I worked late into the night. In secret, I aligned our system's monitors with sensors in a gleam-suit, which connects to all of my nerves when I wear it. Made several subtle improvements to the technology. Received praise."

His left hand roamed all over Finn's body as his right focused on his dick.

"Careful research attached a name to that man's DNA. Showed me he was married. Had two children. When he was born and the date he died. Using the coordinates of his last address, I brought him into the intermediary quadrant."

Joss continued to rub his erection under Finn's balls and maul his dick as his free hand tore at the CKs, ripping them to the point only bits of material still clung to him.

"That is what this space is called. We dare not have you come to us, in person; diseases that have been eradicated might come with you. So we take our subjects in their sleep and bring them here, then manipulate them into ejaculating. We transfer the semen to a safe storage facility, where it is kept for centuries, until we can access it without concern."

Joss pulled his dick away then groped and rolled Finn's balls in one hand as he continued to stroke his dick.

Finn felt himself responding.

"We take them as they sleep so they can pass this off as a dream. This way we do not disturb the continuity of history. But I? I chose to capture that man as he was running. Alone, in the open. And through the gleam suit, I experienced his confusion and fear. Had him remove his training clothes from his lovely body and felt everything he did. Enjoyed having him masturbate himself. Every moment of it dove straight into me to the point that, when he orgasmed, so did I."

Joss put his erection back between Finn's legs and shifted back and forth under his balls.

"But my beast wanted to own his gorgeous ass and feed on his lovely cock and tear him apart for being so beautiful."

He pinched Finn's nips, hard, making him grunt, "No. No. No."

"That is when I experimented in using a surrogate," Joss continued, his voice avid and intense. "A living avatar. I researched records during the timeframe that was assigned to me. Input my specific preferences. And Lowenstein was offered as my match. Such a beautiful young man. So much like my soldiers. I took him as he swam off a beach. Brought him here. Experienced him removing his wet, gleaming swim suit – I believe you called them speedos – and felt him service himself. He did everything I input, including hurt himself. Then I dropped him back on the beach, naked. And every bit of it was glorious."

He bit Finn's other nip, making him cry out.

"I'm letting you scream. I've lessened the control just enough so you can speak, now, and beg, and curse, and whatever you want while I use you."

"Fuck you," Finn snarled. "And you're not...not doing so good...wanking me..."

Joss laughed, cold and hollow. "You'll give me what I want. Every one of you has." He caressed the back of Finn's right ear. "There...now you'll see." He kissed Finn's neck, continuing, "What's especially wonderful is how I can now both caress my subject into complete surrender and feel those caresses, at the same time. Hold you and feel being held. Increasing the beauty of each encounter a thousand-fold.

"Once I knew this, I brought Lowenstein back. Used him against that young man on the plane. Brought them both to the intermediary quadrant and, oh, Finn — the explosive feeling of both stripping him and being stripped. Hurting him and being hurt. Raping him and being raped. Ejaculating inside of him and him ejaculating. His terror as he died and Lowenstein's horror at watching it. It was beauty beyond measure. What worked best was, I didn't need to worry about returning him with injuries. Or even his clothes. The crash took care of that."

Finn snarled with revulsion. "You raped a man who was about to die!? Terrorized him!? You're mad! A fucking serial killer!"

"Finn, Finn." Joss's voice was chiding. "How can you kill someone who died hundreds of years ago?"

He tore the last of the CKs away and ran his hands

down Finn's legs to remove his shoes, making him howl in anger.

"But Lowenstein was weak and after four more uses, his emotional control disintegrated. As I said, Hallsworth was a much better surrogate. I've used him dozens of times. Each one more beautiful than the last."

Joss rose behind Finn and slipped his index finger deep into his rectum, making him cry out, massaging his prostate as his other hand stroked the length of Finn's dick.

Finn cursed him in every way possible but could do nothing to stop it.

And to his horror, he had grown hard.

Joss chuckled, his finger still working inside Finn. "Told you."

Finn howled. "You're bloody evil!"

"Ah, ancient human morality. This is right and that is wrong. What nonsense. When your needs cry to be met, there is no such thing as evil, only satisfying them."

Finn felt himself nearing madness from the finger-fucking and cried, "Stop it. Stop it! I don't want to hear any more! You're going to kill me, so just do it!"

Joss pulled out his finger and stopped massaging Finn's dick. "That's what Schröder said, before I did." He slipped around to face Finn, toying with his nips. "But you have nothing to worry about. I can't let you die." He brushed his lips over Finn's. Bit the lower one. Drew blood. His tongue followed the trail of it down Finn's neck to the hair on his chest. He licked it and kissed it like a greedy beast. "We need what you have, and I will take it whenever I want. However I want."

He rose, lifting Finn's legs up to set onto his shoulders.

"But to your credit, I haven't gone after another doomed man since I had you. Because all I can think about is having you, again." His hands massaged Finn's ass, tender and easy. "And again and again. Which makes no sense. As I said, you're not to the level of beauty that my soldiers are." His hands whispered around to fondle Finn's dick and balls, again. "But I don't care."

Finn snarled, furious and terrified. "Then be done with it!"

A vicious grin came to Joss's face. "What's the fun in that? But since you insist..."

He rammed himself into Finn, making him scream from the sudden sharp pain. His fingers dug into Finn's sides. He bit Finn's nipples as if he was trying to tear them off. Licked at the blood on his chin. His hands grabbed everywhere, sometimes caressing, sometimes slapping, sometimes tearing, sometimes digging in his nails. He pulled at Finn's dick, harder and harder. All but forced it to become harder and harder as he pushed into Finn's ass and back and in and back and in and back and in and back like a madman.

Finn tried to fight him but was too immobilized by the nothing-air so could only scream in pain and curse and spit as Joss slammed into him, harder and harder, growling like a mad dog, gulps of laughter exploding from him. There was no fade into pleasure, this time. Joss's groping and biting grew more and more vicious. More and more painful. Moved down his body and onto his thighs. Drew blood.

Suddenly, Finn felt himself fire his load. He received none of the rush. Didn't feel the build or the beauty of it; he was too hurt and horrified at what was happening. But he definitely ejaculated. And once again, he realized a cover of some kind had been placed over his dick and his semen vanished into it.

Joss pulled out of him and Finn felt the nothing-air force his mouth open and he was shifted to where his face was before Joss's crotch and he could see the man's dick was thick and red and close to exploding. Then the man slid his dick past Finn's lips and over his tongue and deep into his throat and fucked his mouth, all the while crying "Yes, yes, yes," as Finn did everything he could to keep from choking to death. The feel of the man's pubes against his face was sickening. Having the man's balls slap against his chin was pushing him to madness. He was close to vomiting. He wanted to bite down and tear the damn thing off, but the nothing-air wouldn't let him.

Then Joss cried out and filled Finn's mouth with his own semen. Pushing in harder and deeper, if possible, until Finn could feel it spilling past his lips and trailing down his chin to mingle with the blood from his lip in a way that was sickening.

Then he stopped.

Joss's dick stayed in Finn's mouth, erect but softening.

Finally...finally...finally he staggered back, almost in a daze. He groped Finn's softening dick and fondled his balls, saying between gasps for breath, "Be glad...you're important...to them. Now that they...know what...what I can bring them from you...I can do whatever I want...to anyone..."

Finn gazed at him in growing horror. He was barely able to whisper, "No...you said...I was all you wanted..."

"You are." Then Joss gripped his own dick and pissed straight into Finn's face, chuckling. "But I also said...Rob and Stu, you called them...they're unfinished business. Soon as they come looking for you...I'll take one...then the other...and this time...they'll never be found. They don't need to be. They're already dead."

His chuckles grew harsh and vile as he finished urinating and vanished, leaving Finn still caught in the nothing room. Near madness.

Finn woke, lying half on his side. The sky above him was thick with clouds but dawn had broken through. He was quaking from the cold and it hurt him to even so much as breathe, still he managed to force himself to half-rise and look around.

He was lying on straw. A slow, careful inspection showed it was layered thick, and brushing a little aside revealed dirt that had been pounded solid. The straw bunched up against massive walls built of cut stone that had been whitewashed a dozen times. At one end, a low squat wooden door had been cut into it, flush with the stones.

Slowly, painfully, Finn examined himself and found he wore nothing but his torn undershirt. Bite-marks were all over his torso, groin and thighs, blood still whispering from some of them. And from his lip. His entire body felt as if he'd been torn apart and sewn back together. The foulest taste was in his mouth and he could smell Joss's piss. His mind was wrapped in chaos.

He gagged, gulped in several deep breaths, then tried to stand, but a wave of nausea kicked him back to half-sitting-half lying on the ground. He finally managed to force himself to crawl over to the door...only to find it had no latch inside or even hinges he could see. He pushed against it, but it did not budge an inch.

Finn sat next to the door, leaning against the wall, and croaked, "Help. Help! Please." But his voice was weak and cracked. He was certain it barely carried past the stone walls.

He fought another wave of nausea and felt hopelessness rise within him. He had no idea where he was. What day it was. If Rob and Stu were still alive. He was close to losing himself in tears but refused to allow it.

He made himself rise to his feet, in stages. The walls were at least twice his height and he could see nothing that would serve as a foothold were he even capable of climbing. He was completely trapped.

Half-leaning against the wall, he forced himself to stumble around the perimeter of the floor and count off the size of it — about ten meters long and five meters wide. Judging from how cold the stone was, he figured it was about the same time of year, and maybe even still the same day. A couple of times a foot would step upon sharp rocks hidden in the straw, but he embraced the sudden sharp pain because it kept him from falling into despair. He also noticed the straw was relatively dry, so it hadn't been rained upon in a while.

Finn stopped. Leaned into a corner.

Dry straw burns.

If he could find some way of starting a fire, the smoke might bring someone.

At the very least, it'd warm me.

He slowly took off the remains of his bloody undershirt and tied it around his waist, then he began brushing straw into a corner, moving like a man three times his age. He piled it high then picked up two of the rocks that had jabbed him. He struck them together, but they were too damp from the soil to bring a spark. He dug through the straw and found a couple of thick twigs. He inspected the rocks but they were very smooth, so he looked around for more and found one larger stone with a small crevice in it, half-buried in the dirt.

He bunched some of the straw around the stone then lay the thickest twig he had along the crevice, laced more straw around it, positioned his hands around the second twig, as though he were praying, then rubbed his hands back and forth, making the twig twirl as he pressed it against the first one.

He kept at it for several minutes, fighting nausea, making himself ignore the pain and weakness in his limbs, not letting himself even think of stopping.

C'mon, you want to. You will. C'mon, you want to. You will.

Then finally...finally...he saw a whiff of smoke drift from within the straw. He crouched down and huffed on it, over and over, close to hyperventilating before a soft gleam of red took hold...and a tiny flame jumped up.

Finn jolted and grabbed more straw to sprinkle over it, letting the flame grow until he was able to load it with heaps of straw. In moments, he had a roaring fire going in one corner of the enclosure. Crackling and burning and filling him with warmth and beauty and hope. Its smoke rising higher and higher. He all but danced before it...until he grew light-headed and had to lean against the wall to keep from fainting.

He continued to heap more straw onto the flames...but far too soon he was grasping for mere strands and the fire was growing smaller. Then no more straw was left and the fire burned out. Light smoke still wafted from the ashes, but not enough for anyone to pay attention to. He sat back in his corner. Wrapped his arms around himself. Hoping. Waiting. Praying, even. His mind unable to focus on anything but the belief that someone had seen the smoke. For hours and hours it seemed.

Hoping.
Waiting.
Praying.
Believing.
Then the door slammed opened and an old man poked his head into the enclosure.

Finn yelped.

The old man yelped and vanished, then two younger, more powerful men scrambled inside, followed by the old man. They looked rough and wary and held cudgels, and all three gaped at Finn as if he weren't human.

He finally managed to croak, "I...I'm Detective Sergeant. Sergeant Finley. Winterbourne. Of the Clayton-Merrill Police. Could you please...call...local constabulary? I think some men I...I was working with...are in danger..."

****

Within half an hour, the local constables were on-site with a medic, and Finn was being treated for his injuries, as well as hypothermia. It turned out the constables knew Stu and were able to call his mobile phone.

But it went straight to voicemail.

They told Finn he was at the opposite end of the island from Stu's house, so they sent another car out to do a check, but it wouldn't be there for nearly hour. Finn had to fight to keep from collapsing into panic.

The story he gave them was, he'd been working on a drugs-related case in Clayton-Merrill and it wound up having a connection to someone unknown in Terlich. He'd learned the house being used belonged to Stu so had come up to question him.

"Why not call us for to do it?" asked one constable, a doughy man of medium stature.

"I don't suspect he's part of this," Finn said, "so didn't want to raise suspicions. The house in question has been empty for some time and was recently undergoing renovation."

"What about the *cousin* of his?" a thin, blond constables asked. "Come up from Aberdeen, was it, but a year back?"

"Naw, Leeds," said the other. "It's Aberdeen where he sells his goods."

"They aren't who assaulted me," said Finn. "It was a dark man, tall and lean. I don't think he's from here. His accent was Geordie."

A tall sturdy man arrived, his rough features caught in a careful gaze. "He give ye them bites?" he asked.

Finn looked at him, confused. Saw he was nearing forty and his expression was not one of trust. He introduced himself as the local DCI and waited for a response.

Finn forced himself to say, "His assault on me was. Was sexual. He said, if I didn't back away, next time he'd castrate me. And Mr. Haller. And his cousin."

That made the two constables stiffen in uncertainty.

The DCI just frowned. "How'd ye get in the pen?"

"Dunno," said Finn. "Passed out. Woke up in it. Like this."

"Then how'd ye start the fire?"

"Boy Scouts. Twig. On a rock. Straw."

"Yer lucky McGreggor were out to his flock," said the first constable. "He's what saw the smoke."

Finn nodded then looked at the medic tending to him. "Do you have someone who can do a...do a rape kit?"

The medic, a man well into his fifties, didn't flinch.

"The clinic in Leryll, maybe."

"I want that bastard's DNA. I'm betting it's on file. In our system."

"I'll call ahead."

Finn was taken to a temporary mobile building, where the doctor in charge took swabs everywhere Finn told him to, placing each in a tiny plastic bag. He called in the coroner to complete the exam with photos of Finn's injuries, which included a fresh scrape to behind his right ear, then he was allowed to shower. Which he wound up doing twice in order to even begin to feel clean. They gave him hospital scrubs and slippers to wear.

And through it all, neither Stu nor Rob could be found.

The DCI drove Finn out to Stu's house to meet with the constables who were already there, and they searched everywhere.

No one to be seen.

They found clothes still slung over chairs and the bed slept in, bringing a tight smirk to a beefy constable's face. No sign of a struggle. A cold pot of coffee on the counter. The sheets, blanket and pillow were still on the couch, so the DCI seemed willing to accept Finn's story of having come up to do a quiet check on a criminal link.

Finn changed into his suit and a pair of training shoes he'd brought, then the beefy constable called him outside and pointed to the words he'd dug into the dirt. "What's this, then?"

Finn wandered over, his aches and confusion making him move like an old man. "He's the one."

"Got a full name?"

Finn shook his head. He felt a hole expanding deep in his heart, and every passing minute made it worse, but he refused to let himself fall into despair. Refused to think about what the silence meant. What had probably happened to them. That each had been grabbed by the bastard, brutalized to death and their bodies hidden away, forever. The very idea was too hideous to accept, so he relied on his one bulwark to keep the hounds of grief at bay, for the moment – that he was a police officer who had seen a great deal of mankind's worst brutality to others. He could control his emotions, for now. Wait until he was sure both men were gone...and then give way to grief. He thanked Nan for that ability.

As she had often said, "When it's happened, it's happened. You either accept it, deal with it and move on, or you don't."

And in a case like this, if they were dead, he couldn't change that. The truth of the situation was too stark and cruel for him to pretend otherwise.

But he could make damn certain he found out some way of catching the son-of-a-bitch who did this, even if he was a thousand years in the future, and by God he'd make him pay.

****

Finn stayed on the island another 48 hours, but there was no word from Rob or Stu. He even scoured the house one more time to see if they'd left some cryptic message meant only for him, to let him know where they'd gone, but he could find nothing.

By this point, the DCI was of the mind that Rob was either part of that drug gang and had fled to avoid prosecution, or that he and Stu, both, were food for the fishes. And taking into account how Finn had been found, he was leaning more and more to the latter probability. What made it worse was, while he never specifically said so, he seemed to believe Finn's coming to the island had been the catalyst for their deaths.

Finn had to agree with him.

It didn't help that the DNA found in Finn's body was a perfect match to Joss Hallsworth, a DCI in Reading who had an iron-clad alibi. Finn just nodded, not bothering to offer an explanation. They decided one of the samples had been corrupted in some way and began a more detailed, time-consuming analysis.

By this point, Blethyn wanted Finn back to Clayton-Merrill so he could explain what the hell was going on, but Finn ignored his calls and messages and texts. Instead, he spent his time using the library's Wi-Fi to research the policeman killed in Munich — Detective Willem Schröder.

He had just turned twenty-nine when he died, less than a year ago, and was a fair-haired man with an open face that seemed inviting despite the stiffness of his official photo. There was only one side-note in the report that made reference to blue lights prior to him being found. Nothing more...until Finn caught a comment in a separate story that a police officer in Hamburg had been looking into the case, stating, "We may have had a similar occurrence."

That officer's name?

Christian Hauptmann.

The man Finn had found as another possible.

Hauptmann was also a detective and the exact same age as Finn, with sandy-blond hair, a few more pounds in weight, and very aware of his own good-looks, according to his photo. He also looked vaguely familiar. But what mattered most? He was still very much alive.

Finn had to see him, and wanted to do so before he even thought of approaching Joss.

The moment he was able to leave, he hopped a plane to Edinburgh and transferred to a flight for Hamburg. A cold front had blown into the city, heading south, reminding him he was not at all dressed for the weather, so instead of taking the tram he caught a cab to the *Poliziepraesidium*, a post-modern building of blueish glass that bore a vague resemblance to a buzzard's claw. He strode inside with his suitcase, where he introduced himself at reception and said in the best German he could muster, *"I need to speak with Polizeioberkommissar Christian Hauptmann, please. It's a matter of some urgency."*

The desk clerk eyed this Englishman, dressed in a suit that desperately needed pressing and ragged sports shoes, speaking his German with a British accent, his battered valise next to him, and tried to get more information, but Finn was a brick wall. So he made a call.

A few minutes later, a strong, well-tanned man came out, looking even better than in his photo. He had a vague smirk of a smile and deep blue eyes shaped like almonds, and was the same height as Finn, with clothing cut in the latest electronica style that showed off his solid body and legs very nicely.

"I am Hauptmann," he said in lightly accented English, his face covered with a *Don't fuck with me* expression...until he froze. His amazing eyes bore into Finn, who looked back at a face that looked familiar...so damn familiar.

"I'm Detective Sergeant Finley Winterbourne, of Her Majesty's police service. I desperately need to speak with you."

A question replaced Christian's attitude, and his smirk grew haunted and nervous. "Come here," he finally said.

He led Finn to an interview room that held only a table and four chairs, then he closed the door and leaned against it with his shoulder, as if to make sure it could not be opened. "It has happened to you," he murmured.

Finn whispered a reply of, "How did you know?"

"Your eyes. I...I see it. Tell me I am wrong."

Finn hesitated then shared every detail of his initial rape, but did not mention Rob or Stu or how they were missing. He felt that would be too much, at the moment.

Christian seemed to sag as the story went on, so that when Finn was done, he looked close to half his size. He almost laughed. "So I am not the only one. I wondered. I looked. But I could not make myself look to see."

"You considered Willem Schröder."

Christian shot him a startled, nearly angry glance. "What do you know of him?!"

"He was...also taken. Like we were."

Christian's eyes closed and he grimaced in pain. "No, if true, it is wrong. It is so wrong. He was a good man. He...he was going to be married. I was to stand up with him. His fiancé still is devastated." He rolled around to lean his back against the door. "We trained at the *Mittlerer Polizeivollzugsdienst*, together. When I heard what had happened...what I mean is, there was something about it that...that was...I knew it was not right, but..." His voice trailed off. It took him a moment to continue with, "Nein. What happened with him was not the same."

"Are you sure? Blue lights were mentioned..."

"Nein...nothing. Nothing. I found nothing else similar."

"Then why did you look?"

He hesitated then said, "He sent to me an odd text, asking about dreams. Memories. But I had not yet been taken, so...so why do you think this? That he was...also?"

Finn hesitated then said, "Joss told me of him."

"Joss?"

"The man used to attack me. Tall, trim, dark hair. He

referenced an officer named Schröder, the...the second time. Your friend is the only one who fit."

"Second time, you say? For you, more than once?"

"Yes."

Christian's eyes grew haunted. *"For now*? And looking for Willie led you to me?"

Finn nodded. "I saw a note in a news story. I found the police report. When you were discovered unconscious. But the information was locked down, very tight."

Christian tightened.

Finn drew in a deep breath and said, "As I said...I...I've been through this more than once...and wondered if...if you..."

The man straightened himself up, almost defiant, and chuckled, his grin wide and elegant and daring anyone to cross him...and, again, so damn familiar...and said, "I have...I have been taken four times."

Finn gasped. "Four?"

Christian removed his jacket and shirt to reveal deep bite wounds on his sides. Some were almost faded; others, recently scabbed over. His left wrist showed markings from restraints. Still raw and red. "I could not fight back as he...as he tried to tear away my flesh."

"Christ." Finn removed his coat and shirt to reveal his own injuries. Christian shivered at seeing them. Finn continued with, "Restraints weren't used on me. I couldn't move, no matter how I tried."

"Oh, he enjoyed my struggles," Christian said, pointing to a deep bite on the back of his left shoulder. "This is from the week before. There are more on my...on my buttocks. This time, I am taken in my bed. In my father's house. I believed I would be safe, there, but still I...I woke in that space. But I was able to push him away. Kick at him, somehow. Not strong, but enough to hurt him. Which makes him bind me in place. With rope. Thick and rough. The type you find on a farm. I was held across this beam as he...as he beat me. Tore me with his teeth. Used things on me. In me. Put his hands wherever he wanted." His voice grew softer and softer as his shaking increased. "When he finally fucked me...I am terrorized. In pain. Wanting to vomit. But he succeeds. Every time he succeeds. In forcing me to...to...to be like I am a fucking horse he has put to stud."

His voice was barely a whisper as he said, "You are the first person I tell this to. You are the only one who would understand."

Finn gently pulled a chair out for Christian. The man looked around, lost, then flopped into it and gripped the table. Finn sat next to him. Said nothing. Just folded his arms to rest his chin on them and gazed at the tabletop as, inch by inch, Christian clawed his way back to control.

It sounded like this monster was still refining his work. Gaining more and more direct access to the men he chose as his victims, and it was incomprehensible. Snatching men whenever and wherever he wanted. Not only those who were doomed but anyone he wanted. Dragging all of them into a nightmare and torturing them before dropping them back to their lives. Or deaths. Adding to their suffering in ways that were cruel and unimaginable. Anger and disgust boiled in him at the absolute evil of it. So deep and real, he could taste it.

And worse? How there seemed no way to stop it.

That is what hit him the hardest. His duty as a Detective Sergeant screamed into every corner of his body that this must be stopped. But how? How? This beast could appear wherever it wanted, whenever it wanted, control another man to do its filthy work, even if he didn't want to...and from what Finn could tell, that other man need not even be from the same moment in time. So how can you destroy a creature made of nothing?

But there has to be a way to put an end to it. There has to be.

Now he definitely had to speak with Joss. Found out what he knew about being used, himself. It was obvious he was being captured from a few years ago. Was that why he looked so ragged, tired and unsteady, now? Had he gone to sleep, sometimes, and thought what was happening was merely a nightmare? Or that he was losing his mind? Was there another reason he'd been chosen for use as the abuser, aside from the beast wanting to have looked like him? Joss was attractive, but the description offered by the creature for his perfect man sounded stronger. Bulkier. More muscular. If that's what he liked, why not use Rob as his avatar? Could understanding this dichotomy be an answer to finding a way to stopping this...he could think of no other word to use but *beast*?

Of course, now Finn could see Rob's and Stu's concern about being caught in the open alone was wrong. Christian had been taken while he was sleeping in a house. The first young man had been taken from an airplane about to crash. No, his friends had been safe because they were thought dead, and Finn had stupidly led the beast back to them. Revealed that they were...how'd he put it? *Unfinished business*? That meant he was responsible for what had happened to them.

I killed them. I got them killed.

His insides churned. It was all he could do to keep from breaking into sobs of grief, and he was so relieved Christian remained silent.

After several minutes, the man sat back, exhausted, and whispered, "I am sorry."

The sudden words jolted Finn. He made himself straighten up. "For...for what?" he said, shifting to look at him.

"This loss in emotion is not normal, for me. I am stronger than this..."

"Stop it." The words were sharper than Finn intended, but what Christian said cut deep into him. "Nothing about our situation is normal."

Christian stared at the table. "I know this, but...but what...what do you feel...about what has happened?"

Finn took a long time to answer. "Bewildered." Christian cast him a confused frown so he continued, "Prior to the first attack, I was after a girl to marry me. Then I suffered a rape that was horrific and painful and yet...I...I'm almost fine with it. I had no trouble making love to a man barely forty-eight hours after it happened. Which makes no sense to me. And what's more, I'm no longer attracted to women."

Christian shrugged. "It did not have that effect on me. I am already of the Rainbow Family. But I have been with no one, since. I...I cannot."

"I think your reaction is the more expected one."

"But as you say, what is normal in a situation such as this?"

Finn shrugged. "Are you open about it? Being gay?"

Christian's smirk regained a foothold on his face.

"Why should I not be? Yes, some of the officers were uncomfortable, but they see I do my job and have no interest in them, and I am accepted. In truth, female officers prefer to work with me. *No macho stuff*, one said. I...I had someone I was seeing. Someone close. He was very nice. But when this began, I backed away from him." He huffed a soft laugh. "Him, I have known since five years and can say nothing to; I know you five minutes and tell you everything."

"Christian, we share a bond. Granted, this is not something we chose. We were selected by some vile creature who's not only a...a...a demonic sadist, he's a killer by proxy. I know of five men who've died after he was done with them...and he's bragged of more...but it seems that you and I...well, there's a reason we're not being eliminated in the same way and...and I have a theory. I think I know why I'm not but...well...what I need to know is, could you and I be related in any way?"

Christian slipped into deep thought. "You're English."

"It needn't be a close connection. Just...might we check to see if our DNA is of the same line or...or similar? Third or fourth cousin, twice removed, I don't know. Just...something that links us. I don't really know my full ancestry, beyond my grandparents..."

"The man who takes me...he says something about that. What was it? My ejaculation is *wanted* or *needed*. No, I was too hurt to...to...listen..."

"My attacker said something similar, to me."

Christian stared at Finn then bolted from the room, leaving him in place. He returned a moment later with two packets of swab-sticks.

Finn nodded and took one packet then ran the swabs over his tongue and the insides of his cheeks. Christian did the same.

"I will make this the priority," he said, resealing the packets, "so we should have a preliminary result very soon. Maybe an hour."

He vanished out the door, again, motioning for Finn to remain in place, then returned with cups of coffee and some rolls. He dumped tubs of milk and packets of sugar on the table. "I do not know how you like this..."

They sat, and Finn noticed he used two sugars and

three tubs of milk. Like Nan had.

And Rob.

As he stirred, Christian said, "There perhaps is something to what you ask. I am not native German; I was born in London. I am adopted by a family here, as an infant."

"Not by a British family?"

"No." He gave a soft chuckle. "I was *purchased*."

"An English woman sold you off?!"

Christian nodded. "My parents both had forty years and were childless. They were put in contact with a young couple, and I am now here. What is funny is, the year after I am here, my new mother has my sister, and then my brother. We were raised as full siblings, but when I become eighteen, I ask my parents why this has happened. The only answer I receive is, *They did not want you to live in London.* I do not understand it, but it is what it is."

"Do you know the name of the couple who sold you?"

Christian shook his head. "Only a man and a woman. It was handled *privately*. But how did my mother describe them? I think the English is, *Not completely there*? She tells me I am better off here. When I consider your politics, I agree."

Finn hesitated. "Your birth date..."

"I just became thirty years."

"The fifteenth of last month. Like mine. Oh, Christ..."

Christian stared at him. "How do you know this?"

"Your file." Finn shook his head, his breath soft. He could not believe what he was thinking. "And...and my parents left me with my grandmother, when I was an infant..." Then it hit him.

Christian had Nan's smile and Uncle Niall's chin.

"Oh, bloody hell...no, no, no, could you be...could my parents have...?"

Christian raised his eyebrows, slowly nodded and leaned forward, his eyes locked on Finn's. "I am thinking, yes, perhaps we are brothers."

"Not twins!"

"Not identical."

Finn burst to his feet to pace. "No, no, no, no, no, it's preposterous! How could this happen? How could they even do it? Hide you from me and my grandmother, both?

Make it work for even the idiots in the bureaucracy? I mean, I have a copy of my birth certificate. There's no mention of a twin or anything!"

"Is it required?"

Finn stopped cold. "I have no idea." He dropped onto the chair, stunned. "I read for a degree in law, but I don't recall this ever being addressed."

"It may be something to look into, once our test is returned."

"If it says what I think it will," Finn murmured, "and I have no doubt it shall, now. But that may offer a partial explanation as to why you've been used so many times. Joss said my semen was also needed. Christ."

Now Finn told Christian everything else he had learned, all about Rob and Stu, and what had happened to him the second time.

At the end of it, a short laugh burst from Christian and he said, "We are brother rats in a laboratory. I do not appreciate this, considering my country's history." His phone buzzed and he answered it, "*Hauptmann. ... Ja. ... Sehr gut. Noch etwas zu wissen? ... Vielen Dank. Tschüss.*" He ended the call and looked at Finn. "The preliminary test is done. Brother."

Finn hesitated then began to laugh. Christian watched him.

"My bloody parents," he choked out, still fighting back the laughter. "*Our* parents. Sold you and dumped me. Guess I wasn't worth the price, having been *born with issues!* Bloody fucking hell, how could they do that?"

"We could ask them, can we not?"

Finn choked and shrugged. "Have to find them, first. Last I heard, they were in the Andes, but that was years ago, when Nan died. My grandmother. *Our* grandmother. I suppose I could ask my uncles, but there's no guarantee they'd know anything. They didn't want much to do with my father. Never said anything, just...never said anything."

"You say you were sick as a child?"

Finn nodded. "I was born with a congenital heart defect. An artery wasn't aligned quite right. Rapid breathing. Cyanosis. It was repaired...pretty much repaired when I was three. Can't even see where they cut into me, anymore...unless you look for it. Nan saw to it that I grew healthy and..." He sighed and looked at Christian. "You have her smile, you know."

Christian grinned. "Do we look at all like our parents?"

Finn wiped his eyes and looked at Christian. "Your face takes after Uncle Niall's. Your figure, like Uncle Cormac's, from the snaps I've seen. I'm told I take more after our mother. I...I've got photos uploaded onto a site. I...I'll show you." He lay his face in his hands. "Oh, Christ, I feel cut off at the knees. No foundation, anymore. Everything about me, up to a week ago, seems unreal. Like it was a novel I've read or...or happened to someone else."

Christian looked at him for a long moment then said, "I think you have been alone for many years, Finn."

He shrugged. "Never really noticed. Or cared. Got my uncles. Cousins. Friends. But now..."

Christian rose to his feet. "May I introduce you to my parents? And to my brother and sister?"

Finn looked at him. "Do they know what's happened to you?"

"Enough to understand I need their support," he replied in a careful voice. "And they give it. When I introduce you as my brother by blood, they will offer it to you, as well. I know this."

Finn smiled. "I'd like to meet them. And I'll introduce you to my Uncles Niall and Cormac and their families. *Our* uncles. Have a massive reunion."

"Very well, but first we take a trip to Munich."

"Munich?"

Christian nodded. "My sister is with the *Alles Wissen Institute*. She can help us to have our genome mapped, very quickly. Perhaps this will answer questions we may yet have."

A thought almost made itself known to Finn but then vanished, leaving behind a vague sense of uneasiness. Still, something about his DNA was pushing this situation and the more he knew about himself, the better, so he said, "*Sehr gut.*"

****

Christian met with his superior to arrange for some

time off as Finn called Blethyn to let him know he'd be delayed returning.

"*Delayed*?!" the man snarled. "For how long?"

"I...I don't know, sir."

"Winterbourne, what the devil is going on here? Why do I have a DCI from bloody Scotland worrying me for details over a drugs investigation I know nothing about, but in which you are supposedly involved? And telling me it regards two men who are missing and now presumed dead!? For God's sake, I've got the bloody Home Secretary howling at me about this and — "

"I was assaulted, sir."

"I know! They informed me...of...that." Blethyn's voice grew hesitant. He continued with care. "Finn, the particulars of your assault were not...weren't shared, and...well...are you all right?"

Finn's voice grew soft. "I...I don't know."

"Weren't you attended to after the...after the assault?"

"Yes, sir. And we went through the entire process."

Blethyn was silent for so long, Finn wondered if the call had dropped. Then he heard a long slow sigh. "I see." His voice grew tender. "Do you know who did it?"

"I think so, but I'm not sure, yet..."

"*Yet*? Where are you, Finn?"

"Germany."

He heard Blethyn take in a deep breath. "I want you to come home. Now. Leave this to us."

"I can't, sir."

"I want you to come home. I know an excellent counselor, and you will be allotted as much time as you need to heal..."

"I...I will, sir. Soon."

"Finn, it's not a good idea to investigate a crime against yourself. Especially one of this nature. Leave that to us. Come home."

"I'll call you when I know more, sir."

"Dammit, Winterbourne!"

Finn ended the call and turned off his phone. He noticed Christian watching him from a nearby doorway.

"All is good?" he asked.

Finn nodded. "Shall we go?"

Christian shrugged, led Finn to a new BMW with a

rainbow stripe on its tail and drove them to *Finkenwerder Airport*, where they strode up to a sleek business jet. In answer to Finn's shocked expression he said, "I called my father and told him our trip was urgent, so he arranged for us to use the company jet."

"Just like that?"

"It is his company; he may do as he wishes." He eyed Finn's suit. "Munich is quite cold, at the moment. Shall I have us met with a coat for you?"

Finn shook his head. "I'm English. We're born cold." Then he stowed his bag into the cabin's closet.

Little more than an hour later, after a flight that was completely silent but punctuated by careful looks at each other, they landed at *Oberpfaffenhofen*, in Munich. A Mercedes met them and took them straight to the *Alles Wissen Biochemie Institute*, a sleek, modern building that gave off such an icy feeling, Finn felt as if he should have accepted that offer of a coat just to ward off the frigidity.

"Bring your valise with you," Christian said to him. "We leave with my sister."

Finn nodded and pulled it from the trunk. They headed down a path, but it did not lead them to the main doors; instead, it approached a nearby entrance that was all but hidden by a garden of roses.

"They're blooming late," Finn said, absently.

Christian glanced at them and smiled. "You should see them with snow on the petals. They are the result of experiments to develop plants that ignore the seasons and grow wherever they are planted."

"GMOs."

Christian opened the door with a pass-card. "No matter how you feel about it, the way the world is going this may be the only way we all get fed."

"There's always *Soylent Green*," Finn smirked.

Christian cast him a happy look. "You like the science fiction?"

Finn nodded. "Have since I read my first *Marvel Comic*."

Christian's smirk returned. "I prefer *Dark Horse*."

"Oh, they are bloody good; if only they were as prolific."

Christian chuckled and slung an arm over Finn's

shoulders, saying, "I think I like you, Finn."

Then they entered a large foyer that reminded Finn so much of a high-tech igloo, with all the white and chrome and blue glass abounding, he actually shivered. They were met by a tall, imposing young woman in a crisp smock, who looked like the perfect Aryan beauty...except for an odd sense of other-worldly focus in her eyes.

She and Christian greeted each other with huge smiles and chatted in German, for a moment. Finn caught enough to know they were making brother and sister comments so stayed back until Christian mentioned who Finn was. Her smile froze and she looked at him.

Christian laughed and swept an arm around, in beckoning. "Finn, here is my sister, Mikala. Mikala, here is my brother, Finley James Winterbourne."

"Please, it's just Finn." He offered his hand.

She took it, finally grinning. "Welcome. When first I saw the results of your test, I thought it mistaken. But now I see you, and your foreheads are the same. Your noses. The shapes of your skulls. Ah...and your hands. Christian, place your right hand next to his."

Christian did, and Finn was startled. "They're almost identical," he said.

Mikala snorted a laugh. "*Almost*? We shall soon see."

Finn jolted and slung his suitcase onto a nearby chair. He dug in and found Rob's old y-fronts still tightly wound in a laundry bag. He showed them to Mikala.

"These were worn by another man who might be related to us. Can you get a DNA sample off them and check?"

She gave him a condescending smile. "Of course. The technology has advanced a little, in the last few years."

Sure enough, within the next two hours, Finn and Christian found they were fraternal twins, and Rob was close enough to be a first cousin. "Perhaps even a half-brother," Mikala said. "I would need more sample to work from. How do you know him?"

"We only just met," said Finn, "but now he's missing and I'm...I'm concerned."

"You should be," she said. "There's an odd sequence in his structure that you share, but it is not in Christian's. I will need more time to understand it, perhaps determine what it means, but it appears to be a recent mutation."

"Are there any other issues with my DNA?" Finn asked.

"None I can see, so quickly. I will do more in-depth, but at the moment it's a very clean map. No etiologies, yet. Euchromatic. Actually, quite lovely. Would you be willing to allow us a unit of blood for further testing?"

"You wanted only a half-unit, from me," Christian huffed, smirking.

"Yours has a few more heterochromatic areas than does his," she replied. "His is a good base for further research in — "

"Oh, my God!" Finn stumbled back. Almost stopped breathing. "All of this goes into a databank, right? Names and information and...and..."

Mikala frowned. "Finn, we need not use your name, if you prefer, but the information, yes, it does. It would be made available to any who wanted it."

Christian stiffened. "Mikala. Willie also let you do this."

"Willie? Schröder? Yes, when first I began here, I needed a subject and he was willing to pretend he was you. I think he liked me. So sad, what happened..."

Finn and Christian exchanged a look as Finn said, "Oh, Christ," and the blue light swirled around him and —

Joss grabbed his face with both hands as he growled, "What're you doing!?"

Punishment

Finn was in the nothing room, hanging from his hands, and this time he felt like he was bound by rope. His feet were held apart. He could twist and turn but could not gain a foothold or raise his legs.

Joss's fingernails dug into his skin, drawing blood. "Why are you at *Alles Wissen*?! What're you trying to do?!"

Finn snarled and spat, "Whatever I can to stop you!"

Joss let go and stepped back. Finn could see he was shirtless, his chest pumped, the hair on it swirling clean and even as it dove down to his trousers. He laughed. "Stop me?!"

He backhanded Finn, hard.

"Your arrogance is comical. Your future is my past, so I already know what it is. And the fact that I can still reach you shows it hasn't changed. So what you're doing is worthless, childish, and doomed to failure."

Finn made himself laugh, in response. "You sound like a bloody Bond villain! And not one of the best."

Joss gave off a vicious smiling growl as he said, "Oh, you need to be punished."

He slapped Finn. Then backhanded him, again. And again and again and again. Blood trailed from Finn's nose and that bite in his lower lip.

"I can't have you die," Joss finally snarled, his grin nearly maniacal. He gripped Finn's throat and squeezed. "You're my only protection against my overlords. You and your *brother*. I know you're too much of a man to kill yourself. You'll keep thinking you can find a way to protect the others I plan to have fun with. A long line of them. Beautiful young men who'll die too soon. So many wars. So much terror and hate, in your time. I could do a different one every night for a hundred years and not touch even one percent of them, and no one will ever know."

"You're bloody mad!" Finn choked out.

Joss released him, let him cough and gasp for air.

"That's not possible. Insanity has been engineered out of our genetic code," he chuckled. "What you call *mad* is merely me being honest."

"You're not infallible," Finn spat at him. You've made mistakes."

"Have I?"

"Took the wrong man! Willem Schröder. You thought he was Christian, didn't you?"

Joss eyed Finn, almost wary. "He was given to me to find. It's not my fault this was through a clerical error."

"But that's the link, isn't it? You still have access to the records at *Alles Wissen*, and his...the way his information was entered, you thought he was related to me."

Joss caressed Finn's left eyebrow, almost tenderly. "To be honest, I did have doubts the information given me was correct. Which was confirmed, once I had him naked. It's noted in your file you do not possess a foreskin, meaning it was probable your brothers did not. So I decided to see how far I could go and still bring forth his semen. This would prove to my overlords it was not my error that brought this about. Which I did. Five times. I would call it a glorious success."

"Five times?! " Finn nearly spat. "Success!? Torturing a man like this five times!?"

"It was in the name of science. Gathering information to use. It's not as if he mattered. What's the death of a man who's already going to die when it's done for the betterment of all?"

Finn jolted. "You...you killed him, yourself."

Joss smiled. "The autopsy report says he died of smoke inhalation before his poor body was burned to a crisp."

"Did you set the fire?" Finn growled.

Joss hesitated then said, by rote, "Finn, if one disrupts the path of history, one might make things worse instead of better."

"But...but why do you have to come back to us to get fresh DNA? All the information you need is already recorded."

Joss frowned at him. "Why would you think that?"

"At university, I learned about the HGP, a Euro-centric

mapping of the human genome. In an ethics class."

He shrugged. "That doesn't answer my question."

"It was connected to other databases throughout Europe. North America. Africa. Dozens, maybe hundreds. You told me you've been accessing old files, looking for certain types of men. That's what led you to Willem and Christian and...and a man in Argentina and Stuart and Rob and God knows how many others. "

Joss shrugged. "What of it? This is information that is five-hundred years old. Hardly reliable."

"But it's there. It's giving your overlords the links. You just took it a step further and cross referenced with...with death records of the time. Found men you liked who died, and you went after them, as well."

Joss smiled. "I'm not the first to do so. An associate made their connection with Ted Bundy, then stupidly manipulated him into killing a woman who wasn't supposed to die. The change in our history's path was noticed by our analysts, and my associate is no longer part of the program. I won't let that happen to me. I'm careful to choose men who I know have died. Of course, if they actually die a moment or two earlier in ways that cannot be detected, who's to know?"

Revulsion exploded through Finn. "You act like it's a sick *get out of jail free* card. *How can you rape and torture a man who no longer exists? How can you kill a man long dead?* Thirty years of DNA testing was done for the HGP. Hundreds of thousands of possibilities — "

"Millions," Joss murmured as he turned away from Finn.

"So you don't need to do this! Why even start it? You had all the information you needed, so why go after raw DNA from this time period? Is it because somewhere along the line your scientists broke the chain and need to start over?"

Joss laughed. "You think you're working this out. So did Christian, but he's just as much a fool as you. I'll prove it to him, next time I use him."

Then he spun around to whip a cat o' nine-tails across Finn's chest, tearing open his shirt and slicing into his skin.

Finn howled in pain.

"Unless you can make me happy," Joss murmured,

sauntering up to him, a vicious grin on his face. He ripped the shirt completely open, then tenderly fingered Finn's nipples as he said, "Now that you know he's your twin, what will you do to keep him safe?"

"You...you can't kill him..."

"I said *safe*. From me." He shoved the handle of the whip against Finn's lips, smearing the blood on his face as he whispered, "Will *you* feed the beast inside me?"

His lips brushed against Finn's. His tongue licked at the blood.

Finn shivered in disgust.

Joss trailed his hand down the blood on Finn's chest and belly. Slipped inside his trousers to grope him. "Will you take me in your mouth? Draw my cum from me as a lover would? I think it would be joyous to experience this as both the sucker and the suckee."

Finn gulped and was just barely able to shake his head.

"You'd best think about it," said Joss as he wrapped his arms around Finn. He trailed his lips down his neck and to his left nip. Sucked on it as he murmured, "Will you beg me to let you do this to me? And masturbate yourself? And ejaculate as I cum in your mouth?"

He kissed the wounds on Finn's chest. Licked his right nip.

"Will you do this to protect your brother?"

Joss's lips followed the trail of blood down Finn's torso.

"Keep me from using Christian, like this? Is he worthy of your full protection?"

His fondling grew harsh and painful as he ran his other hand up and down Finn's thighs, sometimes pushing the whip handle's nob up against Finn's scrotum.

"Or would you rather I take him? Again? And again? And use my little toy in more ways than merely a whip?"

He guided the handle up Finn's torso, brushing it against one nip then the other.

Finn cringed at every touch but still forced himself to say, "Like you did with Rob and Stu? You will anyway!"

Joss rose, his eyes deadly, and pushed the handle against Finn's mouth. He stepped back to look long and hard at him, strung up and fighting to keep from collapsing into terror, then he snarled, "You don't trust me. That hurts."

He sliced the whip across Finn's torso. And arms. And legs. Over and over. Working around to his back and ass.

Finn howled and tried to avoid the vicious straps. Blood flew everywhere. His suit disintegrated to shreds of cloth. Blood coursed down his body and legs and was smeared all over him as Joss whipped him and whipped him. Front. Back. Sides. Thighs. Finally, he drifted into shock and stopped even trying to fight.

That's when Joss stumbled back, his chest heaving as he caught his breath. His muscles gleaming with sweat. He stretched and shifted his neck to work out the tension in it, then tossed the whip aside and approached his bloody victim like a hesitant lover.

Finn's hands were released, letting him collapse to the nothing floor. Joss tenderly removed the last shreds of the suit and shirt and briefs. Untied his shoes and rolled off his socks. Left him lying there as he backed away into darkness, for a few moments. Then he brought forth a clear basin of gleaming water and a cloth. He knelt beside Finn. Rolled him over to lie back against him...and cleaned the wounds on his chest with a tenderness that bordered on mourning. Sorrow laced his every movement. It was heartbreaking, how gentle he was.

The fluid tingled as it touched Finn's injuries. The pain whispered away. He began to weep as Joss shifted him forward to wash his back, always soft and almost loving as he cleaned blood away from shredded skin. Then he focused on his rear and his thighs, lingering around his crotch.

Once he was done and the now-red fluid was put away, Joss kneeled to embrace Finn from behind, as tender as a lover. Tilted his head back and around to look at him. Kissed him.

And to his numb shock, Finn kissed him back.

Joss's lips pulled away, just a little, as he whispered, "I told you I would obsess over you. You feed the beast inside me. You are all that I want, now and again. Will you serve me?"

Finn hesitated. Joss cocked a smile.

"Will you take me in your mouth to keep your brother safe? Will you do whatever I want? Whenever I want? May

I come to you in the night to be with you? To hold you? To keep you? Will you give yourself to me? Freely? Completely?"

Finn continued to weep.

Joss whispered his fingers up Finn's body to caress his neck as he murmured, "Do you now trust me to keep my word?"

Finn drew in a long slow breath...and nodded.

Joss kissed him, again, then rose to his feet.

And Finn was allowed to kneel before him.

And open Joss's trousers to reveal him.

And take him in his mouth.

And do absolutely everything he was told.

Realigning Plans

Finn woke on a beach under a blinding sun. He was lying on his back and something gritty was stuck to his lips. He felt vague and unsure, and he could not move without pain. As he regained focus, he noticed dozens of people standing around watching two men in bright vests hover over him. One saw that he was awake and asked him something in a language that could be French or Italian or maybe even Swahili.

He managed to croak, "Where. Am. I?"

Then men glanced at each other and the first one said, "English?"

Finn nodded...and his head exploded with crashing boulders of pain. He gasped, then heard the first man nattering on in the language and a woman finally said, "I know the English."

She appeared beside Finn, listening to the man, then she turned kind eyes to him and asked, "You are called?"

He felt a wave of weariness sweep over him but managed to say, "Fin...ley. James. Win...ter..."

And he woke in a hospital room, a nurse checking him. She saw his eyes open and hurried away.

Then he heard a voice cry, "Bloody hell, *City Boy*'s back!"

And Rob appeared in her place.

Stu was right behind him!

Finn couldn't believe it. He wondered for a moment if they were ghosts or angels. But then Rob caressed his head and Stu gripped his hand, he knew they were real.

Alive!

Both of them!

And neither looked like they had been touched by Joss.

Finn laughed with relief...then coughed and choked.

A brisk, middle-aged doctor appeared, a streak of

white in her hair, and she brushed them aside to check on him, speaking with a light accent as she said, "Mr. Winterbourne, how are you feeling?"

"It...it's Finn...just Finn," drifted from him.

"That is good to hear, *Finn*. It almost sounds as if you are cognizant, again."

"How...how long...out?"

"You've been in hospital now two days. Do you remember what has happened?"

Joss rammed his dick down Finn's throat as he came, and Finn gagged and spit and Joss beat him with the whip's handle and bent him over to fuck him.

Finn grimaced. He shook his head. "Blank. Where...am I?"

"Ajaccio."

"Corsica," Rob said. "They found ya on the beach, near the *Carrefour Market*. Ya were pretty bad off."

"Very bad." Christian appeared on the opposite side of the bed, his light smirk touched with more than a little relief while his elegant eyes cast wary glances at the other two.

The doctor rose and said in a voice that was more than authoritarian, "Now, gentlemen, you will have to leave. My patient needs rest and — "

Christian showed her his warrant card. "I am with Hamburg's Polizei, and this man was kidnapped from — "

"I don't care who you are or what has happened. I am his physician and he is my first priority. I will be examining him, and if I believe he is capable of answering your questions, I will let you know. Until then, away."

Christian's smirk shifted to a feral grin, and Rob's eyes grew dangerous.

Finn noticed and croaked, "Christian," making the man turn to him. His voice cracked and growled as he continued, "You met. Detective Inspector. Robert Paul Hoskins? Manchester police?"

Christian's eyes whipped to focus on Rob, startled.

"And Stuart Haller? Of Scotland?" By this point, Finn was out of breath.

"I...I have only just arrived," said Christian, shaken.

They looked back at him, suddenly wary.

"Rob, Stu," Finn said, gulping in more air, "this...this is Polizeioberkommisar. Christian Hauptman. It...it turns out...he and I...are brothers. You should compare notes. On your cases. Give...give the doctor time...to do her job."

Rob exchanged a surprised glance with Stu before focusing on Christian, making himself smile and saying, "Y'know, I could murder a pork chop, right now. Up for it?"

Christian's eyes never left him as he murmured. "It is against my upbringing to — what is the American phrase? — *talk shop* as we dine, but I believe the occasion supports it."

"I saw what looks like a great caf' 'round the corner."

"Their food is greasy and horrible for you," the doctor said, herding them away. "But I am certain you will very much like it. Speak with me before you return."

They all sent Finn one last glance before exiting the room, with Rob pointing a strong finger at him and barking, "Don't go anywhere."

Finn managed to chuckle. "Try not to."

The next three hours were taken up with blood-work, x-rays, and a battery of other tests to check Finn's physical condition. He was also met with by a victim's advocate because the initial examination had revealed injuries that were too consistent with sexual assault for them to ignore. Throughout this, he learned in dibs and drabs that he'd been found lying on the beach, naked and bleeding. The initial thought was he'd either fallen or was pushed over the side of one of the ferries from Toulouse or Marseille, but the local constabulary's consensus changed to him having been on a private yacht and, considering his injuries, not by choice. Then sometime during the night he'd been dumped on the beach by his assailant, who scurried back to his boat and had probably left the Mediterranean. Now they wanted to speak with him to find out who it was. The doctor let them in, first.

It did them no good. Finn told them he remembered nothing from the point he landed in Munich. Their queries about the events under investigation on the Scottish Isles were met with the same information he'd given the DCI. Then he told them they would need to speak with Christian about the rest of it.

"There was little to share with them," Christian told Finn, later. "You and I were investigating human trafficking when you vanished. I promised to send them a report, when I return to Hamburg. It may slip my mind."

This was after he Rob and Stu returned to Finn's room with sandwiches and wine, for dinner. Now they were sitting around Finn's bed like college chums at a cricket match.

Finn learned Rob and Stu had seen the warning scratched in the dirt. Fearing he'd been killed, Stu had packed rucksacks with a few clothes, *borrowed* a boat from a friend and all but dragged Rob onto it. They were now moored in the harbor.

"He's not happy about me bringing it down here," Stu said, "but there's nowt he can do, now."

They hadn't realized till they passed Gibraltar that they were also thought dead, so Stu had contacted his DCI buddy and let him know they were fine and in hiding.

"That was yesterday," Rob said. "Hadn't seen the news till then, when we heard 'bout ya bein' found."

"They had just identified ye," Stu said. "There was a snippet on last night's late telecast with yer photo in it. I know French enough to make out ye were here and not dead, so we headed straight over."

"Had to use my old warrant card to get in the country, but it worked."

Finn leaned against his bed's headboard and sighed. "He knows you're alive, now. I led him to you, and I am so sorry..."

"For what? How were ya to know? By the records, I *am* dead."

"As was I," said Stu. "It took a fortnight to have that corrected, like. And now here we are, untouched since."

"When he'd come and took us whenever he wanted," said Rob.

"So why hasn't he come for us?" Stu murmured. "It has to be deliberate, for some reason. His timing's been too precise for others."

"What if it's not?" Finn asked, his mind drifting in a gentle haze. "He's working off information that's centuries old, to him. And he acknowledged some of it was...was wrong."

Joss smirked at him, saying, "Schröder was a clerical error."

Finn gasped and dug his fingernails into his forearm,

using the pain to keep himself focused.

Christian noticed, and his voice was careful as he said, "But, Finn, he was able to capture you in *Alles Wissen* moments after we arrive. How can he do this?"

Finn looked at him, half-smiling. "I think it's a physical connection. To you and to me, to all of us. Through our DNA..."

"Then he could capture any of us, here, from earlier in our lives. Why not do that?"

Finn sighed. "I don't know. Perhaps when the target dies, either in fact or by error of input, the connection is broken. Or it could be about aligning with certain events or...or not altering the timeline of history. Or simply a flaw in the design. All I can tell, so far, is he used our DNA to track us down and take us."

Stu sagged. "It's as if, once he's had all his fun and yer dead, he releases ye and can't re-establish the connection."

"So I should perhaps die in order to live?" said Christian. "I don't think I'm willing to try that, yet."

Finn was about to argue when —

Joss fucked him, hard, like an animal, beating him with the whip, drawing more and more blood and sending daggers of pain into him.

Finn doubled over, breathing hard. Stu bolted to his feet. Christian froze. Rob jumped to beside him. "Finn? What? What is it?"

"He's remembering the torture," Stu whispered.

Rob glanced at him then looked at Christian, who gave him a slight nod as he said, "From the second time. And third."

Rob sank back into his chair.

Finn regained enough control to sit back up, his breathing almost back to normal. Finally, he softly asked, "Rob, did he...he take you a second time?"

Rob looked at him. "I dunno. Gettin' hit by that car knocked out part my memory. Maybe I'm glad for it."

Finn nodded. "When Joss mentioned the plane crash. His first sadistic assault. It seemed the intensity of it is what helped with the connection..."

"All right then what if his timing *is* not perfect?" asked Christian. "What if he captured Stuart a day early? As you said, he is relying on agéd records that are not precise.

Input by humans who make mistakes."

"But I don't understand why he'd choose me," said Stu. "I'm not like the lads ye described. Plus, I'm older by years."

"How old is your father, Finn?" Christian asked, then added, "*Our* father?"

Finn shrugged, still weak. "Fifty-seven; fifty-eight."

Christian turned to Stu. "And your age?"

"Thirty-eight, next month."

"It's a possibility..."

"But we can't be related! I know my father."

"One never can be certain." Christian's smirk was back in place as he motioned to Stu and Rob. "I would like to take swabs and samples of blood from you both. Send these to my sister, to see." Then he hesitated and looked at Finn. "But I must admit I am concerned. After listening to your story, I wonder if that would be an intelligent thing to do."

"We're all already in the databank, in some way or other," Finn said. Then he cocked his head, nearly smiling. "Christian, could you ask her if anyone in Newcastle or Reading contacted *Alles Wissen* for your DNA results? And see if they also accessed the files for others? Say within the last four years?"

"You think your friend Joss may have more to do with this? That he is not merely used as a vessel?"

"I don't know. Just a thought."

Christian nodded and looked at Stu and Rob. "Your answers?"

Rob held his arms out, akimbo, saying, "Take it."

Stu shrugged a wary yes.

"I will arrange this." And with a nod to them all, he left.

"*Despite all my rage, I'm still just a rat in a cage, eh?*" said Rob, quoting *The Smashing Pumpkins*.

"Ye may not be far wrong," said Stu. "Something Martin said when he...after he had me...the first time. *Hope yer the one.* I didn't think much of it, till now, but he was weeping as he said it. Makes me wonder if there might be something to it all."

"You weren't the first man he did this to," said Finn.

"Well, I'd like to make bloody sure you're the last," Rob said as he sat on the side of the bed. His voice was thick with emotion. "I was so sure ya were gone for good."

"As was I, you. I haven't done much of a job protecting you."

"Are we dead, yet? I mean, outside the bureaucratic shite?"

Finn had to smile, at that.

Joss choked him, saying, "I'll take them when I want them."

Finn flinched.

"Will you do what I want to protect them?"

Finn nodded.

Stuart noticed and knelt next to the bed to lean against the mattress. "Ye learned much, Finn, and knowledge is power, inn'it? Change the world. At the very least, ye took a weight off us. Who knew being dead would let ye keep alive?"

A nurse appeared at the door to say, "Time, gentlemen."

"Visitin' hours're done." Rob kissed Finn's hand. "Back in the mornin'. Ya'll be here, right?"

"I'll try."

Rob ruffled his hair, then he and Stu reluctantly left.

Finn let out a long, leisurely sigh of relief and lay back. Perhaps Joss would keep his promise. Perhaps he would leave Christian alone, so long as he wanted Finn. Not go after Rob and Stu, again. The next time he was taken, he would make they were part of the deal, and he would do anything Joss wanted, no matter how degrading.

Because he could also use this acquiescence to elicit more information from the man. Work out a way to end this horror.

Finn let a smile cross his face. He was back on track to being a cop. A good cop, who never backed down. Like Nan never did. He felt relieved and chill enough with himself to drift into the best night's sleep he'd had all week.

****

Late the next day, Finn was declared well enough to be released from the hospital. He still had had a limp, and he had to face a slew of reporters seeking his side of the story, all of whom went away disappointed since he insisted he could not remember what happened. Christian backed him up by refusing to discuss the case they were working on *due to potential legal ramifications.*

Finn settled into the same hotel as Christian, then they met in his room to go over their notes. But before they could do anything more than begin talking, word came back from Mikala.

"Ye got it to her fast enough," said Stu.

"I had it hand-carried in my father's jet," said Christian.

"Your da's jet?" Rob asked.

"Yes."

"Bloody hell, and I thought *you* were posh," Rob said to Finn. "So...results?"

"You are, in fact, half-brother to me and Finn. As is Stuart."

"Half-brother?!?!" Stuart snapped in disbelief. "You. Me. All four of us? Bollocks!"

"Finn," said Christian, "you know of our father better than any of us. Is this truly possible?"

"All I knew of him was letters he wrote Nan, when he was at King's College. I've never met him."

"Cambridge?" asked Stu, wary. "When was he there?"

"Why?"

"It's where I come into the world. Me mum was at St. Catherine's. Matriculated there and become a teacher. Moved us to the island, and there I grew up."

"What about your Da?" asked Rob. "Weren't he around?"

"Not much. He was RAF, at Lakenheath. Got a transfer but mum wanted to settle; he didn't. So they divorced when I was but a year. I'd see him, now and again. Still keep contact."

"D'ya look like him?"

Stu shook his head. "I favor mum. I've a call in to her, but it's exams so no telling when she'll respond."

"I look like my mother's father," Rob smirked. "And my folks're still together. Got a sister, two brothers and...OH!" He flopped back on the bed to growl at the ceiling, "And they think me dead! So how do I find out what the fuck happened? HOW it happened? If that crap's right."

"It is," said Christian. "I know my sister; she would

not say this if she were not positive."

"I've met her," said Finn. "He's right."

Rob laughed and pulled him down beside him to wrap an arm around his neck. "I joked about this bein' incest, and the truth is, I still don't care."

Finn grinned at him and patted his belly.

Christian looked away, tense, as Rob winked at Finn and said, "Little lower, next time." Then they both sat up.

Stu watched them, not smiling, then said to Rob, "Yer quite the animal."

Rob blew a kiss to him then shifted his gaze to Christian. "You on board with it?"

He took in a long slow breath then said, "I am, perhaps, more cautious than you in such matters."

"One-man man, eh? We'll see." The look he cast Christian was beyond lewd.

Mikala had also run the DNA retrieved from Finn's assailant and it matched Joss. Who was on duty more than a thousand miles away. On top of this, she learned that the forensics lab in Newcastle had accessed *Alles Wissen*'s database several times over the last three years. The final contact being less than a month prior to Rob's assault. In Reading there had been but one request.

For Finn's.

"A few days before I was taken," he said. Then he looked at the date the initial results had been mapped and shook his head. "This was from a test Nan set up. Our grandmother."

"Most of these requests from Newcastle were to compare genetic codes from as far back as twenty years," said Christian as he ran over the list.

"That's still well after the HGP wound down," said Finn, "but Hap-Map was on-going."

"There were only seven positive matches for Englishmen, two of which were the boy in Leeds...and Stuart."

"I'm Scottish!" Stu snapped.

"The other five?" Rob asked.

Christian gazed on his notes before saying, "All have died. Two motor vehicle accidents. Train crash. One in Iraq; one in Afghanistan."

"None in a plane?"

"None of these. But here is the difficult part...all were related to us. Not as close as half-brothers or even immediate cousins, but the basic connection is there."

"Bloody hell," said Rob, "it's like a *Shakespeare* play; kill off the whole family."

"But it wasn't just our family line," said Finn. "They were searching through...well, God knows how many. The first man he went for was young, athletic, married, killed in a plane crash. Probably within the last four years. Christian, could you ask Mikala to run a cross-reference of details on that sort of death with hits on DNA data at *Alles Wissen*?"

"They got millions of samples on file, don't they?" asked Rob. "That could take weeks. Months."

"But I think it has to have been done within the last four years. Not sure why, but it's like he's got to show he's done his search at a particular time through a particular databank to keep from being stopped by his own board of governors. His *overlords*, as it were."

"You think he's got back-up from 'em?"

"I don't know. They may not even care, so long as he's bringing them what they want."

"Our cum," said Stu. "That's brutal kink, right there."

"But I don't get what good that's gonna do," said Rob. "I never were part of any genetic project."

"You are now in *Alles Wissen*'s database," said Christian.

"Oh, fuck, you're right."

"And you were already in the forensics lab's, thanks to the paternity test," Finn added. Then he turned to Christian. "Do you think Mikala would look, for us?"

Christian was still hesitant, but sighed a shrug. "I can ask her to check. But I should note, this is outside her normal sphere of research."

"Something else to consider," said Stu. "I tracked down Martin Lowenstein in Monifeith, Scotland at a care facility for those who've suffered *serious mental or emotional disturbances*. Maybe his DNA's included."

"We should talk to him," said Finn.

"I spoke with Dr. Behrmann, the head, and she says no use to visit. He sits at the window and watches boats travel down the Tay. Pays attention to no one, not even his wife."

"He has been there three years, almost," Christian said

as he looked over Stu's notes.

Stu nodded. "Looks like from about the time he...he nearly killed me."

"I see...and this doctor will not discuss the case without a court order..."

"That's right, and even then only in the strictest terms."

"Then we interrogate Joss, first," Finn said. "He's still in Reading. I've called. Left messages on voicemail and at the clerk's desk, but he ignores me. I'll have to go there and find him."

"You think that's right to do?" Rob asked. "Might send him over the edge, like Lowenstein."

"But he's the main link between you, me and Christian, and I can see no other way to learn more without confronting him."

"What if it's me talks with him?" asked Stu. "Martin's who took me."

Finn hesitated.

"Haller fought so hard, I don't think he noticed I wasn't Martin. Same for Hoskins, both times. He thought I was someone named Prym."

Finn gasped in a deep breath then shook his head. "No, Stu...it was Joss who took you, from what he said."

"I know what Martin looks like, Finn."

"But you were also traumatized and – "

"Finn," said Christian, "if we are close by and have him wired it should be all right. We might even feed him questions."

"Have you done undercover surveillance?" Finn snapped.

Christian's smirk appeared. "A few times."

"Me, too," said Rob.

"Right," said Finn, "well Stu hasn't, and it can be very dangerous. I was on an operation where an experienced undercover officer was caught out and nearly killed. I don't want that to happen, again."

"And I don't want this to continue," Stu snapped. "The uncertainty and fear and hopelessness. I'm finding yer man and speaking to him about this, with or without yer backing. Are we understood?"

Rob and Christian nodded.

Finn saw it was three against one so sat back with a shrug. He figured he could find some way to keep Stu from doing what he knew could too easily turn into a catastrophe. How he would do that remained to be seen. But he'd sworn to keep Stu safe and if he had to tie up all three of them to do it, he would.

And the wicked little thought that wormed its way into his head was, *Wouldn't that be fun?*

****

The request for more information was put to Mikala under the relatively honest guise they were searching for a serial killer, and something he said while brutalizing Finn made them think one of his victims might have recently died in a plane crash. If so, they felt they could close the circle in on him and end *his reign of terror*. Christian grimaced as he said that, in German. However, it worked. She agreed.

"But you will need to find an adequate excuse as to how you disappeared from her laboratory," Christian smirked. "She thinks it was quite rude of you."

"What did you tell her?" asked Finn.

"That you had to use the toilet." Then he added, with a smirk, "She understood you not wanting to mention it before her, or return after, you being a polished gentleman. I don't think she believes me."

Rob chuckled as Finn huffed.

Christian's father's jet had returned to Corsica, so they used that to travel to England. Because Finn had been clever enough to leave his passport in his suitcase, he had that for customs, and Stu had his own, but it took some fancy talking by Christian to get Rob aboard, since he had not legally entered the country.

"Bloody Brexit," Rob snarled, more than once. "Bastards had no idea what they were doin'."

Immigration authorities finally decided Rob wasn't legally in the country, so if he left, he was never there.

"Is this acceptable?" Finn asked.

Christian gave him a cool look and said, "Don't ask."

He didn't say another word.

During the flight, Finn watched Rob doze off and

smiled at how Christian became locked into his notes, working out diagrams and possibilities. Stu sat across from Rob, glancing between him and Finn, uncertain. Finn sighed and shook his head. Despite his assurances, he felt Stu was still wary of Finn's intentions.

To be honest, Finn was unsure, himself. Brother or no brother, he wanted more of Rob. Almost longed for him. It was only the self-control Nan had instilled in him, a sense of honor and decency that kept him from making another play for the man.

Joss held Finn, tenderly, whispering, "Will you do as I ask to protect your brother?"

Finn flinched. He knew he would do more than was necessary to protect those he cared about, and deep down he did care for Stu almost as much as he wanted Rob. It was not a pleasant place to be, right then.

Stu better make up his mind about what-is-what between him and Rob. It's not fair to either of them to be so unsure.

Finn settled deeper into the seat, still vaguely bothered by something regarding the connection between *Alles Wissen* and Joss's requests for information. Such actions were out of the ordinary if not connected to a specific case, especially if not processed through the forensics lab. So what was the problem? He could almost see it...but then it would dance away from his conscious mind, and it was irritating him to no end. So when Stu rose, came over to him and softly asked, "Can I speak with ye?" Finn welcomed the diversion.

Stu sat across from him, their knees almost touching in the close quarters. He huffed and hesitated. Finn just watched him.

"This isn't easy for me," Stu finally said. "I've never been the sort shares of himself. I chased the birds and said what's needed for them to join me in bed, but never anything of value. It's not my nature. Half the reason I'm twice divorced, I'm told." He snorted. "It's not at all like that, for yerself."

Finn shrugged. "Not exactly. As a constable, I did learn to have a wall of reserve between me and the job. It was needed to keep from falling into...well...despair over humanity. Hate. Disgust. The things men and women do to each other. To children. If you don't keep apart from it, you become one with it. I've seen that destroy too many good people. I suppose it's almost like having two complete personas within yourself — one stoic for public view, one private."

"And that's how ye handle what...what happened? Stoic?"

Finn grimaced.

The whip sliced through his suit and cut his skin. Blood flew and he fought to keep away from it.

He hesitated then forced himself to say, "I know what I've been through, and I still feel the...the physical effects of it, and I know that I'm holding my deeper feelings at bay. But we are, for want of a better word, on a mission, and I keep myself focused on that. Once it's done...if it's done...I may well join Martin in his care facility."

"Doubt that. Yer strong. Not like him. But then, he never was one to be solid and there, at all times. When he took me, the first time, he did not want to hurt me. That's what almost makes it livable."

Finn jammed his eyes closed.

Joss cried, "No...not him...not to him..."

He took a deep breath and sighed. "Do you think it...it was...because he knew you?"

"A wee bit. But most, I think it was because he was never that way. Hurtful. Cruel. He could be a wild lad. We both were. Did drugs a few times together. Tripped around the Mediterranean our gap year. But never did a dark side of him show. We were friends. Almost brothers, of a fashion."

"And the scars on you?"

"That beast made him do it, the second time. I saw enough of what was done to yerself to know Martin could never do that to anyone, no matter what the need. I think that's what put him in that care home. May well have destroyed him."

He tightened, then leaned forward to rest his elbows on his knees, his eyes on the floor. It took him a long time to say, "I don't think Rob could understand this, but..."

His voice trailed off.

Finn was gentle as he said, "He cares very much for you."

Stu snorted. "Feels responsible, is more like."

"Could that your version of a wall? Denying the right of someone else to love you?"

Stu cast a sharp glance at Finn. "*Love* me? He's a man, and I'm his age plus six year, but he's more *my* father protector than me his. It's just...I feel safe with him. Safe! It's mad."

"No, it's not. He's a good man."

Stu nodded, his eyes locked on Finn's. "He brought ye to talk to me, didn't he? Said as much, that night. And we started to, didn't we? Like he thought we would."

Finn nodded.

"I have to say, I felt good with ye, the day we met. I put it down to us sharing...sharing that experience. But now? It was as if I...it's mad, but it's as if, once I actually looked at ye, already I knew ye. It spooked me, good."

"I understand. I felt an affinity for you, as well."

"I was never afeared ye'd take Rob from me. How can ye take someone away when ye haven't made them yer own? No, it's that I was confused at how easy Rob was with ye. I kept telling meself it's about nowt but the sex ye both had, and truth is I *was* a bit twitched by it, but it's not that. So I've been watching ye both and now I see it. Ye both *are* brothers. His glass, the way he holds it when he uses one. It's like you. When yer writing something, the way ye focus is like him."

Finn frowned, suddenly self-conscious but now seeing that Stu was right. They did have mannerisms that were identical.

"He tell ye he grew up in Nottingham?" Stu continued.

Finn shook his head.

"His mum was a home-care nurse. Worked the Peak District to Lincoln to Leicester."

Finn jolted. "The spiritual center in Darby. That's where my father met my mother. They were there for two, three years."

"Would that be when Christian and yerself come about?"

"Possibly. They came down to London once I was born. Nan didn't even know mum was pregnant till I was dropped off to her. Then they just...they just left."

"Shite, Finn. Not out for parent of the year, were they?"

"They weren't my parents!" he snapped. "They only bore me. Nan raised me, all on her own. My grandfather died before I came along, and my uncles were at university. Nan was my parents. She steadied me. Supported me. She was more than just my blood."

"She did good by ye," Stu said with a gentle smile.

Finn just took in a deep breath and thanked him with a smile.

"Now Rob and I are of yer blood, as well," Stu continued. "But he feels it more'n me. When ye vanished, he went near mad trying to find ye. Run outside, all over in the morning light. Wearing nothing more than his unders. Till he saw that note in the dirt. And he sank to the ground and wouldn't move, no matter what I said. All he'd do is say over and over, *I've killed him.*

"I was tore up, but not so much that I didn't know we had to get away. Hide till we could make sense of it. Took me more than two bloody hours to get him on that boat. Keep us off from everything, for just a wee while. Regain our bearings. But he wouldn't hear a word I said...not till finally I told him what happened to me."

Finn drew in a deep breath. Stu nodded.

"All of it. Every bloody detail. That's what it took for me to open meself to him...being afeared for him. Wanting him back to as he was. And it did bring him out of his state, hearing how those...*experiences* scarred me. Torn me apart. By the time we reached Gibraltar, he was almost back to himself, swearing he'd let nothing harm me.

"Then we heard about ye. And verified from the hospital it was true. And that night...as he held me...he sobbed. And I held him and...and for the first time, I felt...I felt this...this overpowering love for him."

Finn let out a long slow sigh then said, "I'm glad."

"Are ye?" Stu asked, gently. Then he put a hand on Finn's knee. "Don't answer. I can see it. Yer eyes show to yer soul, Finn."

"I...I'm sorry."

"No, it's me who is," Stu said as he leaned back and looked out the window. His voice grew so soft Finn could barely make out the words. "Ye connected with Rob in a way that I still haven't. That I can't. And I know I hurt him for not taking that final step, with him."

"I wish you'd stop berating yourself over that."

Stu cast him a wary side-glance. "But us now being half-brothers...what complication does that bring?"

Finn shrugged. "It's not my place to assign my version of morality to others. I only know it matters not to me."

"Morality. Legality. Are there such things, anymore?" He absently traced a circle over the window. "All me certainty is gone. The first time I was taken. Out by me house. When Martin come to me, in that blue light. Took me to that room of nothing. And I felt meself being caressed by the nothing-air...I hated every second of it. The way I was disrobed horrified me. And excited me. Martin holding me face and saying he was sorry. He didn't want to do this to me. I both hated him and was glad he was doing it.

"But, God, how I cursed him. Threw every foul word I knew at him. Hated him. Hated his hands on me, touching me in places only women had touched me. Places where no one ever had. Hated the feel of him against me. In me. Hated how it bloody hurt. And when it was done...Jesus, I hated how much I'd enjoyed it. Enjoyed being with a man.

"I fought to convince meself it was nowt but a nightmare. A hallucination. Acid's supposed to have that effect, on occasion. Even long after ye stop using it. I kept telling meself that's all it was."

Finn ejaculated as Joss came in his ass, laughing.

He closed his eyes and said, "Yes, it is rather confusing."

"I think that's why I can tell ye. I didn't know it till recent, but Rob's still closed off. I'd seen the scars on him, but I'd thought them from being hit by that car. Now I see, he's worse off than me. He can't even face what happened the second time. What's sick about it is how it makes me feel good, knowing this. That's what I don't think he'll understand."

Finn had no idea how to respond so remained silent.

Stu picked at a thumbnail before finally asking, "When the two of ye were together, could ye tell me if...ye found that having...that having a man's hands on ye, when ye wanted them on ye...well, was it different from a woman's?"

Rob was holding him. Nuzzling the crook of his neck with his face. Then kissing him, tender and loving.

Finn sighed. "Not really...but it was." He took in a deep breath and let his eyes drift to the window. "It's lovely how...how you almost feel as though you're the one surrendering, instead of your partner." He grimaced. "No, that's not quite right. I don't want to say it's as if you're equals; it's more a case of...well, you don't feel the need to hold back." He huffed. "Which is ludicrous."

"But that's just it," said Stu. "Never had I been with a man before, not once. Martin hinted at it, a few times at uni, but it never went past that. After it happened? I wanted to, again. I'm bloody raped and I want to be with me rapist, again? That put me in a right state, it did."

He was silent, for a few moments, then continued, "I wasn't supposed to be on that ferry. I had nothing to do in Aberdeen. I think...in the back of me mind...I think I was planning to go over the side. My brain was shattered. I had no one to talk with. I mean, what could I say? *Hi-ya, I got alien abducted and buggered, to boot, and I'm looking for a repeat. Wanna shag?* I was at a complete loss. Couldn't understand anything of me life. Could only see how poorly I'd done by meself, all those years. And by others. Then that wave hit and near rolled us over, and I thought God took matters out of me hands...except I was back in that bloody room to be used by Martin. Hurt by him. And it...it made me both angry. And...and happy.

"That time...it was hideous. And he didn't fight against the control he was under. He tore into me, tore me shirt and trousers. Shredded me budgie hamper. And when he entered me, it was with anything but tenderness. And I bloody responded, again. And he laughed. And he...he finished off in me mouth and...and then suddenly I was deep in the water. Drifting down. Thinking, *Just let it go.* But me daughter — yeah, she's got another da, but I'm her father — she filled my mind and I couldn't release me hold on life. Not then. So I pushed back to the surface. Spent two year working on letting go. Fucked every woman I could just to prove I was still a lad, but found no pleasure in it, anymore. No satisfaction."

He chuckled and half-sang, "*I can't get no...satisfaction,*" then chuckled some more. "*Stones* had it right.

"That was the story of me life," he continued, "till Rob found me. When I learned it wasn't just me. That others had been through the same thing. That he had. I was relieved. That's not right, is it?"

Finn shrugged. "I can't say."

Stu sort of nodded. "Yeah. But knowing that helped me stop trying to let go. As did Rob caring for me. Knowing this beast thought me dead, that's proven to be just as helpful, even though he now knows Rob and I are still alive."

"If he could connect with you, he'd have done it long ago and..." Finn let his voice trail off.

Stu cast him a crooked grin. "And I'd not be here. Nor would Rob. Me two coppers. No, *three* brother coppers, each other's security detail, and mine own. I feel royal."

Then he took in a deep breath and said, "This Joss, he's also a copper?"

"Yes."

"Did he also fight abusing ye?"

Finn hesitated.

Joss whispered, "I'm sorry...I'm sorry..."

"The first time."

"But not the ones after?"

"You need to be punished."

Finn hesitated. "I don't know...the last two times didn't sound like him." He saw that Stu was just watching him, so continued, "He was far too angry with me. Like I was interfering with some plan of his..."

Stu leaned forward, more intense than Finn had ever seen him. "Then it *would* be better for me to approach him. I'll ask any question ye want, but I want to face him, on me own. Face a man who's able to live with being part of this. Let me do it, Finn. I want to become strong unto meself, again. Become Rob's full equal."

"You already are."

"In your mind, perhaps; could even be in his, but there's still that frightened little child, in mine. I want him to stop being so scared. That's all I want."

Stu rose and went to sit on the floor, next to Rob. He let his head rest against the wall as he put a gentle arm across Rob's knees.

Rob shifted, opened his eyes to smile at him, took his hand and pulled him up into the seat with him, embraced him and nestled his head against Stu's chest. Soft. Tender.

Loving.

An amazing warmth wrapped around Finn's heart, touched with a hint of loss. No question now; Rob was Stu's, and vice versa. Finn's night with him had been nothing more than a momentary refuge. A letting off of steam on Rob's part. Connecting fully and completely with another human being, for a moment. Finn would still be part of Rob's life, but never would he complete it, not like Stu would. And while this made him sad, it also made him happy for them.

And brutally angry.

To think of how that beast in the nothing room had hurt them. And would happily try to kill them, again. It brought a sense of divine purpose to Finn's heart that he'd never felt before. When he'd said he'd do everything in his power to protect them, to end the threat, he had meant it.

But now he knew that if he had to die doing so, he would.

Without hesitation.

And by God he'd find a way to take that monster with him.

Confrontation

Half an hour before they landed, Christian beckoned Finn over and turned his laptop to reveal Joss Hallsworth's personnel record. They spoke softly, in German.

"How did you get this?" Finn asked, stunned.

Christian just looked at him, almost smiling. Then he said, *"What do you see?"*

"Two extended absences. For health reasons. Six weeks. Then three months."

"The first, just after three years ago for two weeks; the second, a year ago for five. Comparing to Mikala's information, two men died prior to his first absence; three died within the year prior to his second. All of them in the criminal justice system, whom no one would care about. That young man in Leeds, was the last. After that..."

"Were there any recent absences?"

Christian shook his head. *"Nothing in the past year. Willie was six months ago; my...my first, a month after."*

Finn looked at him, so he continued with, *"I was on the Isar, under the Kabelstag Bridge on the beach where Willie was found. It was hot and people were about, so I was in short pants and had stripped off my shirt, pretending to enjoy the ice cold water while I searched the area. Then I was taken...and returned to the base of the Bavaria Statue, kilometers away."*

"Was anything missing?" Off Christian's confused expression he added, *"Clothing that had been torn away?"*

"My new pair of Hugo Boss."

"The same happened to me and also to Rob and Stuart. He's keeping something from each one of us, as a souvenir."

"A remembrance of our time together?" Christian said with a nasty twist. *"How is this even possible?"*

"The same way they can keep our semen, I suppose."

"This is what the serial killer does, yes?"

Finn nodded. *"The first time he had you, did he hurt you?"*

"It was rape, Finn. He did not even attempt to make it easy. No beating. No teeth. But it was forceful and painful. When I ejaculated, he laughed." It took him a moment to continue. *"The cruelty was a later part of the process."*

"Joss is involved in this," Finn said. *"I don't know how, but it's too consistent with a sort of willingness on his part."*

Christian eyed him, wary. *"You are thinking something."*

"I think we should just have Stu lead him to us, then we question him. That would be safer, and I seriously doubt we need worry about Joss breaking down like Martin did. If anything, I think he'll become more dangerous. Better if there are four of us facing him."

"Do you think he even has answers, or that if he does he will give them to us?"

Finn shrugged. *"We won't know till we ask."*

Christian nodded then motioned to the laptop. *"Do you notice something else about his career?"*

Finn looked. *"He advanced to DCI very quickly. He's but a few years older than us."* Then he stiffened. *"He became DCI a month after his second absence? That's unusual..."*

"Perhaps. Perhaps not," said Christian, smirking. *"Tell me, Finn, do you believe in the devil?"*

Finn chuckled. *"Oh, of course. What we have here is the gay 'Rosemary's Baby', with him laying out lads to be buggered by his master in exchange for career advancement."* Finn glanced at Stu and Rob. Both of them seemed asleep. *"No, as fantastical as it sounds, I'm more inclined to believe it does have something to do with the future."*

Christian's eyes were focused on Finn. *"So instead we look to H. G. Wells, yes?"*

"Yes, we're the Eloi and Joss is a Moorlock."

Christian grinned, tenderly. *"I think I would like to have had you as a brother, growing up. Someone I could share with. Talk to."*

Finn looked at him, uncertain. *"Didn't your parents let you speak with them? Your brother and sister?"*

Christian shook his head. *"My mother and father are of a generation that thinks talking of your issues is...unseemly. Mikala and Georg are younger so...I had to build up friends like myself to not feel completely alone."*

"I wish you could have known Nan," Finn said, with a gentle warmth. *"She believed holding things in was a road to*

illness, so held back nothing."

"She must have been good to have raised you so well."

Finn smiled. *"She'd have loved you."* Then he continued in English. "Do you find it odd we both wound up police officers? And Rob, a half-brother who's also a cop?"

Christian's half-grin covered his face. "You think we carry a copper gene?"

Finn shrugged. "Be worth researching."

"I think that is what began our troubles."

They shared a chuckle then Christian's expression grew warm and almost loving, and he said, in German, *"You are doing much better than I expected, after what happened to you."*

Finn hesitated.

Joss filled his mouth with urine.

He cringed then sighed and said, *"I'm not doing well, at all. I just try not to think about it. I try to keep my focus on finding a way to end this..."* He thought a moment, then continued with, *"...Well, for want of a better word, evil."*

Christian nodded, his eyes locked on Finn. *"And if we do, then what?"*

Finn looked at him for a long moment. Saw concern and caring in his eyes. Felt comfortable and safe with him. So finally said, "I've no idea."

****

The Reading area was experiencing a lovely period of wind and rain when they landed at *Blackbushe,* so Christian had an assortment of Burberry macs in various styles and lengths brought to the field, along with an SUV for them to use.

"If you prefer an umbrella, please say so," Christian told them. "But I have never found them useful in weather like this."

Finn took Christian aside to murmur, "Are you mad? Those things are fifteen hundred pounds each!"

"They are not a gift, Finn; they are merely to wear. My father's company keeps a supply on-hand for clients and his workers to use. We all know how English weather can be."

"What does your father do?"

"Pharmaceuticals. He has a large plant near here."

Finn jolted. "Is he aligned with *Alles Wissen*?"

"I doubt it. Mikala would not work there if he was. Not due to a family rift, but from purity. She does not want her research to have even the least hint of being compromised, and to work for your father brings that notion forth without fail."

"What about your brother?"

"He works with our father, learning the business."

"But you don't."

Christian cast him a cool smile. "I like what I do."

Finn shrugged, then chose a classic trench coat in tan that reached down to mid-calf. Stu took a jacket with a hood and Rob chose a bulky mac that fit over his hoodie. Christian put on a simple overcoat with a wide collar...and to Finn's eyes, he looked as if he were born to wear it.

As they were about to get in the SUV, Christian received a text and smiled. "Mikala has a few possibilities for us."

The list was just three names with descriptions and other information on them. The one that stood out? Devino Corey, from Cape Town. He was thirty-two and a mixture of Zulu, British, Dutch and East Indian. A striker for the Port Elizabeth team, he was entered into the *HGP* as a child. He died on a flight that crashed between Johannesburg and London, when he was en route to meet with Surrey about signing with their team, nearly four years ago. His wife and both daughters died with him.

As Christian drove, Finn brought up the man's photo via Google. He was nice-looking, with dark-tanned skin, sandy hair, green eyes and a big smile. Photos of his matches showed he was in top shape.

Stu watched the screen over Finn's shoulder and gave a soft huff. "He was at Edinburgh."

Finn looked at him. "Is that where you attended uni?"

"Aye. I took a gap year. Looks like he'd have been incoming when I was." He looked closer at the photo. "I'm thinking I read about this lad..."

A quick check showed an article in the university's paper concerning rape accusations against Corey, made by a young female student. He was arrested and threatened with trial. Using his phone as a hotspot, Finn opened his laptop and logged into the national police database to pull up the old arrest record. It showed a DNA sample had been taken and sent to forensics for testing. Noted in the file was that the results had not matched samples taken from the woman, so he was not her assailant. She had insisted he was, going so far as to file suit against him and demand another DNA comparison.

Which was handled by *Alles Wissen*.

The case had finally shut down when another man was found to be the rapist — a buff lad of a construction worker who died in a nasty work-site accident, a year later.

His DNA connection had also been verified by both the forensics lab and *Alles Wissen*.

"We may've found another victim," Finn murmured.

He pulled up the record for Finbar Caramin to find his DNA was handled in the exact same way, this time in regards to a murder investigation and despite forensics claiming Caramin's DNA had not matched samples gathered at the crime scene.

"Why'd they do that?" said Rob, looking over Finn's other shoulder.

"Who requested it?" Christian asked.

Finn located Caramin's arrest record and found Joss had put in for the DNA results, while still in Newcastle.

Finn took in a deep breath. "Two days before he died."

Robb huffed. "But why's he askin' 'bout Caramin when there's nothin' to connect him to that murder?"

Finn scrolled through the other arrests Joss had made to find another request to the lab, asking that the DNA of one Stuart Haller be sent to *Alles Wissen* for comparison to DNA from another criminal.

Finbar Caramin.

"Here's the link," Finn said, in near wonder. "I don't know if the first contact was through our lab or your sister's, Christian, but this is where they find their victims."

"One such place, perhaps," Christian murmured.

"It had to have been through the German lab," said Stu, "because I doubt Martin was ever in trouble with the police."

"Same for Willie," said Christian, "and Mikala has been with *Alles Wissen* only since two years."

"Can you ask her to find if Martin has DNA on file?" Finn asked. "Perhaps cross reference it with ours? See if there's any connection to us?"

"Finn, I am driving. You send it."

He sent her an email and got an immediate response, in German, which made him chuckle.

"What's she saying?" asked Stu.

Rob laughed. "She's askin' if we want her to check the whole world's, next. She's not happy to do it, but she will, 'cause her curiosity is up...and she expects an explanation from you?" He nudged Finn, with a twinkle in his eye. "You sure you didn't dump on her?"

Christian chuckled. "I think she likes our Finn."

"That'll prove awkward," said Finn, secretly pleased.

They located an electronics shop en route into the city and within half an hour had a nice range of surveillance equipment. It was all set up under Rob's and Christian's expert eyes, and supplemented by Finn's knowledge. A camera-pen was clipped into Stu's shirt pocket, and that fed into Finn's mobile phone. They ran a number of tests around an abandoned building in Coley Park to check the image quality and see how far its range was.

Throughout, Finn huffed, "It's better than what we have in Clayton-Merrill."

He tried calling Joss twice more, with the same lack of result, so they headed for Castle Street and parked across from *Thames Valley Police Reading Station*. The plan was simple — Stu would enter the ugly, modern, red brick building and ask for Joss, referencing the murder Caramin was accused of as the reason. He would lure the man out the front to be met by Finn and Rob, Christian would drive up, they'd *guide* Joss into the back and bring him back to Coley Park for serious questioning.

So Finn and Stu got out and crossed Castle Street as Rob strolled behind them; Christian parked a bit farther down the road, to keep an eye on Cusden Walk, a passageway between the police station and Magistrates' Court. All three now had their phones connected to the spy pen's relay so could both see and hear what it recorded.

"If anything about this doesn't feel right," Finn told Stu, "walk away. Don't even think about it. Understand?"

Stu nodded, took in a deep breath and headed inside. Then Finn waited by the steps leading up to the main entrance as Rob calmly sat huddled against the rain, at the base of a flagpole.

The first voice heard was the desk sergeant. "May I help?"

"I need to speak with DCI Hallsworth, thanks," Stu told him. "It's regarding a case he's investigating, in Leeds. I'm Stuart Haller."

"Can you give a bit more information, please?"

"It's best if he and I talk in private. Sorry."

"I need more than that to bother him, sir. He's a very busy man."

"Right, then...tell him it's about the blue lights I saw."

"Very well."

"Oh, why'd you say that?" Finn growled, feeling something was going to go wrong. "It's supposed to be Caramin's murder case."

The phone showed only the usual rush and bustle of people going in and out of a police station until he heard, "I'm Hallsworth. Who're you, again?"

Stu turned and Joss appeared on Finn's phone...and the man froze at getting a good look at him. To Finn's shock he seemed even more haggard and wary than from last Monday's photo.

"Stuart Haller. I've come to speak with ye about Finbar Caramin."

This comment shook Joss, even more. "It...uh, it's teatime and I was just going for sushi," he said, his voice barely even. "Come with?"

"No, don't," said Finn, tight and uncertain.

"Where's that, then?" asked Stu.

"Just on the plaza," said Joss. "Out the back."

"No, Stu," Finn muttered, "walk away," as Stu said, "It's nasty out, but never do I turn that down."

Joss rushed him to a rear door. "Come on, then. I'm hungry. We can talk on the way."

"He's made him," said Finn as he bolted to the entrance. "I'll follow them. Rob, Cusden Walk!"

In the door's reflection he saw Rob race for a side passageway as Christian slammed the SUV into gear and did a U-turn.

Where's he going?

"Desk sergeant said it was lights you wanted to see me about," Joss was heard saying as Finn entered the building.

He could see they were now outside.

"They come at ye from nowhere," said Stu, "then yer in a room of nothing facing a beast ye thought ye knew. I'm wondering if ye knew my beast, as well?"

"I...I'm not following you."

Finn used his warrant card to get past the barriers then stopped a constable, held up his card and said, "Back door to the plaza?"

"That hallway, sir," she replied.

Finn raced down the corridor as the woman called after him, "Is anything wrong?"

Stu's voice was soft in Finn's earpiece. "His name was Martin Lowenstein. Friend at Uni. He come at me in that nothing room but a few year ago."

"Martin." Joss's voice was steadier. "What happened to him?"

"Ye knew him then?" There was a moment of silence, then crackling as the phone showed them approaching a block of solid buildings. "He had a...a psychotic break. He's in a care facility, unable to function."

Finn burst through the back door to find an open space that had dozens of people walking around, huddled against the rain, only a few umbrellas about. Some were smoking, others chatting and many now looked at him, wary. No sign of Joss and Stu, and their voices were soft and crackling.

"He did seem weak."

"When I knew him, he was decent and kind."

Rob appeared beside Finn, breathless from running, his hoody soaked flat against his skull.

"People change," said Joss. "I've seen that happen far too much."

Finn looked at his phone and saw them heading down a pedestrian walkway. He shifted to the left, looked, and despite the rain caught a glimpse of the back of Stu's head. He nudged Rob. "There!"

They raced after them.

"Wasn't that the sushi place?" Stu asked.

"There's a better one down here," was Joss's reply.

"Ye like to get wet, do ye?"

Finn and Rob were barely able to keep both men in sight on the busy pedestrian mall. To the left were the tall

Queen's Court and a hotel; to the right the mall and an office tower. It looked like Joss was leading Stu to a major thoroughfare at the end of the walkway.

"How 'bout you tell me what're you really talkin' about?" Joss said.

Stu hesitated then said, "I know Finn. And I was taken before ye were part of this."

"That's not quite how it...it worked...oh, bloody hell..."

The pen showed Christian appearing through the rain, at the other end of the walkway, headed for Joss and Stu.

"You're here," Joss muttered.

"What's that?" Stu asked.

Finn pulled Rob to a halt as his phone showed Joss spinning around, and he looked up and their eyes locked on each other.

Then Joss saw Rob, and even from a distance Finn could see his look shift to that of a wild animal that's been trapped.

"No!" Joss cried. "No, I saw you die! I watched you die!"

Stu glanced around, confused. "Ye saw them — ?"

Joss grabbed his coat, snarling, "In here."

"What ye doing?!"

Joss pulled a pistol and shoved Stu through a mall entrance, snarling, "Go!"

People saw them and scrambled away, screaming in shock and horror.

Finn and Rob pushed through the panicking crowd.

"Why up the stairs?!" Stu cried.

"GO!"

Finn slammed in through the same door, followed by Christian and Rob.

"How're you *both* alive?" Joss snarled. "I saw him hit! I saw you go in the water!"

Not far inside was a door marked Stairwell. Finn yanked it open and heard footsteps and the soft echo of Stu saying, "What're ye talking about!? Ye saw me dying?! You!?"

Finn bolted up the stairs, with Christian and Rob.

"How'd you do it?" Joss snarled. "You a good swimmer? Make it all the way back to England?"

"Another...another isle. Took hours."

"Bloody son-of-a — Winterbourne!?" Joss's voice echoed down the shaft.

Finn stopped on a landing, breathing hard, Christian and Rob a few steps above him.

"Sir," he called, "it's Finn. We just want to talk."

"Too late for that." His voice lowered to a growl as, "Keep going," crackled through Finn's earpiece.

Rob began creeping up, but then they heard Joss spit, "Christ, not now!" And Stu began to howl in terror!

Finn jolted and the blue light swirled around him and he cried out and —

Christian grabbed his hand and —

Finn felt as if he were being pulled by a tornado, close to being torn in half as the light boiled around him. Clawed at him. Made him howl in pain and fear and he felt he was being drawn away but —

Christian had too good of a grip on him and was hanging onto the bannister as Rob jumped back down to grab Finn's other hand and the both of them were screaming something at him as the nothing-air roared over him and around him and fought to rip him away from them...to free him from their grip until —

It stopped.

Finn collapsed and his head slammed against the corner of a step, cutting him. Blood trailed down his face. His mac and trousers were shredded, as if they had been sliced.

Christian was still gripping his hand, shaken, saying, *"My God, what was that?"*

A horrified Rob released his other hand. "It...it was this bloody whirlpool of light whippin' 'round you, grabbin' at you and, Christ, you okay?"

Finn could barely focus on anything, until he noticed...

Joss and Stu were silent.

"They're...they're gone," said Finn. "Can't hear..."

Rob howled and bolted up the stairs.

Christian turned up the volume on his phone and they could just make out Stu saying, "Jesus, why didn't it take us? Why?"

"It only wanted me, not you," Joss grunted. "C'mon."

"Where ye taking me?"

"Shut up!"

"But why're we up the roof?" Then Stu grunted, as if he'd been hit.

Christian clambered after Rob.

Finn forced himself to his feet, wiped at the blood on his face with a sleeve of the mac, then forced himself to follow them.

He heard the door to the roof slam open and Rob scream, "Leave him go!"

Joss's voice howled as it echoed down the shaft, "How can you be here?! You're dead! I watched you die! That car hit you straight on!"

"LEAVE HIM GO!" Rob roared.

Now Christian's voice echoed down the stairwell, "DCI Hallsworth, please, we wish only to speak with you."

"And you and Winterbourne." Joss's voice sounded like he was close to hysterics. "So it's here. It's finally here."

Finn reached the top level, near exhaustion, blood still trailing from the cut, his legs trembling. He stumbled outside, and through the driving rain could just make out Joss was holding Stu by his hair, a pistol to the man's head. They were backing to the far end of the building, a low barrier all that would keep them from falling.

Rob and Christian carefully shifted around to flank them, both in soothing postures. Alarms were sounding and patrol car sirens whooping, far below, just audible over the wind.

Finn was too weak to do anything more than call, "Joss, please, we're only trying to stop this and — "

"How?!" Joss screamed, near tears. "You can't! There's nothing there to stop! They don't exist! How can you stop something that doesn't exist?!"

"Then...then tell me something, tell me something, please." Finn made himself walk away from the door, despite his limp, as upright as possible, his voice calm and soothing. He wiped rain from his eyes as he said, "All...all we want to know from you is...is how did you justify it?"

Joss looked at him, confused. Rain coursed down his face. "Justify...what?"

Rob and Christian continued to maneuver around Joss and Stu, moving closer and closer as carefully as they could.

Finn kept Joss focused on himself. "How you justified all those searches for DNA matches through police channels. That's all. How'd you do it?"

"I...I didn't," Joss said. "I didn't need to. It was...all of it was already there. All I did was pull it up."

"But you made requests from *Alles Wissen*. They're a private German research facility. You had to give a reason for going around forensics. Justification. The Home Office requires it."

"Finn, they're tied into the forensics lab. So are others. I just pulled up what they...what name they give me." He almost seemed ill as he continued, "What name the beast give me. Find out where the guy is and...and...oh Christ..."

He looked like he was about to break into sobs.

Rob put on his most soothing voice as he asked, "Forensics partnered with labs researchin' DNA?"

Joss gulped in a couple of breaths, ignoring the rain pouring down his face, then he said, "Have been for years. Mapping out who commits crime. Who looks to fight it. See if there's...there's a genetic reason. All mapped out. So easy to locate...for me..."

"But that research has been on-going for decades," Finn said, still gentle, "with nothing yet definitive to back it up."

"It's still source material," Joss said, his voice almost blending with the sound of the wind. "Looking for specific men who...who were going to die...going to die..."

"So all you've done is...is help them with this, right?"

"Help?" Joss's face grew maniacal and he ran the hand holding the gun trough his hair as he laughed. "You think it's that simple? I thought you were smart, Finn. I thought you were smart..."

Then he shoved Stu to the floor.

Dropped the gun.

Took a step back.

And tumbled over the side.

Rob cried out and he and Christian raced to the edge.

Finn rushed to join them but the blue light swirled over him and —

He was floating in the nothing room, completely dry, the nothing-air caressing the mac off of him. Soothing him. Tracing itself up and down his entire body and face. He could not avoid any of it.

Whispers of *finally...finally...*echoed around him.

Then Joss was before him, as trim and lovely as Finn remembered. His shirt and trousers fitted. His face unlined. His dark eyes boring into Finn's, hurt, defiant, angry, joyous.

"Finally," he growled. "It's your turn now."

"What do you mean?"

"I'm falling apart. Self-destructive. Been on the border of madness for months. My wife left. Took the kids. They're better off. I become a monster. A beast. All for nothing."

"For nothing? You weren't forced to do what you did?"

"Just when I replaced Martin. And you. First time."

Finn felt his nipples being pinched through his shirt and realized he was doing it to himself. He fought to stop it but had no control.

"What the bloody hell? " he cried. "What's going on?"

He unbuttoned his shirt, despite his best efforts, and lifted his undershirt to give full access to his nips. He flicked at them and caressed his pecs and trailed down his abs to his trousers.

"No...no, not again...not again!"

Joss sighed. "It's not like that. It's going to be like Martin. When I was chosen. Now you're chosen."

The nothing-air forced Finn to fondle himself through his trousers...then unbutton them and unzip his fly. And every moment was like daggers of exquisite need slicing into him.

"I was shocked when Martin took me," Joss continued, moaning in pleasure. Finn saw he was caressing himself, as if he were alone.

Finn felt himself being maneuvered closer to Joss to fondle him.

"Tore me apart, nearly," Joss murmured. "He was psychotic, by then. Close to breaking. He did break, over the man after me. Haller. So the beast had me take over from him. I was supposed to've died preventing a kidnapping, but it kept me alive. To make the transition complete, I had to take him. Violently."

Finn found himself taking Joss's shirt in hand.

"No," he said. "I don't want to do this...I don't want to do this."

"You can't stop it," said Joss as Finn tore his shirt open

to reveal his well-defined chest swirled with hair and two erect nipples. "That it's me able to talk to you, again, means the shift's begun. Its control is shifting to you. You can't stop it. Like a drug. This amazing drug that overpowers everything."

Finn toyed with Joss's nips. Pinched them, hard.

Joss groaned then said, "I'm so glad it's over, because it feels so nice...too nice to control someone else. Use them in ways you never thought you could. No repercussions. Even as what you're doing is destroying another human being. Destroying. Destroying."

He was close to weeping.

Finn fought the urges.

This isn't real, this isn't real. I can't be enjoying this.

But then he was sucking one of Joss's nips, and between his own caressing and the nothing-air's, he was growing erect...and he could feel an intense need encompassing him.

Joss moaned, again, as if remembering a lovely moment. "He fought me, Martin did. Cursed me to even a greater extent than you. Screamed and howled as I beat and buggered him. And when I left him, he couldn't move. He couldn't move..."

"I won't do it," said Finn, fighting to pull his hands away from Joss. Instead, they trailed down Joss's hair and across his navel to the top of his pants and slowly undid his belt...and Finn felt himself go breathless with anticipation.

"Now you'll see. You'll see. You'll start out hating it. Fighting it. Disgusted with yourself. But after you've done it a few times, you'll become numb. No moral concerns. Nothing but joy at the prospect. The mere thought'll fire you up. All reservations will vanish. You'll look forward to each time. Each time you become one with the beast..."

"But this...this isn't how you look, now."

Joss chuckled. "Yeah...this is how I look at twenty-seven. Brings that body back to now. Uses me. And suddenly I've *recovered a new memory*. What you do to me, here...I'll recall it. As I die."

Finn unbuttoned Joss's trousers and slipped them down his hips to reveal black bikini briefs holding a growing bulge. Hair fanned out around it.

Finn closed his eyes and forced himself to say, "But

why you?"

"Something Martin said. *Didn't want to see me die.* I knew what he meant, and I wasn't ready to go, so I told it I...I could find it what it wanted. Information to find the lads it liked. Said I'd let it...let it use me if I got notes to help me solve crimes. But I had to live. Worked. Made me the fair-haired lad to the Home Office. Shot my career along."

Finn's right hand fondled Joss through his briefs as his left hand pinched a nip. "Using your access to our forensics lab and *Alles Wissen's.*"

Joss was breathing faster, his voice almost trembling. "Mainly. A couple others in Africa and South America. Easy to search from the list it sent. Lads it wanted. Didn't ask why."

"But you had an emotional collapse. Twice."

Joss grunted. His hands were slowly pulled behind his head, erotically, leaving his lovely chest open and vulnerable. "Because of that kid in Leeds. Stupid little punter. First time I took him, he thought he was tripping on something. That made it fun. I think he was into pain. Had enough tats. But the second time they had me take him, he was racing 'round in that bloody car, trying to get away from pursuit. Little shite. I did so much to him. Tore into him. Was brutal to him. He was just a wanker. Total little bastard."

Joss clenched his body as Finn slipped a hand between his legs.

"Then he was back in that car as it crashed. And I saw him die. Saw the steering column crush into his chest and glass slice his face and fire explode and he...he never knew what hit him. But he did know what I did to him. As he died, he knew. I was the last to have him and it felt good. Sickening and good.

"When that memory came to me, it was after I heard about him. Now I knew these weren't dreams; they were reality. Every other man that I'd seen...seen die was reality. I thought that's how they're hiding what they were doing."

Finn ran his lips down Joss's treasure trail, licking at it with his tongue.

"I had to take leave," Joss continued. "Used exhaustion as my reason. Brass understood. More dreams came at me. It was using me against men I'd looked up for them. Men who were criminals. Some petty, some bastards, all wankers without cause. Who died soon after. And the bastard made me watch each one."

Finn felt Joss press his legs together to hold his hand in place. His eyes were filled with need. Want. He managed to say, "But Stuart did nothing wrong."

"He was a jack-the-lad. No meaning in life. Brutalized him. Happy to drop him in the water, to drown, but after him, it expanded. Wanted men who *had* done nothing. Wanted each one, twice. Finally wanted Hoskins...a fellow cop. Similarity in genetic structure to Haller. I finally figured out there was something more they were after. Someone."

The fire racing within Finn was unimaginable in its eroticism. Its insatiability. He dared not say another word for fear he'd reveal how much he was enjoying this. Loving it.

"Hoskins," Joss continued, "Rob." He chuckled. "Brutalized him. Hurt him more, second time. Then put him in front of that car to be smashed to bits." His voice became a whisper. "I saw it and felt his death explode through me and I finally knew what this was about. They loved seeing men get killed. Watching them be torn apart. I'd been getting information on men who were about to die in horrible ways, just so they could watch. Christ...I had to take more leave, to calm myself down."

Finn maneuvered Joss's trousers down to his knees, caressing the hair on his legs. Slim but taut. Good form. Almost golden. He slipped his hands back up Joss's legs to cup his ass. Not the biggest ever but enough to hold.

Joss grimaced and forced himself to say, "It kept happening over and over. A cop in Munich. Over and over. Put back...as that fire started. I watched it engulf him. Burn him."

Finn pulled his own dick out of his briefs. It was raging.

"Then was Christian," Joss continued. "Over and over. Each time I braced myself, thinking this is when he'd die...but he didn't. What's sickening is...by then I loved it more than I hated it. Loved the power and the release of it. Loved the fear and pain inflicted. And they told me I could keep using him. That he wasn't set to die. He was useful."

Finn's hands drifted around Joss's sides and up to pinch his nips, hard. He nuzzled Joss's neck, nibbling at his skin. Slipped his erection between Joss's legs.

Joss moaned, and Finn could feel the man's dick press hard against the thin cotton holding him in place.

"I liked him," Joss said. "But I didn't make it easy for him. Didn't even try to. Then you were chosen. I must've given them a fight, because that's when they said you'd take over for me. I was horrified. Angry. And so bloody glad."

"No," Finn was finally able to make himself say. "I can't, I won't."

"Yes, you will. You'll see."

Finn growled and heaved a deep breath...then tore Joss's briefs off to reveal a dick that was hard and ready. Finn caressed the length of it. Toyed with the foreskin. Made Joss squirm. Then despite himself, he lifted Joss's legs onto his shoulders, found his hole with his fingers, and rammed into his ass.

Joss howled in pain.

The feeling of Joss surrounding him was beyond nirvana, to Finn; it was now the beginning and end of life. The meaning of existence. He began to pump in and back and in and back, feeling even more out of control with every thrust, as Joss gasped and squirmed and grunted in pain...all of which added to the carnal demands in them both.

By this point, Finn had lost complete control. He ran his hands over Joss wherever he wanted. Groped him in any way he wanted. Bit at his tits and nibbled at them and sucked on them and kissed them, loving the feel of his chest hair on his face. The sensation of his balls bouncing against his pubes was like a hit of cocaine. He gripped Joss's dick and began to pull on it as his mouth found Joss's and they kissed.

They kissed.

Hard.

Like animals, long and deep, tongue to tongue, devouring each other. Then Joss bit Finn's neck and Finn bit his thigh. Deep. Drew blood. Not even thinking about it.

Joss growled and grunted and snarled and shoved his ass hard against Finn and came, his semen shooting up and back over his chest, slapping all over him, not vanishing. He tightened around Finn's dick so hard and sudden, it exploded inside of him, over and over, as if it'd never cum before.

Finn kept pushing, trying to dig deeper into the man as he bit Joss's left nip so hard, he screamed and Finn felt like he had blanked out, for a moment, but then he saw —

Joss falling away from him.

Falling.

Falling.

Fully dressed and drenched and older and laughing as he plummeted through the driving wind and rain, closer and closer and closer to the pavement and Finn screamed as he watched Joss slam against it, his body shattering, blood spewing around him as his eyes froze into death and —

Finn was back at the forest near Clayton-Merrill, leaning on his left side, half propped up on an arm, his clothes in full disarray. A soft rain whispered down on him. Cold. Cruel in its tenderness. He touched his lips and saw blood on his fingers, so rolled onto his back. Paid no attention to how wet the grass and ground were. Let the rain wash over his face.

Softly wash the blood away.

But not the horror of what he had done.

Not the horror of watching Joss die.

Because Finn finally knew what had driven Martin to madness and Joss to self-destruction.

He'd become part of something that was crushing a hundred, maybe a thousand men for no more reason than to satisfy its depraved carnal needs. Just before they were caught in a hideous death.

The very idea filled his heart with revulsion...but also overwhelmed his body with a want that was vile and demanding and all-encompassing.

Because now he'd been implanted with the idea that watching a man die in a horrible way was a form of sexual pleasure.

And God help him, he loved it.

Disbelief

The days following the suicide of DCI Joss Hallsworth were brutally invasive for Finn. He was kept in isolation, his requests to know what was going on with Christian, Rob and Stu consistently being met with silence. He knew none of them were suspect in Joss's death. During one interrogation, he was shown CCTV and the camera pen revealed Joss had grabbed Stu and forced him up the stairwell. Cell phone video shot by people in the hotel and Queen's Court caught him dragging Stu across the roof, Rob and Christian flanking him, with Finn not far behind. Some even showed him pushing Stu aside before stepping back and falling to the street. So the question was, *Why had a well-regarded Deputy Chief Inspector done this? And why were a DI who was thought dead and a German police detective confronting him?*

The brick wall they were running into with Finn was unacceptable.

What was especially disconcerting to all was how one video caught him just vanishing in a flare of light, only to be discovered in a field more than a hundred miles away not an hour later. The only possible explanation floated by the *IOPC* was that he'd been taken off the roof by helicopter while everyone was focused on Joss's suicide, then ferried there and dumped.

But again the questions were, *How, why, and by whom?* And comparisons with the Corsican and Scottish police reports only added to the confusion. Not even Blethyn could get Finn to talk, despite being angry and, even worse, disappointed in him.

"I ordered you to return to Clayton-Merrill," he'd snapped in the face of Finn's silence. "What's happening here is far outside your level of expertise and well into the realm of pure insanity. I've got bloody MI5 setting up to interrogate you, and they will find out what the hell you've really been up to, my lad. You and your teammates. Christ, Finn — a Scotsman, a German officer and a DI everyone thought was dead?! Sounds like a bloody joke, just without a punchline."

All Finn could say was, "You're right, sir."

"Oh, I'm more than right, my lad. I know how those spooks work, and by the time they are finished with you, you will be singing a different tune."

Finn nodded, then a thought hit him. "Will there a record of this on my file?"

"With those bloody bastards involved? You'll be lucky if you're even allowed to exist, anymore."

An idea began to tug at Finn as he absently murmured, "Then it might *not* be on my police record..."

Blethyn sighed, hesitated, then put a kindly hand on his shoulder. "Depends on them, not us."

"Is there anything I can do?"

"Finn, no one can influence MI5's decisions. Sometimes I doubt even MI5 can influence themselves, they're so arbitrary."

Which gave Finn a glimmer of hope. Maybe...just maybe...he saw a way to end this.

After two days of being kept incommunicado and interrogated by cold blank men and women from the Home Office, he was called into a windowless room to meet a pair of men in bland fitted suits. They reminded him of Tweedle-dee and Tweedle-dum, in looks; in manner, they were two of the heads of Cerberus, and Finn was fairly certain the third head was watching everything via CCTV.

"Let's go over what we got, first," said Tweedle-dee in a carefully controlled Estuary accent. "You get jumped the middle of nowhere. Suddenly, you're callin' DCI Hallswor'f and off to Manchester to investigate the dea'f of DI Hoskins..."

"Not exactly," said Finn.

"Summarizing," Tweedle-dum shot at him, very Cornish.

"Can you tell me how DI Hoskins is doing? I've not been allowed to speak with — "

"We ain't 'ere to talk about your boyfriend," snarled 'Dee.

"Brother," Finn snarled back. "Half, to be precise. Same for Stuart Haller. And Detective Hauptmann is my fraternal twin, so my concern is familial."

"Yeah, we got the report from *Alles Wissen*," said 'Dum. "Your Da was a real player."

"I've no idea what he was," Finn snapped. "I never knew him, so he could have been nothing more than a donor to a sperm bank. Now...are Rob and Christian all right? Is Stu well?"

"We're not part o' their interrogation — " 'Dee started.

Finn cut him off. "I'm a Detective Sergeant, not some mass murderer or terrorist, so I would appreciate not being treated as such! That will only increase the difficulty between us, in place of cooperation, when all I'm asking is if three men to whom I'm related are in good physical and emotional condition! Something you could find out with a bloody phone call and which would make me far more inclined to work *with* you instead of against you, as even a non-rank interrogator would appreciate!"

The Tweedles exchanged a glance then 'Dum got up and left the room. 'Dee focused on Finn.

"Now...let's continue..."

"Doesn't your mate need to be in on this?" Finn asked.

"He knows what I'm sayin'," 'Dee sneered. "This is just preliminary. So...you jumble up to Manchester, snoop 'round Hoskins' dea'f, and suddenly you and he connect. *As brothers.*" The sneer was in his eyes as well as his words. "Then you're off to the Scottish Isles, where you come up naked in a sheep enclosure, evidence showin' you was sexually assaulted. And the DNA matches Hallswor'f's." He gave Finn a glare that was both quizzical and hostile. "How'd you get it? How'd you get his DNA? 'Cause there's no way he could've done what you say he did."

Finn glared back. "Perhaps I'll explain once you're done and your mate is back."

'Dee all but growled. "You hop off to Hamburg, connect wi'f Haup'mann, as *brothers*, day trip it down Munich, and vanish. You turn up on a beach in Corsica, next day, severely beaten. No question about that; we've seen the doctor's report and photos. You, Haup'mann, Hoskins and Haller fly up Reading and confront Hallswor'f. He grabs Haller hostage, forces him up 'a roof of an office tower, words're exchanged...and he does a high dive."

He leaned on the table, his eyes boring into Finn's. "What'd you five discuss?"

Before Finn could spit an answer back, 'Dum entered and sat at the table.

"Hoskins is in Manchester, currently under investigation for falsifying his death. Thus far, it doesn't appear he's actually committed any prosecutable crime, but his case is also being looked into by colleagues of ours. Haller is discussing his actions with a *friend* he has on the force, up there."

"Careful," said Finn. "That *friend* is a DCI and very Scottish."

'Dum huffed. "Hauptmann's been sent home and is currently being raked over the coals by his superiors."

Finn leaned back in his chair and let out a sigh of relief. "I'm glad to know this."

Both Tweedles frowned.

"There's a lot here don't add up," snapped 'Dee.

"Without question," Finn said, absently nodding.

"Videos caught the lot of you rushin' up that roof. Caught Hallswor'f holding Haller hostage. Caught Hoskins and Haup'mann trying to talk wi'f him. Caught you showin' up behind 'em. And then you're gone...and Hallswor'f jumps. What were you sayin'? How'd you get off that roof?"

"Where did you hide from the cameras?" asked 'Dum.

"I didn't," Finn replied.

Then he leaned his elbows on the table, clasped his hands, and rested his chin upon them...and told them every bit of what he'd been through.

Once he was done, both men had unreadable masks on, not letting him know if they accepted his tales or were ready to order a lobotomy. Hesitant about how to proceed, he waited.

Finally, 'Dum leaned forward and said, "You read a lot of graphic novels, right?"

Finn nodded.

'Dum turned to 'Dee and asked, "Was a chem-screen run on him, any of the times he was found?"

"Last one's all."

"Have one run, again." Then 'Dum looked at Finn. "If

you got no objection."

Finn shrugged his assent.

'Dee left to get a medic as 'Dum rose and came around the table, saying, "Let's see this injury behind your ear."

As he carefully checked the half-moon scar, pressing against it, Finn noticed a number in the upper corner of the file, on the table — *14102020-Winterbourne*. He smiled.

'Dum stepped back and gave Finn a long look of appraisal. "Solid bone there. Nothing that even begins to look like a puncture. Yet you think this all happened to you."

"Something did," Finn countered. "You've seen the reports. Medical records. Much of what I proffered is verifiable."

'Dum nodded and sat back at the table. A moment later, 'Dee entered with a medic and three tubes of Finn's blood were quickly withdrawn.

"I want it compared to blood that was drawn earlier," 'Dum told the medic. "Verify it's all the same."

The medic nodded and left.

'Dum turned back to Finn. "No more questions."

"For now," 'Dee sneered.

"We're sending you to a quiet place as we sort through the *information* you gave us. A facility in Monifeith. You'll discuss this with our doctors, there."

"To see how mad I am?" Finn smirked.

Or keep me out of pocket.

'Dum just looked at him then said, "We'll be back with you when we're ready."

Then he and 'Dee left the room.

Finn had the feeling they were going to consult with MI6 to find out if they *had* been conducting experiments with stealth devices and drugs and mental conditioning. He'd heard rumors they'd undertaken such things in the interest of being ahead of the curve when it came to futuristic warfare, and smirked. Helicopters that couldn't be seen or heard. Drugs administered to bring on hallucinations that could be controlled in some way. It still sounded so very James Bond.

But he gave them no argument. He was being taken to the facility that housed Martin Lowenstein, and not for one second did he think this was not deliberate. He wondered if

Martin's psychotic break was real or if he was merely being kept there, just as incommunicado. Or perhaps Finn, himself, was going to be made *catatonic*, like Martin was.

That comment about a lobotomy might not be so far off the mark.

For a moment, he strongly considered making a break for it and heading for Germany. But his inner cop took over. This would give him a chance to see Martin for himself. See if he would share his experience. See if the plan building in his brain might work.

Or if he was only going to make things worse.

****

That night, Finn was ferried to Monifeith in an unmarked helicopter that was so quiet he had to fight a smirk.

Perhaps this verifies the silent chopper angle.

They landed under a moonless sky gleaming with diamond-like stars, using the open car park of a long, low facility atop a hill that overlooked the River Tay. 'Dee and 'Dum escorted Finn straight inside to a plain but pleasant room that had a bed, nightstand, and table and two comfortable chairs by a window that looked out on the ships passing by. Not as cozy as his own flat but hardly unlivable.

The media had been going nuts trying to contact him, now that they were connecting the dots of his recent experiences, so the information door had been slammed shut. The official story provided by the Home Office was that he was *taking much-needed R&R after what had become a particularly brutal and long-term undercover case. He was now in a secluded location so could not be disturbed as he recuperated. Once recovered, he would be made available to the media.*

Finn knew that could be read a hundred different ways, including one where he'd just never reappear, but he didn't care; he actually looked forward to the possibility of peaceful contemplation.

Two white-smocked individuals met him in his room — Dr. Lambert, an owlish man with a slightly stooped back and piercing eyes, and Dr. Behrmann, a round matronly woman past retirement age. They greeted him with assurances they were at his disposal, day or night. He assured them right back that he would avail himself of them. He remembered Behrmann from Stu's research, and figured they were there to pick his brain and keep him from telling anyone else about his experiences.

Meaning it might be possible MI5 actually believed him.

He had no trouble settling in, once he was alone, because he'd only come with the now rather worn clothes on his back. A nice set of sleeping pants and shirt lay across the bed, with slippers on the floor. He had a feeling that as soon as he changed into them, he'd find they were all he was allowed to wear.

He sat on one chair's arm to look out at the Tay. This was hardly a lovely view, even in the darkness. Ugly lights glared on the opposite shore to reflect in the water, and there was a roadway at the bottom of the hill, between the facility and the river bank. What was interesting was how it actually made him feel not only trapped but weary. The last week had been one of the worst in his life, and now not really knowing anything about Rob's, Christian's or Stu's situations. Not being allowed to leave Clayton-Merrill's CID. Showering in the men's dressing room under watchful eyes. Knowing they were seeing for themselves the damage that had been done to him. Alternating between his suit and articles of clothing he'd left in his locker.

When I was off to meet Prue. All showered, shaved, and so long ago.

He was tired of rinsing out his underwear and socks, so if those vanished he would not miss them. He stripped and got into the sleeping clothes, then collapsed on the bed and was asleep almost before he was under the comforter.

The next morning, he woke knowing he had dreamed but could remember none of it. Soft sunlight drifted in and the smell of a decent fry-up ignited a serious need in his belly. Mere moments later, a bright young nurse bopped in with a tray.

"Up already?" she chirped.

Finn grinned. "Best sleep I had in ages."

"That's good. So first let's have our brekkie, then we'll hop 'round the gym for a wee exercise. Dr. Lambert thinks it's really important, and ye look like ye enjoy keeping fit."

"Not of late, Finn smiled. "I'd been living off carry-out."

"Well, that'll change. Yer slated for Dr. Behrmann at half-ten and Dr. Lambert after dinner."

She set the tray on the table next to the window and hopped out, saying, "Need anything? Just call for Keely."

"Thanks," said Finn, but she was already gone.

Under the plate covers were poached eggs, sausage links, beans, tomato, mushrooms and black pudding, accompanied by a massive pot of tea. Milk and brown sugar were also on the tray. Toast was already buttered and jam was in a small bowl. And every bite was on the level of what Nan used to work up on cold winter mornings.

"Have to start your day right, don't you," she'd often said, even when he'd protested he wasn't hungry. "Now, Finn, if I know you, you'll have not but a cheese sandwich and Coke for lunch, and I refuse to allow your growth to be affected by poor nutrition. Eat up."

He had, every time, and he'd felt very grand when he was adult enough to graduate from porridge to a fry-up as glorious as the ones she made for herself...even though the first month he was unable to eat all of it. But Nan hadn't cared; she'd used the remains to make sandwiches for him to carry to school, wrapped in her homemade scones.

He smiled at the memory.

By this point, he was finishing off the last of his tea, and his eyes were idly gazing upon a barge drifting upriver.

She couldn't have known what my parents did. She'd never have kept it secret. Not from me. Not for twenty-odd years.

But he did want to know why they had done this to him and his brother. He remembered Christian saying, *"I was purchased,"* and wanted to know if this was how they'd financed their travels around the world – having babies for people.

Like a bloody commodity.

Once this was over, he would call his uncles. See if either of them knew anything or, if not, perhaps they could better explain his parents to him. Have any idea where they might be. Track them down and get the answers, firsthand. That would be best.

An hour later, Keely bounced back in, chipper and bright, and escorted him to a state of the art work-out center, where he was left alone for half an hour, still in his sleeping clothes and slippers. He spent the time stretching, not exercising, but even with that little bit, he was sweating and ready to take a long hot shower before meeting Behrmann.

As Keely led him back to his room, Finn noticed a round, tired woman wandering into a door halfway down the hall from him. She looked familiar, but it wasn't until he was rinsing off in the tiny shower that he remembered her from the photo Stu had shown him of Martin Lowenstein — it was his wife.

A new set of sleeping clothes was laid out on the bed, no underwear. Finn wasn't comfortable wandering about like that, but he still dressed quick as he could and headed down the hall.

He reached the doorway Mrs. Lowenstein had entered, peeked inside and froze. She was kneeling next to a shrunken figure of a man wrapped in a bathrobe, brushing his wet thinning brown hair. She was so tender as she drew the brush through it, the love she felt for him was palpable. As was the sorrow in her face. Beside her was a basin of water with a couple of wet rags in it. A damp towel was draped over a corner of the chair, and the vague scent of perfumed soap wafted past.

Feeling he had intruded on something private, despite her not noticing him, Finn backed away and returned to his room.

He sat in his chair and watched the door, letting the realization that Martin was, in fact, catatonic settle over him. What Joss had told him about their last time together was now confirmed, and it built a massive rage inside Finn. The mere idea that an innocent man could be so used and brutalized by anyone was sickening.

The last time he'd felt such anger was in Brighton, during an investigation into the death of a twelve-year-old boy. His father had been off working an oil platform in the North Sea for nearly a year and had come home to find his only son identified as female. An argument had exploded, with the child's older sisters trying to intervene while their mother just cowered, and the man had beaten the child to death. The girls were also injured.

Their mother was still cowering when Finn and his

superior had arrived. The father was unrepentant, close to unresponsive to their questions. The only thing he'd said, consistently, was "No son o' mine's gonna be a poofter."

Finn had been able to keep his anger under control as they saw to it the girls and their mother were removed to a shelter, but when the child's body was being wheeled out in a bag, the father had laughed and spit on it, snarling, "Shows you!"

That is when Finn had grabbed the man and slammed him against a wall, howling, "You did that to your child! Your CHILD!"

"He were no child o' mine!" the father had shot back.

The only thing that had kept Finn from breaking the man's neck was the DCI's hand on his shoulder, saying in a calming voice, "We'll deal with him, Winterbourne. He will be dealt with."

Finn had hesitated and the man had snarled at him with a wicked grin. "No' much a man, 'er ya?"

The DCI had shifted focus to him and said, in the same calm voice, "He's more a man than you will ever be, because he has control of himself. And he knows you'll be receiving a whole life term for what you've done, here. Considering how men like you are treated in prison, you'll come to see it might have been merciful, had I let him break your neck."

Finn had forced himself to let two constables take the man away. Then he'd taken some deep breaths and said, "Sorry, sir."

"Don't be," was all the DCI had said. "You merely did what I was thinking. But not again, right? Keep some control."

And so he had.

The memory made Finn cold. He went to the closet, one eye still on the door, and found a nice thick robe to wear. Then he sat back in the chair and willed himself to stop shivering.

After a short while, Martin's wife wandered past, her weariness even more evident. Finn felt like weeping for her.

He waited five minutes then snuck down to the room, slipped inside and sat in a chair next to the man to study him.

Martin had lost a fair amount of weight, almost to the

point of being gaunt, but his features were the same. However, his breathing was soft to the point of not happening, and his eyes were numb to nearly lifeless.

It must have been an effort just to get him into the chair.

Finn leaned forward, rested a hand on his arm, and said, "Martin? Martin. Listen to me. I've been to the nothing room. I know what you've seen. I know what you've done. I understand. May we talk about it?"

Martin gave no response.

"Do you hear me, Martin? I understand. I've been there."

Still no response.

Finn sighed and rose. "I must go. I'll return, tomorrow."

Then he left and kept his appointment with Dr. Behrmann.

Since he knew she'd already been briefed by 'Dee and 'Dum about everything, he confirmed it. In glorious detail. She just sat there. Took it all in, nodding as if he were repeating a laundry list.

It wasn't until he'd been silent for five minutes that she opened his chart and said, "A chemical screen was run on your blood and it turned up some odd references and possibilities. Those are currently being explored. We've also been in contact with *Alles Wissen,* and they've sent us their research into your genetic structure, along with their preliminary conclusions."

Finn chuckled. "Are you suggesting I might have an iron deficiency or not enough magnesium in my system?"

"If only it were that simple," she smiled, without humor. "No, I've had some interesting cases come in, lately, of people experiencing somewhat similar hallucinations and occurrences. Thus far each has been found to have an explanation. We merely need to find what it is for yours. The injury behind your ear and these test results are a good foundation from which to build a diagnosis, once the physical aspects are known. Dr. Lambert is more versed in such matters. Once he's done his examinations and brought forth his conclusions, we'll go from there."

Dr. Lambert turned out to be a very physical physician. He checked every square inch of Finn, including making measurements of areas Finn never had thought should be measured. His main focus were the scars on Finn's body and the injury behind his ear. His initial conclusions were simple. "You show numerous aspects of having been assaulted. Scar tissue around your anus. Whip marks on your body, arms and legs that are still healing. Rubbing around your wrists. Were I conducting a post-mortem on you, I'd say you'd been held and abused over the course of days. Were you?"

Taken aback at the doctor's bluntness, Finn could only nod.

"Your hallucinations are not necessarily uncommon. Nor is the lack of known chemical stimulants in your system. These nightmares can be a way of dealing with the trauma of such an assault. I'll check you in the exact same way, tomorrow. See how the skin is healing. Same for the day after. That should give us an idea as to when this all began."

"I could just tell you," said Finn.

Lambert looked at him with a truly quizzical expression as he said, "Yes, you could, but physical evidence is best when dealing with such matters."

Then he was dismissed.

Over the next three days, Finn ate, exercised, met with both doctors, and quietly noticed that while the fence around the facility might not be electrified and there were no guards with weaponry marching about the ground, there was no way he could easily leave. The drive led down to a gated entry and no one came in or out unless stopping there, first. The orderlies who were always around to help were also well-versed in handling patients who became unruly. Which happened twice — once with a middle-aged man who insisted the Queen was waiting for him to visit with news from Andromeda; the other when a fit younger man swore there were gremlins in his room and that was why he had no tea and by God he was going to Pakistan to get some because that was all that would keep them from coming in the night, taking him into space and wanking him, again, even though he was a good Muslim boy...and on and on...

When Finn approached them to ask questions, he found both had been heavily sedated and Keely was quickly on-hand to lead him away from them. On top of this, Finn's sleep was so heavy, he began to wonder if he was also being drugged to keep him still, at night.

Mrs. Lowenstein would come at the same time, every day, to clean and groom Martin, so Finn got it down to the precise moment when she would leave and he could sneak into the room, sit by Martin and say, "I've been to the nothing room. I know what you've seen. What you've done. I understand. Can we talk about this? Do you hear me? I understand."

He would receive no response, so would sigh, put a gentle hand on Martin's shoulder, and say, "I'll return, tomorrow." And he would sneak out.

He was never there for more than thirty seconds.

On the fifth day he went through the full routine, again, but as he was about to leave, Keely caught him and clucked at him with serious disappointment.

"So here ye be, Mr. Winterbourne," she snapped. "Now ye know, yer not supposed to be in here. This is a serious breach of protocol."

"I just wanted to – "

She took Finn by the arm, saying, "Come along; back to yer room."

But Martin took hold of Finn's right hand!

Both he and Keely nearly jumped through the roof.

"He moved!" she gasped. "Did he move? He moved! His hand!"

Martin's eyes turned to Finn and gained a vague focus. His breathing became a bit stronger. He slowly guided Finn's hand closer.

Keely bolted from the room as Finn knelt beside him. "I'm here, Martin. I'm here. I've been to the nothing room."

"Beast?" whispered from deep within Martin, his voice dry and cracking. His eyes were almost alive.

"Yes."

"Stu...art?"

"He's fine, Martin. Alive. Well. Living in Scotland."

Martin almost wanted to smile, but then his look grew dark. "Joss?"

Finn hesitated and said, "No more."

Dr. Lambert strode into the room, glanced over everything in a flash and pulled up a chair. Keely was right behind him.

Finn started to get up but the man snapped, "Stay where you are." He called to Keely, "Dr. Behrmann?"

"She's coming, doctor."

He turned back to Finn. "He spoke with you?"

Finn nodded. "Couple words."

"More than he's said in years." He took Martin's free hand and massaged it as he checked his limbs. "But this is excellent news. You and I will meet, later, and you will tell me exactly what you did to effect this. Of course, there's some atrophy, despite our best efforts. Let's see if he's capable of rising, perhaps even walking; that would be best for him."

"Martin, will you stand?" Finn asked as he started to rise, but Martin pulled him back down, holding his arm close like he would a security blanket. "Martin, we can talk in the garden."

Martin barely shook his head. "Beast," was all he said, again and again.

Lambert nodded and said, "No rush. We can try, again, later. Are you able to extricate yourself?"

Finn shook his head; Martin had a near death grip on his hand.

"What's he said?" It was Dr. Behrmann's voice preceding her into the room. When she appeared, she seemed more like someone about to meet her favorite TV star than an officious physician. She tried to brush Finn aside but Martin groaned and pulled him tighter, making Finn grunt with pain. The man shifted in a way that made everyone think he'd noticed Finn's pain and relaxed, a little.

"Thank you," Finn murmured. "I won't leave you, if you don't want me to."

Martin drew in a long breath, pulled Finn closer and leaned against him, like a child seeking protection.

"That...was...excellent," said Lambert, nearly overjoyed. "The strength in him."

"What did you say to him?" Behrmann asked.

Finn hesitated then held Martin closer and whispered, "May I tell her? Martin?"

Martin breathed in, deeper and deeper before finally giving Finn the least of nods. "Beast," whispered from him, again.

Finn shifted his attention to Behrmann. She sharpened

her focus on him and gave him a slight smile. That is when he noticed in her white smock was a pen similar to the one Stu had worn. He fought back a smirk.

"Martin and I have shared the same experience," said Finn, "but he was the first. Joss was second. And now I am third."

Martin shifted his head so he could look up at Finn. "Beast?"

Behrmann's eyes were sharp on both of them as Finn gave Martin a look of the purest tenderness and said, "Not if I can help it."

Martin's lips quivered and he looked away. "Can't."

"We'll see."

Then Mrs. Lowenstein rushed in. Martin slowly turned to look at her, and she burst into tears. Dr. Lambert gave her his chair to sit in as she gripped Martin's other hand and wept.

Behrmann spent an hour trying to get Martin to say something more, but he would look only at his wife; Miriam was her name, Finn learned. On top of it, Martin refused to let go of Finn, so he wound up having his dinner and tea brought to him, there. Then a canister appeared for him to pee into.

"I'll get ye a bedpan, if ye need," Keely said. "So long as yer not shy."

"I'll be fine, for now," Finn smiled.

As they sat there, Miriam told Finn all about Martin.

They had been doing well enough until just over three years ago, when Martin passed out while swimming. He was discovered naked on Portobello Beach and could remember nothing of what had happened. Everything was fine, for a few years, but then he began having nightmares. For weeks. They had begun sleeping in separate bedrooms, thanks to his sudden thrashing and cries in the night. Then one morning, Miriam had gone into his room to find him completely unresponsive.

Tests had found nothing wrong with him, physically, except for whip lashes on his body and bites that he could, possibly, have done to himself. Then one doctor had noticed damage to his anus and asked for a rape kit.

"This was a week after he'd shut down," Miriam said, "so I didn't understand why, but the doctor said it verified that Martin was having sex with a man and was probably beat by him. They did a rape exam on him and it showed nothing...but it was so long after. They decided he was secretly gay and ashamed of it, so he was sneaking out to his man to be buggered and punished. They didn't believe me when I said he hadn't."

"But he's been with men?" Finn asked, carefully.

Miriam looked at him. "What do ye know of him?"

"I know a friend of his, from university."

"Stuart. Aye. Martin wanted so to be like him, even after we married. Free and easy with women, he was. Very attractive man." Her eyes wandered to look out the window. "Martin had something of a crush on him." She looked back at Finn. "I know he was with other men. Men who looked like Stuart. But I understood, so he wouldn't sneak off in the middle of the night when he didn't need to. That bloody doctor was judging him. I could see it in his eyes. So I told them they were wrong. That's how he wound up here."

"Who suggested this facility?" Finn asked.

"Couple lads come to hospital and spoke with me. Said he'd be taken care of, and they are good to him, here. I just wish it could be closer to Edinburgh."

"Your children want to see him?"

She smiled. "Arin's the only one old enough to understand or be allowed. The others just want a resolution. Something to happen. They're tired of Martin being first and them second. But I love him. Can't abandon him. Maybe now — who knows, maybe now he'll come back to us."

"I think he will. Is there anything he enjoyed doing that might help? Something I could work with him on?"

"He followed sports – football, rugby, even cricket. Couple programs on *Channel Four* and *ITV* he liked." She chuckled. "He thought *BBC* was too posh."

Finn chuckled. "People toss that word around a lot."

"They say it about yerself?"

"Well...yes, but..."

"It's a compliment, Finn. Ye have manners, and yer way with Martin shows kindness."

Finn blushed and said, "Thanks. I also like cricket; I'll watch some programs with him. Any in particular?"

"Arin, he'd know which Martin liked. Maybe they'll let him come up and watch with ye."

"Ask Keely before you leave. I'm sure she'll be up for it. And I'll stay with him as much as I can. In fact, I think Dr. Behrmann would like me to move in with him."

She looked at Finn for a long moment then said, "Why won't ye tell me why he's like this? Why it happened?"

It took Finn a long moment to answer, "Better if he does."

She sighed. "Do ye really think he'll return to us?"

"He's begun the journey back, now that he knows he's not alone. Will he still be the same man you married? I cannot say."

The next day, Arin, a solid boy of sixteen with golden brown hair and gleaming features, joined them, making Martin slightly more animated. He set up the TV with the names of the programs his father had watched, turned one on, then opened up his laptop and connected to his phone so he and Finn could play some online games. He was surprised not only that Finn knew how to work his way around a rather demanding set of *Demonworld* but that he was well-versed in graphic novels and attended all the conventions.

"Y'ever cos-play?" The boy asked.

Finn nodded. "I was *Thor*, last year, in London. Rather boring, since there were dozens like me. My best was *Nexus*."

"That *is* it! Baron and Rude walk all over like bosses. Got pictures?"

"Pause, I'll show you."

The boy shifted to a search engine and Finn found his page of photos. They laughed about his *Thor* costume...and *Spiderman*, though *Deadpool* brought a wicked nudge from Arin.

"He gets to say *fook*," said the boy.

Finn laughed. Then they found a photo of him in the blue costume with the lightning bolt, and he filled it very nicely.

"Coo...yer his image," Arin said, very impressed.

"I don't know about that..." Finn said, his voice growing soft. "I was nineteen...just ended my gap year, about to start Cambridge..."

"Where'd ye go, ye gap year?"

"A hiking tour of Europe. Educational. Economical."

Arin nodded. "That's why ye got no belly and yer legs ain't twigs. Shoulders're right, too. Where's the visor?"

"My...my hand. Other side. I was about to put it on but Nan snapped this one."

"I carry a photo of you in my purse. "

His voice grew soft. "This one. This is the blue and gold one she had."

"Girlfriend?"

Finn chuckled. "Grandmother. *Nexus*. Set five-hundred years in the future..."

"Yeah. Great art. Stories. I've got some."

"How optimistic it was..."

Then Finn noticed Martin watching them instead of the TV, almost smiling. "Arin, does your father like graphic novels?"

"Not like this. He's more for the serious ones. Political stuff. Oh, he loved *Maus*. I should bring that, next time. We've got a first edition. Signed."

Finn nodded. "Do that, and others."

After Arin left, they were watching a football match on *Channel Four* when Martin shook his head and said, "Referee's blind."

Finn jolted and asked, "What? What do you mean?"

Martin said nothing more, just stayed focused on the TV.

Sure enough, Finn was moved into Martin's room to sleep on a rollaway. Over the next week, they watched sports shows and ate together and were visited by Miriam and Arin, often at the same time, and step by step Martin grew more and more alive. He still refused to speak to Behrmann, but under Lambert's care he began to regain mobility and even went on short walks in the garden with Finn.

Finn was allowed contact with no one else, nor could he call anyone or send any messages. The moment he'd try to do so, Keely would appear and stop him in her sweet chirpy way. He began to wonder if she was a robot, because she seemed to always be there, day or night. He already knew there were subtle cameras around the building keeping watch, and probably microphones. Which was irritating. And angering, because on top of all this no one would tell him anything about his brothers, and he was certain they were being told nothing about him.

The only thing that made the days pass decently were Martin's sports programs. Finn watched more football, rugby and cricket that week than he ever had. Still, the man was improving, if slowly, and Finn was becoming hopeful.

Then on the sixth night, Martin was sleeping and Finn had just got in bed after an hour of wondering if he needed to push harder to make Martin open up. He really wanted to find out what had happened to him sooner rather than later in order to finish his plan to stop this horror, but he'd learned the hard way that pushing for information at the wrong time would only make things harder, in the end. So he just sighed and lay back, expecting to do his usual crash towards sleep when –

The blue light swirled in to surround him.

Catastrophe

Finn was in the nothing room being caressed by the nothing-air over every part of his body. Soft. Erotic. Carnal. Making him breathless with sudden devouring need. He was able to move his arms and legs and look around every direction to see nothing but blue light filtering through the nothingness, and he stood on a floor that did not look like it was there but upon which he could walk. Above him was endlessness.

And for some reason, he was not the least bit afraid.

Until a man appeared before him.

He was taller than Finn and solid. Extremely well-built, with golden-brown hair flowing from his head. A scruff of the same color beard covered a fine chin and danced around well-formed lips to keep his nose from being too small. He wore a black and green rugby jersey that fit tight across his pumped-up chest and shorts that showed off perfect legs laced with the same hair, one calf tattooed with an elegant forest design. A bandage covered his right forearm and socks were scrunched at his ankles atop a pair of new trainers. He looked around, confused and frightened.

And Finn suddenly knew what was going to happen.

"Oh, God, no," he gasped in a voice so soft it barely registered.

"What th' fook?" the man cried. "What th' 'ell's goin' on?"

Finn managed to say, "If I could explain it, I would."

"Who's that? Who's there? Who the fook's grabbin' me? Gropin' me? STOP IT!"

Finn saw the man's shirt shift under the caress of the nothing-air. His shorts drifted up his legs...powerful legs topped off by a pair of white Hilfiger boxer briefs. Perfect form. So elegant and beautiful. The light golden hair on them dancing under the nothing-air.

"This ain' happenin'! THIS AIN'T HAPPENIN'!"

To Finn's shock, an overwhelming passion crashed through him and all he could think to do was reach over and slide the man's jersey up, revealing taut abs also covered in the golden hair. An erotic scream of the deepest, darkest need exploded through him as his fingers touched the man's tight clean skin.

The man seemed to finally see him and snarled, "What th' fook!? Who the fook're you?!?"

Finn chuckled as, "The one who owns you," drifted from him, his breathing deep and intense, his mind nearly shattered.

No, this isn't happening, this isn't happening, I can't be doing this. I'm not like this.

Still, he slipped his hands over the man's neat hairy pecs to find his nipples and toy with them...caress a badger's paw mark tattooed around the left one.

"No, no, no, get the fook off; nobody fookin' owns me!"

It took every ounce of control Finn had to bring himself back to the moment and say, "I...I am so sorry. I'll make it as easy as I can."

Except he wanted the man to cry. To scream and curse and beg and howl in pain. He desired it. Longed for it. Even the thought of it caught his breath in ways he never thought possible and made his heart pound like it was about to explode. He wanted nothing about this to be gentle or kind...so he pulled on the man's nips and twisted them, hard and cruel.

The man howled in pain then choked in anger, "Leave off me, motherfooker! What the fook ya talkin' 'bout? Make wot easy? Who th' fook ARE you?! Ya think ya can do this to me?! I'll fookin' tear ya 'part! If I can get loose...if I can just..."

He struggled to move away from Finn but he was held in place, his hands now behind him, his legs spread apart. Open to anything Finn wanted.

Anything.

I can hold him like this...

Finn cupped the man's crotch and fondled his balls, then his hands traced around to squeeze what felt like the world's most perfect as.

He's mine, now. I own him. I'm going to have him.

"FOOKIN' POOFTER! FOOKIN' QUEER! LEAVE OFF ME!"

Finn battled his way back to a hint of control. Forced his hands to let go of the man's ass. Every fiber in his body fought to continue its assault...but Finn managed step back, murmuring, "We have to keep...some kind of...conscious control."

"Wot...wot the fook ya on about?" the man was nearly breathless, from fear. "Ya fookin' grabbin' me all over an' I can't fight ya and you talk 'bout control?! Wot the fook?!"

Finn looked at the man. His elegant chest heaving. His muscles straining. His eyes wild with anger and fear.

A beast roared up from the depths of Finn's soul and he no choice but to tear the jersey open to reveal the man's rich, full, glorious chest. Then his hands shifted the torn cloth off his shoulders. Amazing shoulders leading up to an elegant neck. Every muscle in his body taut and perfect. More badger's paws trailing up over his left pec and trapezius. Begging to be touched.

So he did, and the man's skin shivered in ways so erotic, Finn felt he might pass out from the joy of it.

He could barely breathe. His body was out of control. His hands roamed over the man, front and back and sides and down to his legs and over his ass to maul his dick and balls through his shorts. He was caught in this euphoric high from which he never wanted to return.

Throughout, the man grunted and groaned in fear and shock and anger, howling, "STOP IT! Wot ya doin' to me? Why can't I move an'...an'...WHO THE BLOODY 'ELL ARE YOU? WHY YOU DOIN' THIS?" Suddenly, his voice grew soft and uncertain. "Don' un'erstand. Don' un'erstand. We was off for Bristol. Just headed for...for Bristol. I...I was on the bloody bus. How'd I get...get here?"

"Doesn't matter," Finn whispered.

"Ya gonna bugger me? Ya gonna fook me? How? How ya gettin' t' do this t' me? How'd ya get to...to me...?"

Then he stopped talking.

A feral grin crossed Finn's face as he focused on the man's eyes. He saw confusion and a slowly dawning awareness, bringing a sort of ecstatic wanton need to Finn's heart.

"We...we got smacked," the man murmured. "I think. Got hit. I think. Bloody 'ell. Saw a...a van? A lorry? Run the light and...and, oh, fook, gonna hit us? Fookin' gonna hit us and, shite, am I dead? Is this death? Is this 'ell?"

"It's worse," Finn growled, then he tore the man's shorts off. Stepped back to view him. See how the white Hilfigers added to the beauty of his hips and crotch. He felt the pure cotton. So smooth and erotic to the touch.

The man gasped...and his dick began to respond to Finn's caresses. "I...I'm bein' punished, right? This is 'ell."

Finn couldn't answer. He was unable to formulate any words, in his mind. A part of him screamed that he should stop himself, but he was too locked on watching his hands glide along the man's elegant inner thighs to begin fondling his dick and balls through the white cotton.

"This is 'ell. I did wrong and I'm sent t' 'ell. I'm bein' punished for fookin' 'round...ain't that it..."

"I don't believe in that," Finn managed to whisper as he stroked and fondled the man's dick and it grew larger and fatter under the cotton, its head promising even more perfection, and he yearned for it.

No man should be this perfect. It's unnatural. It's unreal.

And yet, he was. And Finn was nearly breathless with a deep demanding desire, the space behind his heart screaming to be filled with everything he could take from this golden god. The need enveloping him...controlling him was pure and raw and terrifying.

"I...I only believe in this," Finn gasped as he leaned down and ran his lips along the length of the man's growing erection, still trapped in the boxer-briefs, and nuzzled it and licked his balls. He was like an end-stage junkie preparing his next fix. Anticipation held tight onto him. Made every nerve in his body scream to be let go. The hairs on the man's thighs felt so perfect against his cheek, he had to kiss them. Pull at them with his teeth. Bite into his skin to make them one with him.

Draw blood.

The man's cry of pain jolted Finn and he rose, breathless, and stumbled back, shaken and snarling, "No, I'm not. I...bloody hell, I'm not going to do this to him! Not to him!" And he wiped the blood from his lips.

But a massive wave of want crashed over him. All he could see was how the man's perfect nips begged to be kissed.

So he did.

Licked at them. Sucked on them. Nibbled at them. Crushed his own body against the man's and tried to become one with him. Then a startling animalistic urge roared up inside and he bit the left one, growling with lust.

Another shriek of pain brought a laugh from Finn, in response. He grabbed the boxer briefs and tore them open to let the man's long well-shaped dick spring out, ready to be taken.

The beauty of it made Finn stop. He gazed upon it. Touched it, soft and easy. It felt alive and real and was like something he had always dreamed of. Something he had always wanted. He crouched down and slipped his lips over the head and began to lick and caress it with his tongue, sucking and rubbing and making the man jolt and try to squirm under him. He dug his fingers into the man's ass and could feel him clenching and hear him grunting as his dick grew harder and thicker and needier...and it felt so good...too good...too damn good as his fingers rubbed up against the man's anus and probed and pushed.

"STOP! STOP IT! NO! YOU'RE NOT — YOU CAN'T — NO! THIS IS RAPE! THIS IS RAPE!"

"They don't care," Finn growled. "They don't follow our laws." The words tore into him. He jolted. Straightened up. Took a couple of steps back from the man, saying, "No...no..."

But again, all he could see was the beauty of his victim. Not one muscle out of place. Not sculpted but human and real. In such exquisite proportion. There to be used. Taken. To satisfy him in ways no one else could. To be his and then gone, forever. No one else to have him.

Finn was drowning in this sensuous understanding as it washed through his body.

He realized his own dick was raging hard against his own sleeping pants. He pulled them off, releasing himself. His shirt followed. He stood there, naked, more aroused than he had ever been in his life. If anyone had touched him, he knew he'd have shattered into a million points of desire.

He watched the man struggle, before him. Blue light sparkled over beautiful skin, making it seem to glow as it gleamed in his hair. Dark eyes were wide and filled with fear. Intoxicating fear. The kind of fear that brings a sort of drunken happiness to any victor.

He was unable to keep from being caressed. So Finn caressed him more. Unable to keep from being fondled. So Finn fondled him, more and more and more. Unable to end the non-stop ownership of every part of his body as Finn let his hands and lips roam wherever they wanted.

And Finn was unable to think beyond the idea of owning his beauty.

By this point, the man's snarls and howls had become whimpers and gasps at each new violation. He kept saying, "No, no, please, no, no..."

But his now-raging erection contradicted him.

Then Finn lifted his legs and set them on his shoulders. His own dick pointed straight at the man's ass. He caressed the spot where his cheeks parted to reveal his hole. Slipped a finger up his anus...and another...and another, despite the man's screams...his own dick begging to replace them. Every fiber of his being joyously pushed for that final moment of ownership.

"You gonna bugger...you gonna fookin' rape me?" he choked. "You gonna rape me? You some fookin' demon gonna bugger me? Why? Wot'd I do that's so bad? Wot?"

"It's not your fault," Finn said, fighting to keep from drowning in the powerful feelings. He had to dig each word from within, tear it past the chaotic lightning in his mind. "They're using me. Against you. And there'll be others...and they'll take me whenever they want and....no...no, I won't do it! Not to him! NOT LIKE THIS!"

He managed to force his hands to lift the man's legs off him and lower them.

Oh, but the feel of his calves. The skin. The soft down whispering over them.

Just having his fingers wander along them electrified Finn. Ricocheted through every part of his being. He caressed his hands up the backs of those glorious legs. Loved the gentle tickle of the hair against his palms. The smoothness of his skin. The strength and form of his thighs. How his ass curved up and around. It was euphoria just to touch him. Nirvana. He leaned against him, weak and demanding, gasping from the beauty of their nips connecting as his hands travelled up the man's sides and ran across his back and down, again, to feel his ass as both dicks pressed hard against each other.

The man just gasped and moaned, now, becoming just as lost as Finn in the insistent eroticism of body to body.

Finn slipped to behind him. Wrapped his arms around him to caress his abs and chest as he kissed his neck and molded himself against his back and felt the breath whispering in and out of him and the rise of his ass against his own groin.

Then as he brushed aside the man's hair to kiss the nape of his neck, he noticed something small and glowing cupped around the back of his right ear, its light throbbing.

So that's what it's from. Is this how they own us?

But the thought was kicked aside when his dick slipped between the man's cheeks. That sensation, alone, made doing anything to own him completely justifiable.

I will be the last to have you. You will now be mine, forever. No one else's. Only mine.

The thought made him ill...but he could not stop it.

He reached around to feel the length of man's dick...fat and straight and hard as a rock...and he yearned for it to be in him. But even stronger was his need to be inside his victim. He shifted his hands back to maul the two cheeks...pulled them open...made the man's ass completely available. Finn slipped his erection between them. Pressed it against his rectum.

The man grunted and his breath grew faster.

Finn opened him wider and slipped a finger into his hole.

The man moaned in some combination of fear and pleasure.

He used his finger to guide his head to the right point.

Shoved his dick in.

The man cried out in pain.

The beauty of it made him keep going in. Deeper. Deeper.

Now the man screamed.

Finn pushed in even deeper. The reality of this amazing ass wrapping him in its splendor broke down his last defenses. He could barely murmur, "I'm sorry, I'm sorry, I'm sorry..."

Finally, he could feel the man's skin against his pubes. His right hand grabbed the man's throat; his other arm wrapped around the man's chest to pinch and play with one of his nips, and he began to rock in and back and in and back and in and back.

He reached down to fondle the man's dick, and it was like solid stone. He stroked it and groped his balls and ran his other hand up and down his abs as his nips rubbed against the man's back and added to the screaming lightning within him. He felt the nothing-air caress his thighs and toy with the hair on his legs and fondle his own balls and whisper over his naked ass, making him pump harder and harder, bringing him closer and closer to the final explosion.

The man screamed and yelled and cursed and tried to fight but couldn't move as he was mauled and groped and caressed all over and fucked and masturbated and it kept on and on and on and then...slowly, oh so slowly, he began to work with Finn. Push back at him. Grip him tighter with his ass. Gasp in pure pleasure instead of pain.

Each thrust into him was something exquisite. It filled Finn with perfection. Each stroke on the man's dick made him grow even harder. His own balls became even more tender and quivered each time that perfect ass brushed up to them. His nips were crazed by each light lovely touch against that elegant skin. His thighs laughed with joy from the nothing-air traveling over him. He couldn't believe it.

He was...he was *loving* this!?

He was enjoying raping a man he didn't know!?

The device clinging to behind the man's ear glowed brighter and brighter. Did it mean his victim was enjoying being raped?

It does. You know it. You've been there. He loves it.

In and back and in and back, Finn pushed, over and over and over. Each thrust taking him closer and closer to a horrifying nirvana...the sensual demands of it surrounding him, completely, making him lose all sense of time or reality as he kept going in and back and in and back, and going and going and going for hours and hours and he didn't care because he wanted it and needed it and hoped it would never end...

Until he felt a rush build and build and build then explode from behind his balls and hiss through every fiber of his being as each muscle in him clenched and joined with the nothing-air's caresses to make him grunt and howl and cry aloud in a bellowing roar when the rush slammed down his thighs and across his ass and over his nips and up into his dick and –

He was yanked back out of the man's ass just before a never-ending line of semen screamed from him, the likes of which he had never experienced. He could feel every bit of it dance from his balls up through his dick and shoot out like a bullet before it vanished into the nothing light. More cum leapt from him to vanish as the nothing-air worked him till he fired, again and again and again, and that also vanished.

Then he felt the man slam his dick harder and harder against his hand and jolt and shudder and cry out...and jettison his own massive stream of cum. Gasping and whimpering in pleasure and horror and joy and pain. He rammed against Finn, again, sending more and more flooding into the nothing light until he was a quivering, laughing mass making incoherent sounds.

Finn was so lost in his own overwhelming sensations and feelings and exultation, he was just as incoherent.

After a few minutes...or hours, Finn had no concept of time, just then...he slowly...slowly...slowly drifted back to himself. He found he was back in control of his body, now. He looked around and saw a perfectly beautiful man who appeared to be drunk out of his mind, his eyes half closed, his face slack from the overwhelming sensations. Semen gleamed in trails on his torso and legs. His elegant dick still dripped with more of it and had just become limp enough to allow his foreskin to return.

Finn's own dick was still engorged but shrinking back to normal. He embraced the man. Ran his hands over his torso. Kissed him.

And the golden god kissed him back, murmuring, "That weren't 'ell. It were 'eaven. 'Eaven."

"A combination of the two?" Finn whispered.

A soft smile came to the man's elegant face.

Then he fell back.

Finn grabbed for him but he was snatched away.

And dropped almost naked into a bus.

And something slammed into it, shattering glass and sending shards of metal over a dozen men followed by an explosion of flames that enveloped them.

Finn screamed in horror and —

He woke, frozen. He couldn't think. He was barely able to breathe. Could only whimper. The room was dark and cold and quiet...

And someone was lying on top of him, holding him down.

And had a hand over his mouth.

Finn could not understand what that meant. Could not think of what he should do, in response. His mind was blank. He stayed still, shivering, fighting to take a breath, looking at nothing for what seemed like hours before he began to make out –

Martin was lying on top of him, using his hand to keep him quiet.

"The blue light," he whispered, his voice cracking. "Woke me. Saw ye gone. Waited for ye to come back. When they took me as I slept, they always sent me back to me bed. So I waited. When ye appeared, ye started to thrash about so I jumped ye to keep ye quiet. If they hear ye, they'll take ye from me and I need ye here. I need ye. Ye know what happened. Ye understand, a little. Will ye scream now? Will ye still scream?"

Finn was still shaking but managed to indicate a *No*. Martin carefully pulled his hand away and caressed Finn's head with a tenderness that helped him regain even more control. He realized he was naked and that he'd been sweating, despite the room being cold as ice.

"It's happened to ye, right? They made ye hurt someone."

Finn looked away, unable to formulate an answer.

"Now ye truly understand," Martin choked as he rose and moved off the bed, still unsteady. His sad eyes never left Finn's as he shook his head. "Ye thought ye understood, but ye didn't. Not till this. But now..."

He managed to kneel by the bed and take Finn's hand in a gentle caress.

"Yer the beast, now," he said. "I'm so sorry."

The Beast Roars

When Keely came in with their breakfast and to check their vitals, as she had every morning, she found Finn to be shivering and achy, with a fever.

Martin sat nearby, saying in a gravelly voice, "He was...he was restless all night. Coughing. Arin had the flu, recent like. He might still have been contagious."

She looked at Martin, her expression cocked. "Yer chatty, this morning. Our Finn's had a good effect on ye, hasn't he."

Martin shrank a little...but nodded.

"Are ye going to eat all yer brekkie, this time?"

Martin glanced at his tray of porridge then looked at Finn's tray, took in a deep breath and said, "Can I have his? He's not gonna be up for it."

A smile filled Keely's face as she said, "Better than it go to waste. I'll bring more tea, juice and water." She turned to Finn. "Would you like some acetaminophen?" Finn managed to nod. "All right, and I'll let Dr. Behrmann know yer not up for — "

"I'll take his slot," Martin said.

Keely jolted around to look at him, amazed. "Ye'll speak with Dr. Behrmann?" Martin nodded. "I'll...I'll let her know," she continued, her voice filled with emotion. "Right back."

Then she rushed from the room, tears in her eyes.

Finn looked at Martin and murmured, "Don't...need to...do that..."

Martin knelt by him and caressed his face. "It's time I did. This way I'll be here with ye, when it happens, again. I'll help ye come back. No one else knows what it means, but I do, and I'll help ye come back. Like ye did for me."

Finn gripped his hand and held it close.

Martin also made himself take Finn's appointment

with Dr. Lambert, who was very impressed with his physical recovery.

"He nattered on at how shocked he was I'm so mobile, so quick," he told Finn as they watched sports on Channel Four. Well, Martin watched; Finn was seated in a chair next to him, in fresh sleeping clothes, wrapped in that thick robe, a blanket around his legs, gazing out the window. "Seems I lost more fat than muscle, and he don't understand why. Wants me to start exercising in his office, hooked up to a battery of sensors. See if they can figure it."

Finn barely paid him attention. They were like this through dinner and tea.

Then a pair of sportscasters began to discuss an upcoming rugby tournament in Bristol.

"This'll be an epic matchup," said Martin, almost gleeful.

Finn groaned, "Please...don't want to hear...about it..."

"Thought ye liked rugby, okay," said Martin, reaching for the remote. "No, wait, ye said cricket. Just a recap, okay?"

The first segment showed a team in the locker room happily stripping off black and green jerseys as a reporter spoke with their coach.

Finn cringed. "Oh, no...not them..."

Martin looked at him, saying, "*The Peregrines*? Ye got something against Leeds?"

Finn looked away. "Crash."

Martin grew confused. "Crash?"

"Bus. Team..."

"They were in a crash? When was that?" Martin turned up the sound...then froze. His voice grew soft. "What kind of crash?"

Finn frowned. Looked at Martin. Began to breathe heavily. He turned to watch the program.

The tournament in Bristol was to start in three days, and *Team Leeds* was nothing but bright joyous young men of a dozen different nationalities, all in peak physical condition, who were wild and eager to get started. The coach was handing out the usual blather of how *they'd just do their best* and *these were excellent teams they'd be up against* and the like when a shirtless golden god of a man burst between them, laughing as he cried, "Bollocks! We'll wipe the bloody pitch with 'em all!"

Finn felt like he'd been punched in the gut.

It was the man he'd assaulted.

And in a corner of the screen was a little logo – *LIVE!*

"Barry, Barry! BARRY COWAN, hang on!" the reporter yelled, all but dragging him back to the camera. "You seem sure!"

Barry's face was caught in a heartbreakingly beautiful grin. The badger's paws gleamed on his sleek freshly-washed skin. "We got reason to be."

A black player with lovely green eyes appeared behind Barry and said, "He got a new tat. Every time he gets a tat, we smash 'em."

"Great! Let's see it!"

Barry raised his right arm to show off a bandage. "This debuts on the pitch, first match. Not before. Go to me website – Barry Cowan dot org an' guess which picture is it. Make a donation to Barry's kids 'n watch Friday's match! If you're right, ya get in a drawin' for tickets to Sheffield, in the Sky Box!" Then he danced away.

"There we have it," said the reporter. "*The Peregrines* are off to Bristol, in the morning, and this promises to be quite the show! Now to Newcastle!"

Finn felt like he was floating in nothingness. He didn't dare move for fear he'd wake and find he was dreaming, again. He focused on the screen, shaking, his voice a whisper as he said, "Martin...is this a rebroadcast?"

Martin slowly rose, his eyes locked on Finn. "No...no, the tournament starts on Friday. Here is Tuesday. They're off there, tomorrow."

"Barry Cowan's still alive?" Finn gasped.

Martin gave him a terrified look and said, "Barry Cowan? He...he's their star and that...that charity he fronts for is...and...oh, Christ, Finn. Was it him?"

Finn was gasping for air.

Martin knelt by him. "They took ye early. Sent ye back early. That's it, isn't it? Happened to me, once. Found out the man I...I was used against died the day after...the day after I...and I thought I should've known, should've done something. It was the one before Stu...and then I hurt him and I tried to find him to warn him but I...Joss took over and...and..."

Finn bolted up, nearly in hysterics. "What was it, what was it, what was it? Team. Bus. Back...no, side. Hit. Lorry. Fire. Everyone on board. We've got to tell someone — stop them!"

Finn started for the door but Martin shoved him onto his bed then put a hand over his mouth. "Not a word!" he snarled. "Ye told me what happened to that Muslim lad — he went off hysterical and now he's sedated, and you will be, too, and nothing'll be done."

It was a struggle, but Finn managed to make himself listen to Martin and see he was right. His breathing slowly relaxed.

"But I...I'm a police officer," he finally croaked, nearly weeping. "Sworn to serve. And protect. Have to find a way to stop them."

"Talk it through. Talk! Tell us what ye saw."

Finn rose and ran his hands through his hair, fighting to think. "Team. On a bus. Headed for Bristol. Hit on left...so turning right. On a motorway? Where's their training camp?"

"Outside Leeds," said Martin. "I'll call Arin. See if I can get him before he leaves for here. He can get the address and contact info. Maybe even their schedule; he's good at that. He's due about seven to watch England against — "

"Will he let me use his mobile? I can call people."

"Such as who?"

"I...I dunno, yet! Let me think on it. But I have to do something!"

"Yeah. Yeah, I'll see to it. And he'll have his laptop."

Finn grinned and almost laughed. They had a chance. All they needed was a plan. If something hasn't happened, yet, it didn't need to.

Maybe they could rewrite the future's past.

****

Keely wanted to refuse to let Arin meet with Martin in their room, due to Finn's illness, so Finn went out of his way to show her he was past it.

"Must've been something I ate," Finn told her, doing his best to look hale and hearty. "I dropped a pound in the loo and feel a lot better. Perhaps the fish, last night."

"None else had trouble," she said, wary.

"Yes, but I'm not like anyone else, am I?"

She huffed, checked him over, found his fever was gone and saw no sign of chills or aching, so relented.

"But if ye relapse, don't come at me," she huffed.

Arin strutted into the room then gave Finn the team's contact phone number and his mobile. Finn called them, but after making his way through a dozen phone prompts he wound up with a recording saying they would get back to him. He almost hung up but then words spilled out.

"Look I'm sorry, but I...I'm Detective Sergeant Finley James Winterbourne, of Clayton-Merrill CID, and I'm asking you to not make the trip to Bristol. Please. Something terrible will happen. Do not make the trip. I believe the bus is targeted and will be...will be attacked. By terrorists. We've just received word, so please, do not make the journey."

He hung up, thought for a moment, then flopped into a chair, saying, "I don't have their numbers."

Martin looked at him. "Whose?"

"Stu. Rob. Christian. They're on my mobile." He kicked himself, mentally, nearly laughing. "I suppose I could call Manchester police and ask to speak to the man who's back from the dead, but I doubt I'd get through. For all I know, they've left him dead. Paperwork's simpler."

Arin pulled up a screen on his laptop and said, "The bus hire the Peregrines use is out of York. Call in a bomb threat?"

"That won't stop anything," Finn said. "Merely delay the busses as they're checked. And it would make my first call even less reliable." He leaned back, at a loss. "What were their names? Two men from MI5 interrogated me, and they told me their names but all I can remember is Tweedle-Dee and Tweedle-Dum. How bloody stupid."

Keely came in, startling them. "How're we doing?" she saw the hire company's website up. "So what's this?"

Martin rose, smiling, and said, "Arin's had a lovely idea. Hire a transit van for a day trip down to Edinburgh. Whole family. Finn's never been. We're looking at prices."

"You'll need Behrmann's and Lambert's permission for that, so you'd best include them in the process. No guarantees they'll allow it. Would you like some tea?"

"I would *love* some, Keely," said Finn. "Please."

She happily went back out.

"Arin," said Finn, "can you get a contact number for MI5?"

He pulled up their website, which offered a tip line.

Finn dialed the tip line and said, "It's Winterbourne and it's happened again! I was taken as I slept and used and it was against Barry Cowan, but he's alive. He's still bloody alive and he said things about going to Bristol and that's where they're headed in the morning. You have to stop that bus. They'll be hit by a lorry and he'll be killed, along with others. You have to keep them from going to Bristol. They're leaving in the morning, Wednesday morning, and their training camp's in Leeds. Keep them there. Don't let them go."

Then he ended the call. And chuckled. "They'll probably trace this back to you."

Arin eyed him, wary. "Um...I'm in around loonies and lost my phone, a bit. God knows who said what, where."

Finn smiled. "Stay on our side, will you?"

Arin shrugged and turned to Martin. "Da, what's he about?"

Finn nudged the boy. "Can you find out when the bus is slated to depart for Bristol?"

Arin hesitated. Martin took over the laptop and looked, saying, "There's no schedule for that, but it's arranged to arrive at the training camp by 7am. Allow an hour for loading and typical nonsense, I'd say they'll set off about eight. Ye thinking of calling in that bomb threat?"

"No," said Finn, his eyes locked on the TV screen. It showed a clip of Barry Cowan escaping a scrum with the ball, his powerful legs covered in mud, his shorts pulled halfway off his exquisite ass. "As I said, that won't work. They have to be stopped, not delayed."

"And just how do ye determine to do that?" Martin asked.

"I'm going to Leeds."

Martin laughed. "How? Will ye hire a car from Edinburgh to come pick ye up? I doubt they'd let it in the gate, nor would they allow ye out. We're in a secure facility."

"I need to stop that bus," Finn growled, "not merely

delay it, and I can't do that from here."

"But we don't even know if it was this match. It might actually be a year in the future or on their journey back."

"No, no, it is, it must be. Everything aligns with that. Things Cowan said. The bandage on his arm! I'm sure it's this journey, I know it."

Arin was glancing between them, nervous. "Da, what's he on about? Ye said this is just over a tip ye got, about the Peregrines being attacked but..."

Martin looked at the boy, startled, then grabbed Finn and dragged him into the washroom. He slammed the door, his voice a low growl. "I don't want him to know what this means. Not yet."

Finn nodded, fighting to keep control of himself as he whispered, "I understand. I do understand. But just think of what you saw, Martin. It drove you mad and Joss to jump off a building. I watched him. Every moment of it. All the way down."

Martin's face went white. "All the way?"

Finn nodded. "And...Cowan...there was fire and it...it surrounded him and others and they were screaming..."

Knocking at the door jolted both of them. Martin opened it to find Arin looking at him.

"Da?" the boy asked, now upset. "Is it starting, again?"

Martin hesitated, glanced at Finn, then put a hand on his son's head, murmuring, "No. It's ending." He cast another look at Finn. "It's ending?"

Finn took in a deep breath and made himself sound as reasonable as he could. "If this works. To what degree I've no idea, but I do believe it will put an end to it."

Martin looked between him and Arin, his mind whirring.

Finn dared not move, but his eyes were tearing into the man.

Martin shifted from wariness to confusion to determination before he took in a deep breath and asked his son, "When's mum collecting ye?"

"I drove."

"Ye got yer license?" Martin said, startled but smiling.

"Yeah, a PIP. Mum arranged it."

Martin took in a deep breath. "Ye in the van?"

"No, she got that. Picking up Edith and Eric from

practice. It's been raining so..."

Martin squatted before Arin, his eyes locked on the boy. "Arin, ye know I'd never ask ye to do something wrong, don't ye?" The boy nodded, even more wary. "I want ye to let Finn hide in the boot of Mum's car and take him out of here."

"But there's guards..."

"If they search your car," Finn quickly said, "you knew nothing about me sneaking into the boot. I'll back you up."

"Then when yer to home," Martin said, "give Finn some of my clothes." He looked at Finn, almost smiling. "They'll be awkward on ye, but will arouse less suspicion than ye driving about in that robe." He turned back to Arin. "Give him the spare key to the van. It's in the pantry, on a hook in the door. Let him hide in the garage."

"Da..."

"Please, Arin. We're trying to save a man's life, here. Will ye do this for me? Please? I need to know ye'll do it for me."

"But ye been sick..."

Martin nodded. "I'm better now. And this...if it succeeds, this will finalize my recovery. Will ye do it? For me?"

"Will ye come home, then? Mum's lost without ye."

Martin drew the boy close and held him. "Within a week."

"Then I'll do it," he said. "But how?"

"Visiting hours are almost done," said Finn, looking at Martin. "If you can keep them busy..."

Martin looked hard into the boy's eyes. "Go out the car. Leave the boot unlocked."

Finn added, "When you feel me get in, go."

Arin hesitated then gathered his things and headed out the door. Martin sagged as the boy hurried down the hall. "God, I never want this to happen to him," he said.

"I'll stop it or die trying. That'll kill their beast."

"Don't say that."

Finn smiled at him and lied, "Figure of speech."

"It's a Vauxhall Vectra," Martin finally said. "Silver. Old but in good shape. The van's a small passenger one, so should fly under the radar." He took in a deep breath. "Do ye really think this'll work? Changing the future?"

"It hasn't been written, yet."

"...I wonder..."

Suddenly Martin tore Finn's shirt open and screamed, "They took me, again! Ye bastard! Ye helped them find me! Bloody bastard!"

Finn struggled to keep Martin from hitting him as Keely. "What's the problem?"

"I don't know," Finn cried. "He jumped me and tore at my shirt and he's berserk."

Martin slung Finn against his bed before the orderlies roared in to take hold of him. Finn noticed one orderly's clip was hanging from a sleeve and deftly snagged it as they fought with Martin.

"It's your fault!," Martin kept screaming. "I'll kill ye for it! I'll kill ye! Bringin' 'em back to me!"

"I...I should leave the room," Finn said, as he rose, making his voice shake.

"Yes," Keely said, shuddering. "Wait by our station."

Finn slipped out, quietly scurried down to the main entrance and used the orderly's clip to release the door's lock, then bolted outside. He saw a silver Vectra with its trunk open, slipped over to it, jumped in and pulled the lid closed.

The car started moving, immediately.

Finn listened as they headed down the drive. An alarm began ringing. The Vectra stopped and Finn heard the guard at the base of the driveway ask, "What's up, in there?"

"Dunno," Finn heard Arin reply. "I'm halfway down the drive when the noise starts."

"Another looney gone berserker's most like it."

"My da's in there!"

There was a long silence, then the guard said, "Ye old enough to drive, then?"

"Got me license three month back. Had to show to da, to prove it."

"Show it me."

Another long silence. Finn began to worry they'd be delayed long enough for Keely to realize he was missing. He wondered if he'd be willing to hurt someone in order to prevent what he knew was a tragedy about to happen.

No...he was. He knew it.

So he quietly pushed the board that covered the spare tire aside, under him, and found the tire iron and slipped it out and was working out a plan of action when —

"Independent license. No doubt o' that. Well, careful the road."

And they headed on.

Fugitive

After what seemed like hours, Arin pulled down a short driveway and parked the Vectra. He let Finn out of the trunk to find he was in the garage.

"Ye might want to stay here," the boy said. "I think I saw Mum round the circle when I pulled in. I'll bring the key out."

He scrambled into a side door as another vehicle was heard approaching. Its headlights flared against the garage door, making it glow. Finn crept back into the trunk and pulled the lid almost completely closed. He heard children's laughter and Miriam saying, "Don't forget yer things in the back! All to the laundry."

"Here! Just beat ye to home!" he heard Arin say.

"How's yer father?"

"He's all right Played some games. Finn's a vidiot. I think he cheats."

Finn huffed.

"Be kind. He's helped your father a lot."

"Oh, forgot me rucker in the car."

Arin hopped into the garage, tossed the key into the trunk, grabbed his rucksack and headed back into the house without a comment. Then Finn heard him return and drop his phone in the car, as well, muttering, "GPS."

The house didn't settle down for another three hours, and Arin never did bring out clothes for Finn to wear. When it was nearly 1am, Finn crawled out of the Vectra, slowly opened the garage door then closed it just as slowly.

He found a green Ford Transit Connect Wagon that was at least ten years old, and looked it. The tires were approaching baldness and a crack was in the windscreen. Finn took in a deep breath, clicked off the alarm with a soft *beep*, got in, adjusted the seat and mirrors for himself, fixed his safety belt, and drove away.

GPS told him it was more than 200 miles to get to the training facility and the van had just over half a tank of fuel. A quick calculation told him he might just make it, with no room to spare, so rather than push it he travelled at a steady speed down the A1 along the coast and around Newcastle to the A1(m), nervously watching the needle on the fuel gauge slowly creep down...and down...and down.

It didn't help that on the south edge of Newcastle two cars had collided and blocked the road. That set him back by half an hour and drained more of his fuel, even though he turned the van off, while waiting.

When he was outside Darlington, the fuel gauge warning light was burning and he had close to an hour's drive ahead of him, so he drove into an all-night pull-out and stopped by the pumps. He got out of the car and hurried inside to the cashier.

"I'm sorry," he said, breathless, "but I'm out of petrol and forgot my wallet and my wife's having her first contractions and I just came to get petrol for the drive to the maternity ward and I'll pay you back if you'll just lend me five litres worth. Just five litres, please."

The woman took in his sleeping pants and torn shirt and the robe half-wrapped around him and shook her head and said, "I got yor set. Name's Pegg. Bring me a tenner, next yor through."

"Thank you, thank you, so much. If it's a girl, we'll name her Margaret, for Peggy."

"Name's no' Margaret. Just Pegg, like Simon is."

Finn backed to the entrance, laughing. "Scottie. New *Star Trek*!"

She grinned at him and said, "*Hot Fuzz*."

"*Shaun of the dead!*"

"Arr, yor a fun one! Show us yor bum, no need t' pay."

He whipped aside the robe, spun and pulled the sleeping pants down then swatted his rear. "Cash on deposit?"

"Arr...ya *would* be a fun one..."

"Thanks, again!"

Then he bolted back to the van, put fuel in, and zoomed away.

It was now after seven.

The training facility was on the other side of Leeds,

and getting through the town during rush hour would have been a lesson in pure frustration had Finn not been so hyper he laughed at drivers as he forced his way past them. More than a few did a lot of screaming at the maniac racing around. Finn had to fight himself to keep from acting even wilder. The last thing he needed was for traffic control to come chasing after him. But he was doing good; he was making good time.

Then he was on the A4 and, according to GPS, not five minutes from the training facility, so he risked speeding and weaving around cars.

Let traffic control stop me, now.

Then he was a kilometer from the entrance. Up ahead was the intersection...its light just turning red. Cars were pulling to a stop in both lanes, on his side, blocking him.

I'm turning left, so I can get around them.

Then a pair of blue and yellow police cars pulled across the road to turn right, their lights flashing...

They heard my warning?

...And a bus started across, following them.

"Oh, no, no, no, no, no, it's not eight yet, it's not even eight!" he screamed.

That's when he saw a massive red lorry approaching, in opposing traffic.

Coming fast.

Too fast!

IT WAS GOING TO HIT THE BUS!

He was too late!

A howl pitched from within him!

Then he remembered Barry saying *"Broadsided us."*

Broadsided.

BROADSIDED! ON THE LEFT SIDE OF THE BUS!

In an animalistic rage, Finn crushed the pedal to the floor and the engine roared and the van shrieked forward, going faster.

Faster.

Faster.

He steered onto the left shoulder, skidded a little, then swerved around the stopped cars on two wheels and aimed the van's nose straight at the bus's rear tires and –

Finn woke in the hospital.

Oh, bloody hell, not again.

He felt no pain...until he tried to move. Then daggers sliced into his back and neck and he grunted and froze. Slowly he realized something was holding his mouth rigid.

He was intubated, and it was damned uncomfortable.

He remained as still as he could, giving the pain time to subside, then did a slow, methodical check of himself. A careful shift of his head to the right helped him realize he was also immobilized in a neck brace. He was barely able to raise his arms, but could just make out that his left was covered in light dressing and connected to an array of tubes and monitors while the right one was in a cast. He let his arms drop, already exhausted, then tried to raise his legs...but only his right leg responded. His fingers told him his left thigh was also in a cast.

Bloody hell, what happened?

A Sister strode in, all no-nonsense and looking like she had been that way since birth. "Good morning, Mr. Winterbourne," she chirped in a voice that matched her looks. "Seems you're feeling better."

He tried to say, *What is all this*, but all that came out was a gurgle.

"No need to speak; you were seriously injured," she said as she whipped open the window's curtains to reveal a bright chilly day. "I've put in a call for the doctor; he'll be here in a moment." She put a hand to his forehead. "Excellent. Fever's broken, but let's take a more accurate gauge." She plopped a thermometer under his arm and clipped a sensor to his left index finger, then checked his pulse.

A tall thin doctor entered, looking like he was well into his seventies, with an aristocratic bearing that screamed Eaton.

"Ah, Mr. Winterbourne," he said, his voice very Edwardian. "Good to see you finally awake."

Before Finn could even think to say anything, the doctor put a finger to his lips and began checking him over. "I'm Dr. Willys-Carrington. But everyone calls me WC, and I hope you will, as well. Once you can. In answer to what I am certain will be your first questions, you were extremely restless, so we induced you into a light coma five days ago to allow us not only to treat you but give your body time to settle. Your internal organs were not happy with being jostled about, and you've broken both your right arm and left leg. You also have second and third degree burns on your left arm, the latter of which will require skin grafts. Fortunately for you, they were able to drag you from the van before it was completely engulfed in flames." He rose to his full height and glanced at the Sister. "Vitals are good. I see no reason to delay." He turned back to Finn. "Ready to breathe on your own?"

Finn nodded.

Within minutes, the intubation tube had been removed, more exams done, and Finn's throat more sore than it had ever been.

"Now then," said WC. "Do you remember what happened?"

"I...I hit...a bus?" Finn managed to say.

"Very good," said WC. "And very correct. Then an out-of-control lorry also struck the bus and your van. Fortunately, your vehicle prevented that lorry's tail from swinging around and toppling onto some cars stopped at the opposing light. One of which held a family of five. The damn thing was loaded with canned goods. It would have crushed them instead of nearly crushing you."

A moment of tenderness swept over the Sister's face. "You were very fortunate."

Finn took in a deep breath. His mind was unable to focus. "No...too late...too late...for something..."

"Now, now, now, no more of that or I'll put you back under coma. You muttered it non-stop as we tried to mend you, and it's incorrect. You're currently in ICU, part due to your condition, part in order to keep you away from the media and their invasive questions. You're quite the hero, you know, and subject of some hilariously malicious gossip. But if you're up for it, in a day or two, I know that family would love to thank you, themselves, for what you did."

They checked Finn's vital signs one more time, chirping happily about how well he was mending, but he paid them no mind. His brain was scrambled in ways he couldn't begin to understand, and he was so depressed all he wanted to do was crawl into a hole and never come out, again.

After a couple of days, and sessions of cleaning and debriding the burns then applying the initial skin grafts, two investigators looking into the crash were allowed to talk with him. Initially, they had thought he was the terrorist attacker, as warned about in a phone call, but then they identified him and learned he was the caller. And cameras at the intersection showed not only had the lorry approached the intersection too fast, it was losing control. To all appearances, Finn had deliberately sped up, swerved around the stopped cars, aimed straight for the bus's rear wheels and hit them.

What the investigators wanted to know was, *How had he known that hitting the bus's rear axles would jolt it around enough to point its tail at the lorry, keeping it from plowing into the bus's side?* Which would have been disastrous, considering it then exploded into flames.

Finn wasn't of much use, again. He was still trying to understand why he was in Leeds, unless it was to look more into Finbar Caramin's death. But it made no sense for him to be doing that. Then he was told he had snuck out of the convalescent home and stolen the van from Martin's family, which made even less sense to him. He'd never stolen anything in his life. Well...nothing of real value. They finally left with less information than they'd initially had.

Next to visit was Dr. Behrmann, who wanted to know why he'd deliberately provoked Martin Lowenstein into making a scene. And how he'd been able to escape the facility.

"I'm sorry," he told her, "but I'm still trying to sort things out, in my head. Is Martin all right?"

"It's ridiculous to say this," she said, glaring at him, "but I think your manipulation of him helped bring him back to reality. I've met with him a dozen times in the last week, and everything he now tells me indicates he's on the mend. If I get agreement from colleagues, who're meeting with him, now, I think we may be able to work with him on an outpatient basis. Free up his bed for another."

An odd sense of joy spread through Finn and he said, "I'm so glad. His wife and children miss him."

"His wife isn't so happy with you, after what you did with their van. The insurance isn't enough to get them another."

Finn took in a deep breath. "Please tell her I'm sorry, and that I will see to it the van is replaced with a new one."

Behrmann looked at him for a long moment then got up to leave, saying, "You're a hard man to figure out, Winterbourne. I think you're a poor liar and rotten thief, with more than a touch of sociopathic attitudes that have no basis in reality, but you're also the kindest man I've ever known. We'll talk more when you've returned."

Then she left.

That evening, after dinner, The Sister came in, grinning. "There're some people who'd like to see you. Up for it?"

Finn just nodded. He knew it was that family, and he had no idea how he would handle their questions and praise, since he'd done nothing to deserve it, just stupidly caused a wreck, no matter what everyone claimed. Besides, he was still depressed and it felt like part of his brain was lost in a fog. But as Nan had often said, "Best to get the worst done first."

A moment later, the Sister led in a Muslim family of five, bearing gifts. He accepted the gentle kiss from the wife and neatly-wrapped packages from their sons with warmth – a hand-knitted afghan that reminded him of Nan, and a robe and fresh sleeping clothes.

"Yours were destroyed," said the husband with a shrug.

"We weren't sure your size," said the oldest boy, who was perhaps twelve.

"You're too kind," was all Finn could manage to say.

Then a group of nicely-dressed young men barged in, chattering amongst themselves, all healthy, sturdy, strong, a dozen different nationalities and cultures, with an athlete's swagger to each of them, and wearing black and green jerseys.

The Peregrines.

Some sported bandages and cuts that were healing, one had an arm in a cast, another was in a wheelchair, while a couple more still limped, slightly. With them were photographers and news cameras and reporters waiting with baited breath for what they were sure would be a seven-hankie moment on tonight's news.

Followed by Tweedle-Dee and Tweedle-Dum, their eagle eyes sharp on Finn and the group.

Finn sighed. He had no idea how he was going to

explain this to them and shuddered at the thought of their disbelieving questions, sending him even deeper into a brutal weariness...

Until a golden god of a rugby player trailed in after them, cuts on his face nearly healed, a fresh elegant tattoo of a Peregrine Falcon perched on tree branch covering his right forearm.

Finn's jaw dropped and he gasped, "Barry Cowan?"

Barry stopped and eyed him, half grinning. "I know you. I...I think I know you."

Finn managed to remember to breathe in before he said, "I...I don't see how. We've never met. But I...I know who you are and..." And Finn had absolutely no idea why he would know of the man, because while rugby was okay, he was more into cricket.

Wait...wasn't he also the driving force behind a foundation or...? "A charity," Finn blurted. "You've set up charitable foundations..."

"Yeah, for 'omeless folk, LGBT youth. Met at a fundraiser?"

"Yes, yes, that must be it," said Finn, completely certain that was *not* correct. But it had to have been something like that. He glanced around at the group. "Looks like you're all well and good."

"Fanks to you," said a buff multi-race man in Cockney. "Coppers said your 'it knocked our bus 'round and its tail took th' brunt o' that lorry."

"If ya 'adn't," said Barry, "they think he'd o' tore in the side of the bus, instead. We got jumbled about, couple lads was pretty hurt, but all still 'ere."

"They helped Mr. Amin and his sons pull you from the wreckage," said the Sister. "You were partially trapped. Only life lost was the driver's. Sad, but could've been worse."

"'E were on speed," said a black player with amazing green eyes. "An' I don' mean 'is van."

Suddenly Finn was overwhelmingly happy and laughing and felt like everything was well and good, and he had no idea why. "I'm glad it wasn't too much of a shock," he managed to gasp.

"We made off better'n you," said Barry, nudging his cast.

The Muslim boys and father were in slack-jawed awe of Barry, so he and the team gleefully joined them and let their mother snap photos on her phone. Completely forgotten for the moment, Finn beamed. Then they spent the next hour chattering and thanking Finn and giving him and the boys a lifetime of free passes to their matches, making the news crews *Ooh* and *Ahhh* over the heartfelt moments.

All under the eagle eyes of 'Dee and 'Dum.

Through it all Finn kept trying to remember where he knew Barry from. No question he was a damn good-looking man, even in street clothes and not a pair of Hilfiger briefs...

And why the hell would I make that comparison? I've never seen him in a locker room.

When the reporters starting trying to ask Finn a bunch of questions about the other episodes he'd been through, 'Dee and 'Dum did nothing but put a finger to their lips in way only Finn could see, and he refused to answer anything *due to national security*. The reporters weren't happy, but at least now they had a hook for their stories...including one that presented Finn as clairvoyant...and another that claimed he was from Andromeda, to which Finn had to say, "That's something of a strain."

No one got the joke.

He was in hospital for three more days before WC determined him fit for release. He would still need more grafting sessions, but he could now take care of himself. So his arm and leg were put in mobile casts and 'Dee and 'Dum took him straight back to Monifeith, where they wheeled him into his old room and sat down at the table to interrogate him.

'Dum started with, "Well, Winterbourne, you're quite the lad. Stealing a van, driving all night to Leeds, and slamming it into a bus ten times its size."

"Why'd ya do it?" 'Dee asked, eyeing Finn, deeply wary.

For the first time, Finn could honestly answer, "I have no idea. The last thing I remember was watching the news. Sports, I think...and then I'm in hospital."

"Which show?" asked 'Dee.

"Um...it was on *Sky*...no, *Channel Four*. Martin chose it

and he likes their coverage."

"When?"

"After tea. He and I dine in his room and — "

"So 'tween seven and eight in the evening?"

"...That sounds about right. I think his son was with us."

'Dum checked his notes and took in a deep breath before asking, "You remember any story about *The Peregrines* traveling to Bristol for a match?"

Finn jolted and —

Barry Cowan burst in on his coach's interview and —

"*That's* where I knew him from!" Finn yelped.

'Dee's wariness increased. "What you mean?"

"*The Peregrines*! I don't follow rugby, but I recognized Barry Cowan, and I couldn't understand why, and that's it — I saw a clip on the news. I was going mad, trying to remember."

'Dee and 'Dum exchanged a look that gave Finn pause. Finally, 'Dee opened up his phone, said, "This your voice?" and played a message on it.

"It's happened again! I was taken as I slept and used and it was against Barry Cowan, but he's alive. He's still bloody alive and he said things about going to Bristol and that's where they're headed in the morning. You have to stop that bus. They'll be hit by a lorry and he'll be killed, along with others. You have to keep them from going to Bristol. They're leaving in the morning, Wednesday morning, and their training camp's in Leeds. Keep them there. Don't let them go."

Finn felt his head swim and his breath go shallow. He sensed that if he hadn't already been seated, he would have fallen over. Every nerve in his body tingled. It took all of his concentration to ask, "Will you play it, again, please?"

'Dee did, his eyes sharp and fierce.

Finn could not speak. He remembered nothing about making that call. Absolutely nothing.

'Dee asked, "Wha' 'bou' this?"

He opened an industrial-strength laptop and played a clip from a CCTV camera.

Of Finn's and Martin's room, as each lay in his bed.

And a bright blue light whispered across the lens and Finn's bed was now empty.

Martin rose and went to the bed. Knelt by it.

"Like that for near an hour, 'e was," said 'Dee, "then..."

The blue light whispered past, again, and Finn was on the bed, naked and thrashing as Martin jumped on him.

Finn's eyes slammed shut and he couldn't figure if the sounds bursting from his were laughter or tears. But now he knew.

I remember nothing because there's nothing to remember! Nothing! NOTHING!

He had altered the course of the future and saved not only Barry Cowan's life but also who knew how many others' from that wreck, and the truth of it was so overwhelming, he lost complete control of himself and his whole being felt lifted up to heaven as he wept and laughed and gasped, "I stopped it. I bloody stopped it." Over and over and over and —

The blue light swirled around him and he was back in the nothing room, still laughing and crying from joy.

Finn's euphoria vanished as he realized where he was. He began to shake, half from fear...and half with anger...until he realized his left arm was still bandaged, and the cast still on his right, and his leg was in that cast and he was standing. Physically standing.

Then a form approached him in the nothing light.

"No," he snarled. "No, I won't let you do this with me, again. I'll bloody make you kill me, first!"

The form took the shape of a woman who was tall, slim and controlled, her eyes large and green, almost opaque, with a face that was a meld of half a dozen different races in perfect symmetry. Gleaming black hair flowed from her head to around her shoulders, almost seeming to become part of the shimmering dress she was wearing, and her skin was a golden brown. She would have been beautiful if any part of her held even a hint of emotion.

Flanking her were two men built to absolute perfection, their faces the epitome of masculine beauty, wearing uniforms so tightly fitted, they seemed like a second skin. They, too, came across more as robotic than human. Each held a weapon that was small and sleek, but Finn sensed it was probably deadlier than anything available in his own world.

"What have you done?" she asked, her voice clipped and without the slightest hint of an accent.

"I took back my future," he spat. He found he could move and walk, though still with a vague limp. He saw no floor beneath him, but he didn't care.

She straighten to stand even higher, as if meaning to intimidate him. "You have altered our past."

He snarled. "If it's been changed, how do you know? I didn't remember any of it, myself, and — "

"We finally deciphered the information in your file."

"What file?"

"Some organization with which you were affiliated, after calling so much attention to yourself. They used an antiquated form of encryption; it was difficult to reconstruct."

"You couldn't just go back and watch it being input?"

That almost brought a smile to her elegant lips. Even her guards seemed to hint at a smirk.

"Have you any idea how extensive the past is, for us? And the limitations of this device? There have to be links of some sort for us to map a journey to a particular point. We found that samples of DNA worked best — "

"Sealed in vaults at *Alles Wissen*?"

She almost let herself seem irritated at the interruption. "And many other locations. As for your information, our system is a thousand generations removed from the most highly advanced of yours, so it is nearly impossible to interpret these files within a short timeframe. We first had to know of them, then locate them within our own databanks, understand what they were and find agéd devices in order to open them for translation."

"That doesn't answer my question," Finn shot back. "How did you know your past had been changed?"

Her voice almost sounded haughty. Her guards stood even more erect. "You think our abilities no greater than your own?"

Finn almost snarled a response, but his police discipline kicked in and he decided to let her talk.

"We have statisticians, for want of a better word, who have mastered the science of determining human decisions," the woman continued, "and who can now predict the future with ninety-nine-point-eight-four-three-eight percent accuracy."

Finn had to chuckle. "Isaac Asimov wrote about that in his *Foundation Trilogy*. Do you call yourselves *The Hari Seldens*?"

"Your comment is nonsensical."

Finn shrugged a smirk. His eyes wandered to the two perfect male specimens flanking her. He was fairly certain they were watching him back, though now it seemed more from curiosity than wariness.

"We had our greatest masters apply this science to

you," she continued. "Specifically, between the time of your first genetic testing and your second. They constructed the life you would have led had you not been assaulted, and we found anomalies that were distressing."

"That's a gentle way of putting it."

She hesitated. "You understand what I am saying?"

"Of course."

She nearly laughed. "But you speak English, which is very limited and ceased to be a language of importance nearly four centuries ago."

"You're speaking English to me."

"Through a translation program. Our method of communication is now Esperanto mixed with one based in mathematics. Ĉu vi preferas, ke mi parolu en ĉi tiu lingvo?"

"No, English is fine."

This brought a sense of near curiosity to her. The two guards also focused their eyes even sharper on Finn. He almost felt like a specimen under a microscope.

"You do understand my words," she said. "This makes what happened even worse."

Finn spun around with a howl, nearly making the guards grab him. "What *did* happen?"

She grew closer to Finn, now examining him as if he were a prize horse she was considering purchasing. "Assaulting you changed the course of your future...and our past. Now I see to how great a degree. And how tragic."

"*Tragic*?!" Finn snapped. "Terrorizing men like this is criminal, but to also do it as they're dying? That is an abomination!"

Her eyes met his, and he could see their colors changed as she spoke, growing darker when her words were angrier. "Do not apply your antiquated version of morality to us. The concerns of those long dead are immaterial to our needs. All I can say is, this was not supposed to have been done to any who would remain alive."

"Like me and Christian and Martin, and God knows how many others. What a lovely way to describe an unacceptable level of cruelty. And what about Rob and Stu?! Were they really supposed to die?"

"Haller and Hoskins were errors, thanks to incorrect data being input during *your* time. Their deaths were through no fault of our own. Fortunately, their futures were of no consequence."

Finn nearly spat. "How dare you say that?!"

The guards seemed amazed that he was arguing with her.

"It is the truth. Our statisticians determined Haller to be responsible for siring one child, which he did prior to his assault, and Hoskins was never seen capable of siring children, himself. He would, eventually, have reconciled with his bed partner and accepted her daughter as his own. Now? He will not. It mattered nothing to the greater scheme of history. The daughter will die at age nine in a virulent pandemic that will also kill her mother, the man who sired her, and hundreds of millions of others. The one aspect which has changed, regarding Hoskins and Haller, is how their isolation will protect them from this. Initially, they too would have succumbed."

Finn hesitated. "What sort of pandemic?"

"That is immaterial."

"Well...what about Christian? And...and Martin?"

"Your twin will prove immune. As do you. Lowenstein and his family will move to Aberdeen and will not be much affected. But he has already fulfilled his part in history with his son — "

Finn's inner cop kicked in and he snarled, "Stop it."

She jolted and took a step back, in shock. "I merely try to explain the course of — "

"*Course of history*, to you. Right. Got it. But that's not what you're really doing. You're deflecting. Trying to keep me from figuring out what really happened. I can see it, now. I already know some of it, such as when Stuart was taken. You or your *agent* thought he was me or...or you were looking for me. You directed your agent to him, but kept him within a specific timeframe and – "

Her eyes grew dark and dangerous. "Who told you this?"

Finn snarled at her, "Who do you bloody think? I'm held and tortured and fucked in that bloody nothing room as your agent chatters nonstop and lets all sorts of evil things out and — "

She held up a hand to silence him. "As I said, our device was developed solely for research."

196

Finn stormed up to the woman. The guards almost jumped him, but all he did was go nose-to-nose with her.

"You *admitted* you let him do it!"

Her eyes grew lighter as she said, "We did not know the extent of what was being done."

"Now you're lying."

"No! We had not realized there was a flaw in our system. We developed the intermediary quadrant to isolate subjects like yourself. Study them. Capture them while sleeping. Prevent them from bringing diseases long eradicated back into our world. Unfortunately, it also prevented us from knowing what actions were being taken by our agents, in it. And there were some who...who took advantage of that flaw. Directives have been issued to end it. I tell you in truth – the device was intended solely for research."

"But any device that's developed can be used badly, when in the wrong hands. Surely you knew that."

She sighed, back to being superior. "We have long been able to restructure one's genetic code to prevent certain problematic issues from occurring, and to expand upon others we wished to develop. But we have also learned these manipulations can impact on some individuals in a negative way that is not readily noticeable. Our initial observations were...insufficient to prevent instances of our agents succumbing to the temptation of, for want of a better word, a sociopathic need to harm others. They justified it within themselves by choosing to use those who would have no influence on our past, and they knew this flaw would also hide their abuses from us."

"How many instances?"

"Four, only."

"That you know about."

"All other agents in this program have been evaluated and found to have behaved correctly. Now safeguards are in place to prevent it from recurring."

"You're still lying. Joss told me you knew but agreed to let him keep doing his thing while he searched for me." She grew haughty but Finn continued to glare at her. "Why was I so bloody important that you let human beings be tortured?"

She almost seemed to scowl, then began to pace, her

eyes going dark and light, emotion threatening to break through her icy exterior.

"The human genome was breaking down. If this deterioration had been left unchecked, humans would have ceased to exist within three-point-two centuries. Your genetic code is valuable in the reversal of this. Your ancient sample on file..."

"Thanks to my grandmother?"

"Yes. It was barely readable, but offered promise. And the additional sample we finally determined to be yours, at *Alles Wissen*, was insufficient to work with but, again, promising. We followed the trail of a particular genomic map to Haller, and requested his semen be transported to a safe storage facility."

"In Alles Wissen's vaults."

She cast him a look of pure condescension. "That has already been noted. We had our agent use Hallsworth's capacity as a police office to access records there and establish a particular file deep in their system."

"My own private cum vault, with souvenirs of each rape. How delightful."

She actually glared at him, more than irritated. "There, we could use it in our time. Haller's samples led us to Hoskins, and his led us to Hauptmann. We thought he was the one we needed until we realized he was homosexual."

"What if he is?"

She actually frowned at him, in disbelief. "His DNA is not perfect to encourage procreation. While it is not so difficult to alter the gay gene..."

Finn snarled.

No, Finn, no, let her speak. Let her hang herself.

"...Beginning with altered data has proven inadequate. We found three fetuses out of ten would still develop according to the aberrant gene, and if we removed it prior to joining it with the egg, the pregnancies failed. That is why we had to locate you. Your DNA was crucial to reversing the degradation."

"So I am a fucking lab rat to you!"

"No, not you. Shall I tell you how damaging the actions taken against you were, for us?"

Finn hesitated...then nodded.

"Our statisticians determined that, had you not been

assaulted you would have joined with a woman you were seeing at the time, sired five children, and the youngest of them would have survived the pandemic to discover the beginning of the collapse. Her findings would not have been accepted, at first, but she would have laid the foundation for research into reversing the trend, and we would currently be at the point where our genetic structure was strengthening rather than only just beginning to stabilize. When our agent removed your progeny from our history, it delayed our recognition of what was happening, by centuries. What is fortunate is...by keeping the man you assaulted..."

"His name is Barry Cowan!"

She cast him a look that was colder than any he'd ever seen as she continued, "...Alive, you happened to bring us another chance to stabilize everything within an acceptable timeframe. He will now sire a line of descendants, one of whom will be the first to notice the development of a breakdown in humanity's genetic code. We estimate this is one-hundred and twenty-three years later than it would have been recognized, by your daughter, but is much better than what we had faced. This is why the alteration of your path was of such importance."

"That still doesn't explain why *my* genetic structure matters so much, to you."

"It is helping us re-align our peoples' genome with greater speed and much better results."

"Realign? Wait, wait, wait, wait, wait, are you effectively saying you're impregnating women with my sperm? Like we're actually practicing something from *A Boy and His Dog*?"

Her expression became nonplussed. "Again your comment is nonsensical, but yes. Your semen helps to hasten restructuring of our genetic code. It is remarkably pure and is being used to a far greater good. Had your father not impregnated so many different women other than your mother, we'd have had greater resources."

Finn jolted. "Wait...are you saying I've got more half-brothers and...and sisters?"

"Only five male children were sired. The rest were female."

"Five? Who's the fifth — wait, that architect in Buenos

Aires. Bernardo something. You took him, as well?"

"Yes. But he was also not usable."

"Bloody hell," Finn said. "So here we have it. You made an agreement with this *agent* to let him rape and torture men who were going to die so long as he kept bringing you Stu's and Rob's and Christian's semen...and Bernardo's, for testing. And finally, mine. And now you're happy. How fucking evil."

"Again, with your ancient morality," she huffed. "No one else had as great of success in finding what information we needed."

"So you stood aside. Let things proceed. Even provided him with the equipment to do it." He touched the back of his right ear. "Something here that glowed."

"Ah, this." She held up a small half-moon shaped wire, saying, "This sensor merely connects with your autonomic nervous system to manipulate you into an erection and ejaculation. It's proven very successful. But we thought it minimally invasive; we now believe it also alters your genetic structure and sexual orientation."

"That thing made me gay?" Finn asked, in disbelief.

"That is the indication. However, it seems only to do this if you are taken while awake and aware. If taken in your sleep, it makes no difference. Another anomaly we have been working at correcting. We may be able to reverse the process, if you wish."

Finn jolted. He thought of Prue and how much he liked her. But being with Rob...he'd never felt so complete with anyone as with him. Never felt anything similar for any of the women he'd been with. In a flash he saw that he was pursuing them because he thought that's what he needed to do to build a family, but now he knew that he was mistaken...and eventually he'd have seen that. His Uncle Niall had his husband and his dogs and those were a family, to him. Uncle Cormac, his wife and his cousins were also family. And now Finn had his brothers. And sisters, if he could find them. And a whole new world of possibilities had opened up for him. So he shook his head.

"No," he said. "No, you're wrong; it didn't change me. All it did was draw back a curtain and open my eyes. I'll stay as I am."

"It is probably just as well. Our past has been altered

too frequently, of late. To do it, again, could prove catastrophic."

"Not for me. Your past is my future." Finn stepped back, smirking at her. The guards eyed him, now fascinated. "Maybe I'll alter it some more."

She glared at him. "There is no need for this. We promise you will not be approached, again. Nor will anyone else, even those who would have no effect on our past."

"*Those doomed to die, anyway*, right? How do I know you'll keep your word?"

That brought a look of shock to the guards' faces.

The woman nearly snarled. "It is written into the code. No subject may be harmed in any way, form or fashion. There are no exclusions. And our elimination of the agent who assaulted you and your brothers is being proffered as an example of what will happen if one attempts to circumvent the code."

Finn felt an odd mixture of wariness, joy and uncertainty build within him. "Execution?" he asked.

Her expression shifted to amused, lending her face an ethereal beauty beyond compare. "Executions were ended centuries ago. There are punishments far worse than death," she said.

The blue light swirled around Finn, again, but not before he caught a glimpse of four human forms wrapped in what looked like cloth, similar to a cocoon hanging in mid-air, a dozen hoses connected to each one, with only their eyes showing, wide, filled with pain...and pleading...

Pleading.

Pleading.

Returned, Again

Finn was lying outside an old white house three stories tall with a black roof, done in a square Germanic style. It was snowing and lush evergreen trees surrounded the residence, with open spaces that were as inviting as they were lovely. Three cars were parked on the gravel drive, one of them familiar.

A new BMW with a rainbow stripe across its tail.

"Christian?" Finn whispered.

As if he had been called, Christian burst from the house at a run, wearing jeans, an unbuttoned shirt and no shoes, "FINN!" exploding from him. He ignored the snow and the gravel on the drive as he raced across it, his face caught in unfettered joy. He skidded to his knees and grabbed Finn by his arms, strong but gentle. "Finn. Finn."

Finn gave him a crooked grin and said, "You wanted me to meet your parents, so here I am..."

Christian held him close, nearly weeping, speaking in German, *"I didn't know where you were. Or Stuart or Rob. No one! No one would tell me!"* He pulled back to look at Finn, more closely. *"Are you well? You are hurt. But you are hurt."*

He touched the cast on Finn's arm and then the bandage and seemed to only just realize Finn still had a cast on his leg.

"It's not as bad as it looks," Finn said in his halting German. *"What matters is, it's over. It's over."*

In answer, Christian held him close, again, until he could regain control of himself. *"I...I will call for our butler..."*

"No, Christian, if you'd just help me up. I can walk. Right?"

Christian nodded and helped Finn to his feet then guided him into the house and introduced him to his parents, a very refined elderly couple who, as Christian had promised, offered him their full support...and without even raising an eyebrow at how he'd just appeared at their door. He was given a room on the ground floor, drawn a hot bath by a maid, provided with some of Christian's clothing to wear, and helped to dress by their butler. By the time he was done, he was feeling human, again, and Christian was knocking to be let in.

Finn beckoned him in as the butler left. "This must have been quite the life," he said.

"It was all right," Christian shrugged. "I did not think I was so much larger than you."

"I've lost some weight. Thank you for these. Never worn Hugo Boss, before."

Christian acknowledged this with a smile, then he put his hands on Finn's shoulders and touched foreheads as he said, "We are about to dine, and we would very much like you to join us. Georg will be at the table. My brother, and his family. Mikala will arrive in time for coffee. I should let you know, I have told them everything." He chuckled. "They do not believe me but are too polite to say otherwise."

Finn nodded. "I'll need to let the facility at Monifeith know where I am."

"I wondered if that is where they had taken you, but I could learn nothing. Your MI5 has a very strong lock on any information. It is the same for Robert; I do not know where he now stays. Stuart is home, and we have been in contact. His DCI is trying to locate Robert but is also reaching stone walls. The first I knew anything regarding you was what happened with the bus crash. On the news." He shifted back, his eyes boring into Finn's. "I wonder if...if that is why things have...have ended?"

Finn nodded.

Christian grinned from ear to ear and his words tumbled out. *"I am so relieved, and so proud you are my brother, and I tried to call but only could get voicemail and I would have come to visit Monifieth, but I am prohibited from leaving Germany because my passport is in my superior's desk and the letters I sent to you were returned to me and –"*

Finn put a hand to Christian's lips to silence him. The man took in a deep breath then continued, "Before you leave this house, you will give to me your email address."

"You couldn't find it on your own?" Finn asked, with a

smile as he drew Christian close.

"I tried but..."

Finn pulled him closer and said, "I'll give you anything you want. You've become very important to me."

And he kissed him. Soft. Gentle. Elegant and real. A kiss neither would ever want to end.

When Christian finally sighed, his voice was choking, "I was so afraid for you. You...you will tell me everything, tonight, ja?"

"Everything."

"Then come; dinner awaits."

The meal was five courses grand, and the conversation polite and not the least invasive. Georg was quiet but attentive, a carbon copy of his father in not only looks but manners, as were his two daughters, Anjelika and Lena, and his very refined Austrian wife, Luisa. Finn told them of his life, focused on Nan and her ways, and they seemed to approve.

They told him little of their own.

They had coffee served in an elegant drawing room filled with antiques and fine portraits of family members that stretched back hundreds of years. He saw one of the elder Mr. Hauptmann and Georg, but not of Christian.

When Finn looked at him, questioning, he said, softly, "These are of their bloodline, Finn, of which I am no part."

"But you are, of mine, which is much better."

Christian grinned. "And makes me very happy."

They turned to find Mikala was at the door, watching them. Finn could now see both her mother and father in her.

"I made it just before the snow closed the airport," she said, smiling, then swirled in. "Hallo, Finley. You and I have much to discuss."

The conversation with her was more pointed, especially when Finn suggested there might be secret vaults at *Alles Wissen*. She huffed that it was nonsense...so he let it drop. He had the feeling no matter what he did or said now, he would never know if it made a difference.

Nor did he want to.

As for his disappearance from her lab, he told her Joss was the reason for his kidnapping. He'd been sent an urgent text and called away in a rush to meet an informant, but it was a trap.

"Next thing I know, I'm in Corsica," he said.

Mikala had shaken her head and patted his cheek, saying, "You are not a good liar, Finley. Your eyes are too open and honest."

"Well...that's my story and I'm sticking to it."

"Of course you are," she said with a knowing smile, then she cast a sly glance at Christian. "I am sorry you are not available. You would make a good husband."

"Um...thank you? Now, if you don't mind, I'm knackered. If you'll all excuse me..."

Everyone understood, so he rose to head to his room then stopped and turned to Mikala, "Oh, have you heard? Apparently, a new form of the Black Plague has made itself known in Russia and Asia, thanks to the permafrost thawing."

Christian stiffened. Mikala noticed and glanced between them, saying, "Yes, I know of this."

"So...if it should reach Europe, we'd be ready for it?"

"I doubt it will come this far. Winter is here, and a Russian winter will kill almost anything."

"But if it did? Say...next year or the year after? Or the year after?"

She eyed him, for a long moment, saw that Christian was eyeing her in a sidewise way, then said in a voice that was quiet and meaningful, "We will be ready."

"Thought as much."

He started for his room but Mikala stopped him with, "Finley. I've heard stories about you..."

He chuckled. "I wouldn't put much credence in them. I just get...hunches now and again."

She nodded, her eyes locked on him. "I thought as much."

And they had left it at that.

****

Finn wasn't really tired. Instead of getting in bed, he made a call on Christian's mobile.

A gruff sleepy voice answered, "Yeah?"

"Arin, it's Finn."

Boom, he was awake. "Bloody hell, where are ye?"

"Is your father home, yet?"

"Last night! They let him come home, last night."

"I'm so glad. Will you tell him something for me?"

"What?"

"Tell him it's over."

"What's that mean?"

"He'll know."

"Well, is it what ye were talking about that night?"

"If he wants to explain, that's up to him."

"You're really a wanker, y'know!"

"Yes," Finn chuckled. "A vidiot in the extreme."

"I didn't mean it. Just something to keep mum off guard. "

Now Finn laughed and they chatted a bit more, finally promising to meet up at the next comics fair in Glasgow, then he rang off and called Stuart.

"So yer alive," were Stuart's first words.

"Yes. And would you let your DCI know that I'm willing to return to England and tell them whatever they want, but only of Rob is sent to collect me."

"Ye...ye think he's well, then?"

"I know he is. He's too important not to be. I'll explain it all once he and I are with you."

Stu hesitated. "I...I don't know if I want to know it."

"Even if I tell you it's all over?"

"Can ye be sure of that?"

"As sure as possible." There was a silence then Finn added, "Stu, how're you doing with Rob not there?"

After a long pause, he replied, "Spend most nights in the jail."

"But you faced down Joss — "

"And near made a bollocks of it." Stu took in a deep breath then said, "I'll let him know."

He rang off as Christian knocked and slipped into Finn's room, wearing an undershirt and loose gym shorts.

"Your duties are complete?" he asked.

Finn nodded and pulled him into an embrace. He nestled cheek to cheek, with him. Nuzzled an ear to his nose. Nibbled an earlobe, saying, "I've wanted to do this since I first saw you."

Christian chucked, softly, saying, "Commit incest?"

"It's not like we were raised together."

"True." He kissed Finn's neck and trailed a hand over the cast on his arm. "But you are injured."

Finn chuckled. "I'm not an invalid."

"Nor could you ever be," Christian murmured, then he kissed him with a tenderness that was like home and peace and the best part of life one could imagine.

When he pulled back, his eyes did not leave Finn's. "When I was young, knowing I was adopted I would feel always incomplete. Holding you like this, I feel the opposite."

Finn smiled and tickled his hands down Christian's back, light and electrifying.

Christian held him closer. "Everything that beast forced me to do, I had done already with men. But then...then I could not face it. Until now."

"Now?" Finn whispered.

"I like your kisses. I like the feel of you against me. I want to regain who I once was. Become whole."

"Allow me." Finn guided him back onto the bed and continued to caress him. He pulled Christian's shirt up over his chest to kiss his lovely nips, first the left, then the right.

Christian's hands tickled down Finn's sides, his breath deep and joyous.

Finn shifted up to kiss him, again, loving every point where their bodies touched, especially when his hard dick, wrapped in the cotton of his briefs, rubbed against Christian's unfettered one, under the shorts.

Finn trailed his tongue down Christian's treasure trail, took the drawstring to his loose shorts with his teeth and pulled them down to reveal his pubes. Golden brown and lovely. He nuzzled them with his nose. Bit at them, light and playful. Smiled as Christian's dick flopped about in response.

Christian rose to a sitting position and reached down to caress Finn's ass, then pulled Finn up to kiss him, again, and laid him back to lie on top of him.

"Sorry, guess I'm not very good at this, yet," Finn said, "but I will — "

Christian put a finger to his lips. "This is no time for comment or confession," he whispered. "No need for excuses." He kissed Finn, this time hungry and deep, before continuing with, "You know I am a careful man in matters such as this." Another kiss. "So will you let me decide what we will do, to start?"

Finn looked at him, slowly took in a breath and nodded.

Christian kissed him, deep and loving, and rose to a kneeling position, then lifted Finn's ass to rest on his hips. Finn could feel Christian's erection slide along his pants and up between his cheeks and nearly gasped at the beauty of it.

Christian pulled Finn's trousers open and lowered the briefs to set free his dick, and it flopped back to show how clean and lovely it was, with a nice head fit to be kissed. Which is exactly what the man did, up one side and down the other before slipping his lips over the cap and swirling his tongue around it, sending Finn into spasms of euphoria. This man knew exactly how to give a blow job...a long, hard, elegant blow job...and it was driving Finn mad with desire. He'd lead Finn up to the brink...then shift to kissing him. He adjusted Finn's balls so they were outside his briefs and fondled them, gentle and sure as he dove back down on Finn. He edged him like that for what seemed like hours before finally taking all of him in his mouth and sucking him and stroking him and rolling his balls and devouring him with all his might, making Finn nearly scream when he ejaculated.

And Christian swallowed every bit of it.

He finally collapsed to Finn's side, exuberant, caressing Finn tenderly, smirking and whispering, "It *is* like riding a bicycle; just get back on and it will all come back to you."

"Pun intended?" Finn chuckled.

Christian enveloped him in a protective embrace. Finn reached down to fondle him and realized his shorts were soaked with his own cum.

"Without me touching you," he said.

"Just rubbing against you was as much as I could handle."

"I've a lot to learn if I want to make you as happy."

"Later," said Christian. "Tonight, we are together."

"Tomorrow, then." He kissed Christian and told him everything that had happened.

Everything.

When he was done, Christian kissed the top of his head and murmured, *"My poor man. My poor Finn. You have made me even more proud to be your brother."*

"My lover. My brother. My family."

Christian drew him closer, his sighs filled with joy. Finn smiled and relaxed into his arms.

And both drifted into the best sleep they had ever known.

Finally Understood

Tweedle-dee and Tweedle-dum were on the Hauptmann's doorstep at 9am, the next morning, a haggard but neatly-dressed Rob with them. The moment he saw Finn, he straightened up and yanked him into a tight bear-hug. Not word was said, nor was one needed...even though Rob's embrace was on the painful side.

'Dum had Christian's passport in hand and held it up for him. In response, Christian threw some clothes in a valise, kissed his parents and joined the group.

"Can you do that?" Finn asked. "Just up and run off?"

"I am under suspension," Christian replied. "Until my case is finalized, with my passport I may do as I choose."

They left in that super-silent government helicopter, stopped to pick up Martin, in Edinburgh, and headed on to Stu's home. There, they spent hours discussing everything that had happened.

In excruciating detail.

It ended when they were ordered to keep it confidential.

"If you don't," said 'Dee, "you don't exist no more. Got it?"

"If ye think I'd share this with anyone," said Stu, holding tight onto Rob, "yer barkers. That's what they'll think I am."

"I've told me wife and children I repressed a memory of being assaulted at university," said Martin. "By some Neo-Nazi bastards. It took me over when I saw one of them standing for office. But now I'm healed. And to put sold to it, I'm helping the bloody alt-shite bastard's opponent oust him."

Christian smiled his approval and said, "With my family, my sister believes I am making a joke of her profession, so I will *confess* she is correct. She will be angry, but will *understand*. My brother wishes to know nothing about my life, so I have told him nothing. My parents will respect my wishes, mainly because they will be relieved I no longer wish to burden them with it."

"Nobody knows what happened with me but those at this table," said Rob. "I ain't chattin' it up, and if you lads want to leave me dead, I'm for it."

"Too late for that," said 'Dum. "We got you down for deep undercover."

"Best we can do," 'Dee added, nodding.

"What about your family?" Finn asked.

"They're pretty unhappy with me, *City Boy*. Let's give it a year; see if they calm down, with this new angle."

Finn nodded and turned to 'Dee and 'Dum. "My superior knows I was sexually assaulted," he said, "and believes my actions of the last two months have been as a direct result of that. Which is not incorrect. I've asked for a six-week leave of absence, to *regain my balance*. He's agreed. I see no reason to burden him further with the suspicion I might also be stark raving mad, no matter what the evidence."

"Ain't no evidence."

Finn looked at him, nearly smiling. "I vanished in front of cameras in my room, and also in front of you during an interview that was being recorded..."

"Dunno what ya talkin' 'bout." And 'Dee's expression was a brutal, *Do not even think of saying otherwise.*

"Right," Finn finally said. "What evidence?"

"But what of Finn's actions to protect the bus?" said Christian. "It has been well-reported. How is this explained?"

'Dum said, "We put the story out that he got a day pass from Monifeith and borrowed Martin's van to check into DI Hallsworth's involvement with two other deaths. And we're going with Winterbourne's explanation that he was kidnapped and brutalized while investigating human trafficking, using Hallsworth's suicide to verify it. Also, did you know our Finn took a police-sponsored driving course?"

"Years, ago, yes," said Finn, nearly laughing, "when I considered joining the pursuit team, but what's that to do — ?"

"You were in the right place at the right time. When you saw that lorry coming up too fast to stop, that training kicked into gear, gave you the idea about hitting the bus so as to use its tail to keep it from being broadsided. The rest was blind luck, but...*thanks to your actions*. Repeat it often enough? Press'll believe it, and they'll get everyone else on board."

"You really think so?"

"Yes." And, again, his expression said, *Accept it*.

"What do you two believe?" Christian asked.

Before Finn could tell him it didn't matter, 'Dee looked at him and said, "I believe there's too damn many bloody idiot's out there what would go bonkers over this, an' we don't need to give 'em any more cause to be even more bloody stupid 'n they already are!"

"Of course," said Christian, smiling...but not completely certain he'd understood 'Dee's response.

So that was it. Finn was hailed as a hero, dragged before a dozen press conferences to *explain* it, and presented with a medal by one of the royal princes, with a kiss from their wife.

Everything else was locked away in MI5's vault.

Finn then joined Christian in Hamburg, during his leave, and managed to salve Mikala's huffiness over her brother's *joke*. And how did he manage that?

Well...the Peregrines came to Hamburg for a match with the city's rugby union. Finn took Christian, Mikala, and Georg and his family to watch and then meet the team, whom they invited to the Hauptmann mansion for a celebration, after they won. Finn saw to it Mikala and Barry got to spend time together, and they struck up such a fierce relationship, they were married within a month.

But then divorced five months later.

And remarried, two months after that.

And divorced, again.

And...remarried, again, this time for keeps...and wound up with seven children.

Which made Finn, Christian, Rob and Stu majorly-cool uncles who became even cooler when Bernardo was introduced into the family, pleasing them all to no end. Finn never was able to locate his parents and his uncles were of no help, so he had to start his search from nothing to locate his sisters...and he never was able to ascertain he'd tracked all of them down.

But that was over the next few years.

Prior to all of this, Christian was dismissed from the police force.

"For *bringing the service into disrepute with my wild and unacceptable actions,*" he told Finn the night before he was to return to Clayton-Merrill.

"That's not right!" Finn growled. "It wasn't your fault."

Christian shrugged. He looked almost as ragged as when Finn first met him. "My father said he knew this would happen. I was always too independent to make a good police officer."

"Oh, that's bollocks."

Christian almost smiled. "He offered to intervene, and I thought of it...but in truth, my career is now over."

"Couldn't you get on with another force? Berlin? Munich? Frankfurt?"

Christian shook his head. "We are not as forgiving of such things, as are the British."

Finn sat him on the bed. "Then join me in Clayton-Merrill. With your expertise, I'm sure CID would love to have you."

Christian chuckled. "But I am German."

"Not by birth. And...Christian...I'd like you to be there."

"It is a pleasant thought, but..."

Finn huffed then shoved him back on the bed and fell on top of him, growling, "Don't be dense! I love you, and I want you there. I'll marry you, if that's what it takes."

Christian blinked. "Finn...we are brothers..."

"Only by birth." Followed by a long lovely kiss.

Christian squirmed under Finn, deeply aroused by the man lying on him, and Finn did all he could to intensify it. When Finn finally shifted back to gaze into his elegant eyes, the man could barely breathe.

"I...I have think about this," whispered from him.

He tried to get up but Finn held him in place. "I said I love you. What more is there to think about?"

Then he kissed the base of Christian's neck and drew his lips across his chest to find a nipple, grasp it with his teeth and lick at it through the shirt.

Christian pushed him back to look into his eyes and said, "Are you certain of this?"

"I've already said," said Finn. "And you haven't answered my question."

Christian hesitated then looked at Finn with love, and he smiled and caressed his face and wrapped his arms around him and they kissed in a way that made the world swirl around them in tenderness and joy and protection and peace.

A month later, Christian moved to Clayton-Merrill. Blethyn and his wife greeted him, warmly, and he joined CID as a civilian tech-meister. Finn's fellow officers gave him courtesy and respect, and he felt on top of the world.

What was even better? When Rob and Stu, who had finally become one, came to spend holidays with them, they were just as accepted.

So to Finn's overwhelming joy, he now had a full and complete family.

But there was one last bit of business he had to finish.

He waited a few months, till he knew he and Christian could be totally alone and unnoticed, then they not only dug his physical personnel file out of storage, they hacked into his online file and added a note to each of them.

A note that read *MI5 folder # 14102020-Winterbourne.*

The final link.

To be discovered in 500 years.

Now Finn knew, without question, all was right with his world.

And his future was back in his hands.

THE END

About the Author

Kyle Michel Sullivan is a writer and self-involved artist out to change the world until it changes him...as has already happened in far too many ways. He has lived in London, Los Angeles, San Antonio, El Paso, Kansas City, Honolulu, Austin, Houston, and now resides in Buffalo, NY.

He has won multiple awards for his screenplays and has all genres of books available — from a fable (*David Martin*) to cold and dark suspense (*How To Rape A Straight Guy* and *Rape in Holding Cell 6*, which have been banned a couple of times) to farcical (*The Lyons' Den*) to gay murder mystery (*Underground Guy* and *The Vanishing of Owen Taylor*, a follow-up to *RIHC6*) to tragedy (*Bobby Carapisi*) to romantic mainstream (*The Alice '65*). The Beast in the Nothing Room is his first SF-Horror story.

He uses Tolstoy as his guide and tries to build characters as vivid and real as possible. He has a lot of fun doing it mixed with angst, anger, and amazement ... but that's the lot of a writer.

He's re-published all of his early books himself, in both paperback and ebook with a couple in hardcover, beginning in 2013; anything earlier than that is out of print, except for *Boys Will Be Boys* (which contains a novella he wrote); it was published through STARbooks Press and continues to sell on Amazon.

Other Books by the Author

Underground Guy
The Alice '65
The Vanishing of Owen Taylor
The Lyons' Den
Bobby Carapisi
Rape in Holding Cell 6
Porno Manifesto
How to Rape a Straight Guy

and a fable:

David Martin